THE BLADE OF TRUTH

WRAK-AYYA: THE AGE OF SHADOWS BOOK
TWELVE

LEIGH ROBERTS

DRAGON WINGS PRESS

CONTENTS

Editing by Joy Sephton: http://www.justemagine.biz
Cover design by Cherie Fox: http://www.cheriefox.com

Sexual activities or events in this book are intended for adults.

ISBN: 978-1-951528-34-8 (ebook)
ISBN: 978-1-951528-35-5 (paperback)

DEDICATION

For those who know the magic words to open worlds of wonder are

What If?

CHAPTER 1

The presence of the Guardian still hung in the Great Chamber. The crowd, made up of the Brothers, the Sarnonn, and the People, slowly dispersed, each to their own communities, but with promises given from their hearts to join together to defeat the negativity that threatened everything and everyone they loved. The Brothers' stories of the Waschini intimidating their people hung heavy in everyone's hearts.

Haan led Notar—who had first revealed himself to Oh'Dar near Shadow Ridge—and his people to Kht'shWea, and they all walked in silent reverence for the events they had just witnessed. The two Sarnonn communities would spend the next while becoming acquainted and learning to live together.

The Brothers left for their own villages, and in the back of the Chiefs' minds was the plea from Larara for help finding her lost grandson, stolen away by his father, Berak, whose body had been found with no sign of the offspring.

Nootau and Iella left for the Far High Hills. Lying unspoken between them was the Guardian's statement that Nootau's future did not lie in the leadership of the High Rocks, as well as Nootau's admission of his intention to leave with Pan when she came to retrieve An'Kru in seven years' time.

As for Tehya and Khon'Tor, they were also returning to the Far High Hills, now carrying the news from Pan that Tehya was seeded. For the first time since he had met Hakani, Khon'Tor knew peace in his heart. As he walked beside his tiny mate, he vowed to become the best father he could from here on, for both Arismae and the new offspring promised by the Guardian.

Adia and Acaraho were dealing with heavy revelations. Acaraho was in part relieved, knowing that Nootau knew the truth about his parentage, yet at the same time grieving the truth coming out. The young male would always be his son, and he clung to Nootau's profession that nothing had changed between them.

The pain of the past with Khon'Tor had been healed, but Adia now had a new struggle. Seven years. She would have An'Kru with her for only seven years, at which time Pan would return to take him away. It would take all her willpower to focus on the present moment and not let the specter of his leaving ruin the time she still had with him.

Oh'Dar escorted his grandparents back to their quarters. He could see on their faces that they needed to rest. It had been an extraordinary event, and he knew that it came on the heels of trying to adjust to their new life—one which few Waschini could imagine.

"My mind is reeling," Miss Vivian stated again.

"I know I keep saying this, son," Ben said, "but both your grandmother and I are so very glad we chose to come here with you. It is a far greater adventure than either of us could imagine."

"Something is on your mind, Grayson," Miss Vivian said. "Is it what happened with our attorney, Storis?"

"I believe that Storis's concerns were settled. But I have a bad feeling about that seedy-looking fellow with him, whom he called Tucker. I just hope nothing more comes of it. And, of course, I hate that the Brothers are being harassed by our kind and that I feel powerless to help them."

"We will think about whether there is anything we can do," declared Ben, "while not disclosing our whereabouts or that we are still alive. Something will work out." He rested his arm on Oh'Dar's shoulders. "Why don't you return to the village for a few days? We will be fine here. I am sure you want to spend some time with your beautiful wife."

Looking around in wonder, Notar and his people had followed Haan to Kht'shWea. They had never seen such a massive cave system as Kthama, and to hear there was another nearly as large so close by was equally impressive. Haan did not anticipate any problem but, as a courtesy, had sent ahead his High Protector, Qirrik, to let his people know they were welcoming new members to the community.

By the time they arrived, a small crowd had gathered outside Kht'shWea, with a larger crowd inside the entrance. Haan hailed them and broadly smiled when he saw his mate, Haaka, with his daughter Kalli.

"Greetings!" he called out. "We are blessed today. The Great Spirit has brought brothers and sisters to join our community."

Those gathered had been speculating among themselves.

"Where are they from? How did they get here?" a voice called out from the melee.

"Let Haan speak," said another voice.

"This is their Adik'Tar, Notar," Haan said, gesturing to the male standing next to him. "The Guardian Pan has brought them to us."

Heads turned rapidly.

"The Guardian has been here?"

"She appeared at the High Council meeting at Kthama. She spoke with us about our responsibilities to work together with the Akassa and the Brothers to protect Etera from destruction. I will tell you about it later, but for now, we must welcome our guests."

Qirrik stepped forward, "It will take us a while to allocate living quarters."

Notar spoke. "We are grateful to you and your people, and we will be happy with whatever quarters you can spare. I can explain who are the unpaired males so you can allocate them appropriately."

"To ease your transition," said Haan, "for now, we will keep you all together in one of the sections. Then later, if any of your people wish to move to other quarters, we will do our best to accommodate them."

Sastak, Haan's head female, stepped forward, "We will need to make sleeping mats quickly and locate extra gourds and baskets. Adik'Tar Notar, do you have a head female I can work with?"

Notar turned and signaled for someone to come forward. "This is Lezuan. She will be able to help organize some of our people to help with this."

"Thank you," said Sastak. "I need to know how many mats we need to make and how many of your families will need nests for offling. It will also help us determine where to put you."

Haaka and Qirrik worked together to organize Notar's people into manageable groups and took them to look around inside. The newcomers were amazed at the size of the cave system. As they entered, they looked around, trying to take in the height of the ceiling, the sharp rise of the rock walls.

The living quarters were also far larger than what they were used to.

Before long, organized work details were either gathering or making the additional supplies needed. Chatter accompanied the busy hands as strangers became acquaintances, and Haan's people speculated about the Guardian, what she was like, and whether they might also be blessed enough ever to see her. *The Guardian of Etera was once again among their people!*

Haan gave the newcomers time to settle in before calling an official meeting.

"Adik'Tar Notar, we welcome you. The Guardian, in her wisdom, has brought you and your community to us. This is your home now, though I know it will take a while before it truly feels like home. In time you will become accustomed to our routines and learn where we forage, hunt, and gather water."

Haan motioned to Sastak and Haaka to step forward. "My mate Haaka, and our head female, Sastak, whom you have already met, will be here along with High Protector Qirrik to answer your questions. There are wonders here, amazing historical wonders, which we will show you after you have settled in."

Qirrik stepped forward and explained about the sounding horn for meetings and where they gathered to eat together. He told them of the Great River that snaked around Kthama and Kht'shWea and about the treacherous paths that wound through the rocky terrain. He suggested that they not wander off on their own but let the others show them where to gather and hunt.

When Qirrik had finished, Notar addressed the people of Kht'shWea, "We could not ask for a warmer welcome. You are right, Adik'Tar Haan; it will take us some time to settle in. But do not take our need to adjust as any sign of a lack of gratitude. Clearly, Kht'shWea is a place of wonder, and we are honored to be invited to live with you here.

Some time later, Notar found Haan alone. "Adik'-Tar, I have one pressing question if you would not mind— In the assembly room at Kthama, there were other of your people there who had the same coloring as the Guardian, Pan. Among my people, there is much talk of these, and I ask if you could tell us who they are, and more about the Promised One she spoke of."

"The silver-coated Sassen are Guardians. How they came to be, well, that is a long story," said Haan kindly, "and one I will gladly share when we have time to do it justice. They are here to help usher in the Wrak-Ashwea. You will see them in the community, and you are welcome to talk to them. Thord and Lellaach are their unofficial Leaders. There are twelve altogether, six mated pairs, and the females are all seeded, which is very exciting. As for the offling that the Healer Adia was holding and of whom Pan spoke, he is the An'Kru, the Promised One. We are living in wondrous times, at the threshold of a new age, and your coming here is no doubt part of the future unfolding as it should."

"Thank you, Adik'Tar," Notar said. "We know of the prophecy of the Promised One from when the Guardian visited us in the past, but we have much to learn. I will share this with my people, and we will then wait to hear the rest of this miraculous story."

"We will learn from each other," Haan said graciously.

Oh'Dar was glad to return to the village and the warm embrace of his Acise. She would deliver in summer. Their first offspring, their first child. And now his grandparents would be part of it, would have the joy of seeing their great-grandchild grow and learn.

Chief Is'Taqa and Honovi greeted him, and soon others came running. He looked for his life-walker and was concerned when he did not see her.

"Where is Acise?" he cried out in alarm.

Honovi took his arm, "She is in your shelter. Come. She will be so happy to see you."

"Why is she there? Is something wrong? She was fine when I left for the High Rocks."

"It is just a little spotting, but we are a bit concerned and think it best if she does not move around much," Honovi explained.

Oh'Dar opened the flap and knelt down beside

Acise. He stroked her hair and looked deeply into her warm brown eyes.

"I am so glad you are home," she said. "I am sure Momma told you?"

"If the stress of all this has been too much for you, I will never forgive myself for leaving!"

"It will be fine; I feel it in my heart. Momma had the same problem when she was carrying Snana. I just have to be careful from now on and not overdo things. Ithua said the same thing. Please try not to worry. And please do not tell your grandparents. There is no need to worry them. They have enough to deal with, adjusting to their new life."

There was little talk between Storis and Tucker after the attorney's admonishment that they would have no more contact once they returned to Wilde Edge. The silence was broken only by the sound of the wagon wheels crushing the snow and the crunch of the horses' hooves plodding them forward.

Storis had not wanted Tucker to know the exact whereabouts of the locals' village, yet the man had disobeyed him and followed him there anyway. Not knowing what was on Tucker's mind made the lawyer uncomfortable, and he now knew in his gut that the less Tucker was involved, the better, and regretted hiring him at all.

Storis was right to be concerned. Tucker's mind

was swirling with ways to extract more money. For him, this was certainly not the end of it, and keeping his silence about the locals hiding the Morgan child was certainly going to be worth something.

Tucker's voice broke the silence between them. "Interesting story about the kid, isn't it? And the sheriff's men searched that village, from what I heard. Yup, would be a shame if they learned that those locals had been hiding the boy after all."

Storis's stomach lurched. He knew what was coming but again tried a strong approach. "We have a deal, Tucker. Our business is now over, as I said. Get on with your life; this matter doesn't concern you anymore."

"I think it could. From what I overheard, the Morgans were very wealthy. Probably still are. I know how rich people think; they never let go of everything. They probably have some stashed away somewhere."

"If they do, I certainly don't have access to it," Storis answered.

"Oh, you lawyers are pretty resourceful; I am sure you could find a way."

Storis looked away from the path ahead and stared at Tucker. "Just what are you saying?"

"Do I have to spell it out for you? Unless want the sheriff's men poking around that sweet little village and asking questions no one wants to answer, I suggest you find a way to get your hands on some of that money. Otherwise, I'm going to be meeting with the sheriff when I get back."

"No one cares about that now. It was years ago, and the Morgans are dead for all they know. There's no one left to care about it."

"But they're not dead, are they? Might be interesting to see who is really buried in those graves at the Morgan farm. Oh, yes, you see, I did a little homework a while back. Man like you described, Grayson Morgan, stands out. Pretty easy to learn his story just by askin' around a bit."

Storis clenched his jaw. For a moment, he had a terrible thought about disposing of Snide Tucker before they got back, but he pushed it away immediately.

"Nothing good will come of this, Tucker, causing trouble for good people who have done nothing wrong. I'm warning you," Storis said.

Tucker laughed maniacally. "You are warning me? That's a good one. Well, I won't bring it up again —for now. After all, you're going to need time to figure out how to pay me to keep my mouth shut. Yes, sir."

Mrs. Webb and her family heard that Mr. Storis was back in town and that he was staying at the local inn. Grace asked her mother if she and her brother, Ned, might go with her into town to see if they could find him.

"Grace, if Mr. Storis wanted to visit us, he would. As much as I understand your curiosity about him, it is best that you leave it up to him whether he calls on us or not. I'm sure he is a busy man."

"Your mother is right," her father agreed. "Besides, it doesn't look right for a young woman to be seeking out a single man's company, even one so much older."

"He's not that much older," Grace complained. "Besides, there's no one else here who holds any interest for me. If you don't let me spend time with him, I'm going to die an old maid."

It was true that the lawyer was the only man in whom Grace was interested. He would certainly be able to provide for her and free her from the life of struggle familiar to most of the inhabitants of Wilde Edge. That didn't mean her father had to like it, though.

"If he wants to keep contact with us, he will, so no more of this. You are not going into town to look up Mr. Storis. Now go and do your chores," Mr. Webb said.

Grace went out to the barn to help her brother. "It's not fair," she lamented. "Mr. Storis is nice. He's a true gentleman. Them and their old-fashioned ideas; there's nothing wrong with a girl going after what she wants, is there?"

Ned stopped to lean on his pitchfork, "They just

don't want you to get hurt. Or get a bad reputation. Trust me, if Mr. Storis is interested in you, he won't stay away long. Didn't he say he was moving his business here?"

"Yes! Oh, I do like him so much," Grace sighed.

During the ride back to Wilde Edge, every minute in which he was not worrying about Tucker, Storis thought of Grace Webb. He wanted to stop at their place, but he was covered in trail dust and grime. Besides, he did not want Tucker anywhere around there. There had been enough trouble from that man as it was, and it seemed it wasn't over yet.

When they arrived, they took the hired wagon and horses back to the stable. Storis said he would return later to pay the stablemaster, not having carried any extra cash on him for fear Tucker might have robbed him had he done so. But now, Storis knew that the man had his sights on a much larger payday than a one-time looting would bring.

"Where's my pay?" Snide Tucker said the moment they had stepped outside.

"Meet me back here after dinner. I will pay you and the stablemaster. Then I never want to see you again."

Tucker looked around and then stepped forward and slammed Storis against the stable wall. "You weren't listening, were you? Our business is not done. Not by a long shot. I'll be back here later to get my pay, but as I said, you best be thinking about how you're going to keep my mouth shut about everything else."

Storis broke Tucker's grasp on him and forcefully shoved him back. "Get out of my sight before I do something I'll regret."

Tucker laughed, "Oh, so you do have a backbone somewhere? Well, well, well." Tucker tipped his hat and added, "See you later, lawyer-boy."

Storis went to the hotel and cleaned up. A bath was a rare luxury, but he treated himself to one that afternoon. As he was relaxing in the tub of steaming water, his thoughts returned to Grace. Her smile, her lilting laughter. Her inquisitive and sharp mind that had besieged him with questions about what it was like to be a lawyer. The full lips that begged to be kissed, how she would feel in his arms. In his bed. And that was the moment Storis decided he would do whatever he could to win Grace and her parents' approval of the match.

After he had paid his dues and listened to more threats from Tucker, he took a walk to the Webbs' house.

Mrs. Webb answered the door and was surprised to see him standing there. "Why, Mr. Storis, welcome. Come on in. We are just sitting down to dinner."

Storis removed his hat, "I promise you, ma'am, I do not intend to stop by specifically at dinner time. It just seems to work that way."

Mrs. Webb laughed, "It doesn't matter. You are welcome here. Grace and the rest of the family will be glad to see you." She noticed that Storis's smile brightened when she mentioned her daughter's name.

He stomped the snow from his boots and came in.

Soon they were all seated at the modest kitchen table, passing around the plates and bowls of Mrs. Webb's delicious cooking. Buster was at his station under the table, hoping for scraps to mysteriously fall from above.

"You are a wonderful cook, Mrs. Webb," Storis said.

"Oh, please, it's time you called me Nora, and of course, my husband is Matthew," she said. "So you finished your business trip with that Mr. Tucker?"

"Yes, I accomplished what I needed. And as I said, I won't be having any more dealings with him."

"He said before that he might stop by some time," Mr. Webb said.

"If he does, please get word to me. I don't want him to be a bother to you." Storis couldn't help but glance at Grace.

"Are you still moving your practice here to Wilde Edge?" Mrs. Webb asked.

"Yes. I will be on my way back to Millgrove

shortly to pack up my business belongings. It should not take me too long. Before I go, I'll arrange for some office space in town."

"Will you need any help setting it up?" Grace asked. "I am good at organizing." She leaned over just enough to drop a piece of biscuit to Buster, who was waiting hopefully below.

"My goodness, Mr. Storis," Mrs. Webb said, "I do apologize. We did not raise her to be so forward!"

"It's fine, really. I admire Grace's spiritedness. And please, call me Newell," Storis said. "To answer your question, yes, I could use some help, if that is alright with you, Matthew. And I would insist on paying for it."

"Two days a week to start, but if there is any talk in town, it must stop immediately," Mr. Webb decided.

"Well, then it's settled," Mrs. Webb exclaimed. "Goodness me, both our children are moving out into the world, Ned with his studying to be an animal doctor, and now Grace has a job!"

"I will still take care of my chores here, Mama," Grace said, then smiled at Storis. He smiled in return, in a way that made Mrs. Webb feel she might be wise to start sewing a wedding dress.

CHAPTER 2

Back at the Far High Hills, Tehya couldn't wait to tell her parents about the assembly and the Guardian's visit. After she had explained who the Guardian was, she told them what Pan had said about her being seeded. They were ecstatic, but remembering the horror Akar'Tor had put Tehya through when she was carrying Arismae, who had also almost died after being born, they could also not help but feel anxious.

Vosha asked her daughter, "You do not yet know that you are seeded, but the Guardian knew?"

"Yes, Mama. I am so happy. And the Guardian said it is a male."

Tehya's parents certainly understood that after what Khon'Tor had also gone through with Akar'Tor, both needed good news.

"Then Arismae will have a brother," Vosha said

wistfully. "It is such a blessing for offspring to have siblings to walk the rest of this life with once we are gone."

Tehya thought of her brothers; though she did not see either of them that often, the bond between them was strong.

"I hope things can settle down now," she said. "Harak'Sar asked Khon'Tor to train Brondin'Sar, to help prepare him for leadership. They are meeting tomorrow, I believe. Maybe that means my mate will be able to stay here for a while. I have missed him so, and he needs a purpose to help him find his place here."

Brondin'Sar sat patiently listening to Khon'Tor explain that he would be helping prepare him for his future role as Leader of the Far High Hills.

"I am honored to be counseled by the great Khon'Tor."

"And I am honoured to be counseling you. Your father tells me that you want eventually to succeed him as Leader."

"That is true. My brothers do not, however, which makes it easier on all of us."

"Tell me why you want to be Adik'Tar."

"Because it is in my heart, I have a vision for our people—not just here, but all our communities. A vision of us united, working together more closely for the benefit of us all. We are only as strong as our weakest members, so by exchanging knowledge, goods, and ideas, such as we now do, but more formally between communities through the High Council, we will all become stronger."

"An honorable vision. Your father must be very proud."

"He has said he is," acknowledged Brondin'Sar. "Adik'Tar, I heard that you are to have a son."

Khon'Tor could not stop a smile. "Word travels fast."

"When it is such great news, yes. Everyone—and I mean everyone—is very happy for you and Tehya. We are all very glad you have come to be part of our community."

Once again, Khon'Tor was able to receive the positive words. Whatever Adia had done back at Kthama had truly healed his wounds. With his strength and confidence returning, he felt more himself than he ever had. He no longer felt he wore a badge of shame that others knew his every failing—and they were many who did.

"We are both thrilled, yes. Thank you. Now, let us start by walking through the Sacred Laws. I want you to explain to me what each one means to you."

"The first of the first laws is that the needs of the community come before the needs of the individual," Brondin'Sar started. "I do not take this to apply to everyday situations, but to when there is a serious issue. One where an individual's needs might conflict with the greater good of the People. In that case, an outcome which might benefit the individual but cause great harm to the majority would be set aside in favor of the community."

"Can you think of an example?" Khon'Tor asked.

Brondin'Sar thought a moment. "Let us say that someone had a terrible secret they had lived with all their life. Maybe a crime they committed a long time ago. And they wanted to clear their conscience by confessing it and suffering the pain of the consequences in order to quell the anguish in their soul. To make things right, so to speak. But revealing what happened would devastate others, perhaps even the entire community. In that case, to confess their dishonorable deed in order to gain peace for themselves but at the expense of others would be breaking Sacred Law. However difficult to live with, they would do greater harm in coming forward. In that case, the right thing to do would be to live with their guilt as their penance."

"An excellent example. And in this case, the struggle to obey Sacred Law was internal to the person alone," Khon'Tor observed.

He wondered what had prompted Brondin'Sar to think of such an example, but in his soul, he heard the words of the Guardian. *Son of my father's sons, blood of my blood. Return now to your daughter and to your gentle Tehya and the son who is even now growing peacefully within her belly. Unbind and release the regrets that still hobble your soul, lest they cause you to stumble on the way to your destiny."*

"In my experience," continued Brondin'Sar, "most of the great battles are within ourselves."

"You are wise beyond your years. When your father steps down, the Far High Hills will be blessed by your leadership. Now, on to the second law."

"Honor the females as they walk with the Mother. Females are the givers of life. We are told they are to be revered and protected because it is through their bodies that new life is brought to Etera. In that regard, they are closer to the creative force of the Great Spirit.

"They are strong in many ways but not physically as strong as us males. It is our place to do whatever is necessary to ease the struggles of their lives. To provide for them, help them find joy in every day. We must allow their souls to stay soft, unhardened by the difficulties of life, so they may nurture our offspring and keep them free from fear and strife while they are growing up. The burdens of adulthood should never be borne by young shoulders. We must share times of joy with our females and stand by them in times of sorrow."

"You learned that from watching your father and your mother?" Khon'Tor asked.

"Yes. And recently, watching you and Tehya.

Everyone speaks of the deep love between you, and — Khon'Tor, may I speak freely?"

"Please."

"Since you came back from the High Council meeting at Kthama, something about you has changed. When you first came here, you seemed burdened, as if you were carrying a great weight. Perhaps having given up leadership of the High Rocks, you were lost as to your place on Etera. But all that seems gone, for which many of us are glad.

"But it is not just your record as Leader of the High Rocks that inspires us. It is not just your long list of accomplishments that inspires us. Something you might not think of in this way, such as your relationship with Tehya, is what inspires us. Being a Leader is not just something you do; it is something you are."

"Thank you for your kind words, Brondin'Sar. It is true; I am still finding my place. I am grateful to your father for taking us in. I know it means a great deal to my mate that she is close to her parents.

"Now, on to the third law—"

Harak'Sar sent for Khon'Tor. "My son tells me he is benefiting greatly from his time with you. I want to thank you. Also, a messenger has come from the High Rocks."

Khon'Tor waited patiently for Harak'Sar to tell him more.

"Larara beseeched the Brothers' Chiefs to help her locate her daughter's son. In response, they have sent word of the Brothers' villages with which we have no relationship. There is one such group not far from the route Berak took."

"Does the Overseer know?"

"No, I thought we might tell her ourselves and see what she suggests."

It did not take them long to find her.

"If we have no contact with them, we must tread carefully," Urilla Wuti advised. "They know of our existence, I am sure, but that is not the same as meeting us face-to-face."

"The only way of knowing if the offspring is there is to visit. I see no other way," said Harak'Sar.

"Let me consider this. I may have a solution, though it might be just my wishful thinking."

When the males had left, Urilla Wuti sent for Iella and explained the situation.

"Iella, you have the ability to communicate with Etera's creatures. How far do you think this ability will reach? Would you like to test it out?"

"Tell me what you are proposing."

"You shared how you first discovered your ability when you connected with a squirrel, in a way becoming one with him. All we know about this village is the general location. We could spend days trying to find them. Do you think you could connect with one of the birds of the air, one that could travel the distance and see from above what we are not able to?"

"I believe I can do what you suggest. I have been practicing my abilities. When do you want me to try?"

"Whenever you are ready."

"I will need a good night's rest to be at my strongest. So, tomorrow morning, at dawn? Now explain to me the approximate area where this village might be."

Nootau and Urilla Wuti accompanied Iella out into the forest surrounding the Far High Hills. Iella found a comfortable spot to sit, leaning against a sturdy trunk, surrounded by the towering trees that reached toward the sky. The others sat a distance away and stilled their own thoughts.

The dawn breaking cast rosiness across the landscape as streaks of the warm daylight broke through the fir trees to cast their glow on the newly fallen snow.

Iella calmed herself and looked up, reaching into her soul to form a question, a request. *Who sees me who is willing to be seen?*

Before too long, a hawk circled high overhead. As she had with the squirrel, she felt a surge of love for it. And it was as if her love for it created a connection between them. Iella felt a bit of dizziness, and then she was seeing everything as the hawk saw it from far above. The forest stretched out to the horizon, its soft snow-covered boughs broken by the bare branches of the deciduous trees. She felt the support of the air under her wings, lifting her, carrying her as she rode the currents. She looked down and saw herself propped up against the tree trunk, but in such detail as she could never have imagined. Each strand of her hair and even her eyelashes were as clear as could be. Iella would later marvel at the hawk's visual acuity, far beyond what she could have imagined.

She felt the sharp cry come up and out of the hawk's throat before it split the silence of the sky. She asked for his help, and he immediately banked left and caught an up current, taking her even higher above the trees.

Down below, Nootau and Urilla Wuti watched the hawk circling and circling, then suddenly fly upward and disappear over the treetops. They turned to Iella, who seemed so very still.

"I think she did it," Nootau said.

"I did not think it would happen so quickly," Urilla Wuti said. "It may not take the hawk that long to travel to where the village is, but it could still be some time before he—they—return. We might as well get comfortable."

"Is her connection affected by distance, do you think? The further away the hawk gets, will the connection hold?"

Higher and higher they flew, until the clear blue sky surrounded Iella on all sides. The forest below stretched out further and further, and the speed at which they were traveling was exhilarating. To be weightless, to cast off the binding that held her to Etera's soil, oh, what joy. The air currents passed over the hawk's feathers, creating no sense of chill or cold. It was pleasant, the ruffling of its feathers against the wind, and she felt supported by forward momentum, then twisting and dipping as the current changed, catching the next updraft and rising higher again.

Lost in the joy of flying, it seemed no time before a Brothers' village came into sight. At Iella's bidding, the hawk flew lower, and soon he was circling overhead close enough for her to see almost every detail. It was mid-afternoon, and the Brothers were going about their chores. Iella almost lost the connection when she saw what she could swear was one of the People's offspring. The long wavy black locks were in sharp contrast to the Brothers' straight ones. Her heart leaped with joy.

At her suggestion, the hawk swept in lower and let out a cry, and a few of the villagers below pointed upward. The magnificent bird turned his head, and Iella could clearly see that the offspring was one of the People's.

Having found the village and who she believed must be Linoi's lost offspring, Iella then asked the hawk to help her get her bearings so she could find her way back. Higher again they flew, and this time, he found a nearby river and followed it. He seemed to be pointing out landmarks on the way, too, dipping lower toward a particularly large boulder, a twist in the river's path, an isolated stand of dead trees.

Then Nootau, Urilla Wuti, and Iella's own body came into view again. The hawk let out another piercing cry, and she saw her mate and her aunt look up at them. Iella thanked the bird and gently broke the connection. The next moment she was back in her own body, feeling the cold of the snow under her legs and feet. She opened her eyes, and the others came running over to her.

"We were starting to worry," Urilla Wuti said as Nootau helped his mate to her feet.

"Oh, oh, it was amazing. Oh, the joy of flying, feeling the power of the air to lift you high above— and how far they can see. I had no idea. Life is miraculous, it is, it is," Iella exclaimed. She was overcome with joy at what she had experienced, and it took her a moment to collect herself.

Nootau put his arm around her to steady her. "Did you find the village?"

"Oh, yes. I am sure of it. And the hawk; he knew what to do. He showed me how we could find it by following a river that runs not far from there. I am sure I could find it again.

"We must go back and let Harak'Sar know," Urilla Wuti said.

"And Khon'Tor," added Nootau. "He went out looking for the offspring previously, so no doubt he should be one to go with us."

Khon'Tor said he could be ready to leave anytime; Harak'Sar only had to say the word. But they needed a plan. They could not just go up to the village and introduce themselves. They did not want to alarm the Brothers.

"I believe I can help. Just leave our introduction to me," Iella said. And so, that evening, Khon'Tor, Iella, Nootau, and Harak'Sar's High Protector, Dreth, set out to find the Brothers' village and hopefully bring back Linoi's abducted offspring.

First light had broken a little while previously. One of the Brothers from Chief Kotori's village was fishing down by the river when a squirrel hopped onto a nearby tree trunk and chattered at him. "Ho, brother, what brings you here today?" Pakwa smiled at the friendly creature. Then another squirrel came down the trunk of a nearby tree and joined the first one. They eyed him carefully, tails flicking. "I see you have a brother!" Pakwa smiled again.

Sounds in the brush caught Pakwa's attention. A large buck stepped out of the wood line and stared at him. Then a doe, then another doe. Pakwa had never seen wildlife act like this—as if they were intentionally seeking him out. He set his fishing gear down after a hawk alighted on the top of a nearby dead tree. He was puzzled, though not alarmed—not until a second and third deer joined the first and a raccoon ambled by, also stopping to sit and stare at him.

"What is happening?" he asked into the air.

"Do not be afraid," a female voice called out.

Pakwa swiftly turned to the sound, which seemed to be coming from behind the group of deer.

"We mean you no harm; we come in peace."

Pakwa waited, and slowly a figure came through the brush and walked between the deer. None of them moved; they seemed not to care that she was among them.

"My name is Iella. I am one of the People," the female smiled.

"We know of you. But have never met any of you," Pakwa said, glancing at her. She was beautiful, though much larger than he, and when she stepped closer, he could see there were other differences between them.

"You command Etera's creatures?"

"I do not command them. They do as I ask out of their free will. But yes, they are here at my request to show you that, just as they recognize I mean them no harm, I mean you no harm either."

"Why have you approached me? What is it you want?"

"I want your help. We want your help," and she motioned behind her as if there were others with her. "We are seeking an offspring, one of our own. We believe he may be in the care and safety of your village."

"What is it you want with him?" Pakwa had thought of denying it but realized that this person had some supernatural abilities and might know he was not being truthful.

"Please, we wish to speak with your Chief. Please go to him and ask him to meet us here. Tell him what you have seen and assure him that we mean no harm to any of you. To anyone. Will you do that? If so, we will wait."

Pakwa did not know what else to do. "I will go to him now."

His kind knew little about them, except that they were peaceful and always helpful to those who had contact with them.

It did not take long for him to complete his errand.

"The Chief has asked that you come to the village and bring your friends with you. He wishes everyone to see you and especially the woman who has been caring for Ahanu."

"I understand. No doubt she has grown fond of him and needs to be assured that we mean him no harm." Iella motioned behind her and out of the brush stepped Nootau, Khon'Tor, and High Protector Dreth. The Brother's eyes widened.

"Come—" he stammered, then turned to lead them.

The village inhabitants had been called together. In front stood two males, most likely the Chief and the Second Chief. Behind them was everyone else, including one female holding an offspring clearly of the People.

Overhead, the hawk circled, letting out its piercing cry.

Flanked by the deer, raccoons, and squirrels, Iella and her contingent approached. They stopped a respectable distance from the Chief, not wishing to appear imprudent or disrespectful, but he raised his hand to beckon them closer.

Dreth, Khon'Tor, and Nootau stayed back, but the forest creatures with Iella moved forward the tiniest bit. Iella could see the villagers' eyes dart over them, mystified that they not only accompanied her but were also not intimidated at seeing so many people together.

"I am Iella, of the People of the Far High Hills." She motioned to Khon'Tor and Nootau, "These are also from our tribe. We come in goodwill."

"I am Chief Kotari. This is Second Chief Tawa.

And this is Tiponi, our Medicine Woman. Pakwa said you have come for the child."

"He is one of ours. He was stolen by his father and left to die. We are grateful you found and took care of him. A debt which cannot be repaid," Iella said.

The female holding the offspring pulled him closer, and he laid his head on her shoulder.

Iella could see she struggled under his weight as he was far larger than any of the Brothers' offspring would be at his stage of life. She looked to be of pairing age, and Iella wondered if she had offspring of her own.

Khon'Tor had now also moved forward. He said, "We would have come sooner, but we did not know where to find him. I promise you, he has a loving family waiting for him. His father's remains have been found, so he will be returned to his grandmother."

"What of the mother," the female holding the offspring asked. Then she glanced at the Chief.

"You may speak, Myrica."

But it was the Chief who explained that Myrica had found the boy and was raising him. "She saw the man you say was his father, who abandoned him, and she has concerns for the child's welfare," Chief Kotori said.

"The mother has returned to the Great Spirit, as has the father," Khon'Tor said. "There was great conflict between them. It is uncommon among our people, I assure you, for any of our offspring to be abandoned so."

Chief Kotori looked at Myrica. "When you brought the young one to us, you knew this day would come. It is not good for him to be among us, for his sake, or ours, or his people. He belongs with his own kind."

Myrica kissed Ahanu and shifted his weight in her arms. She walked slowly over to Iella and hesitated to hand him over. But to her surprise, he was not at all afraid, so, slowly, Myrica let her take him, wondering if the connection to the forest creatures extended to children. She tilted her head so her long black hair would hide her grief.

"I assure you," Iella softly said as Myrica looked up at her, "he will be loved and cared for. Thank you for loving him. Perhaps someday you will wish to meet him when he is old enough to understand what you did for him."

"That is kind of you, and it would be good for me, but for his sake, I hope he never learns that his father intentionally left him to die. No child should have to bear that burden of being so unwanted."

Then Myrica slipped away.

Khon'Tor spoke again. "Chief Kotori and Second Chief Tawa, I invite you to have further contact with us. There are several of our communities not that far from you. We are friends of your people. We have a High Council, on which others of your Chiefs sit. We are committed to the good of all our peoples, especially in light of the stories we are hearing about threats from the Waschini."

"We know of these troubles, of the Waschini trying to force many of us off our land, but we understand that your people are unknown to them. What help can you give us since you must now live your lives in Etera's shadows?"

"What you are saying is true," Khon'Tor acknowledged. "We must remain unknown to the Waschini. But we are experts at remaining hidden. We can offer you help by providing watchers to alert you to Waschini riders coming through. And you can meet the other Chiefs and discuss issues with them. You are isolated here, and we offer you community and brotherhood."

Chief Kotori nodded. "I will consider your offer and consult with my Elders. We do not know how to make contact, though."

Iella spoke, "If you come to a decision, speak your intention to the birds of the air, and they will let me know."

"You have powerful magic, but Pakwa said you do not command them," the Medicine Woman, Tiponi, said.

"No, they willingly do as I ask."

Just then, Myrica returned with a woven basket. "These are Ahanu's things. His favorite toys and his blanket. Perhaps they will help him feel at home in this new world where he truly belongs."

With nothing more to say, Iella turned and

walked away, U'Kail in her arms. Khon'Tor, Dreth, and Nootau turned and followed her. Slowly, one by one, the deer, the raccoons, and the squirrels followed the four of them and the offspring into the forest.

The hawk, now perched at the top of a dead oak, let out another cry before taking off.

Nootau offered to carry U'Kail, and, when the offspring didn't object, took him from Iella. Then U'Kail looked over Nootau's shoulder in the direction of the village. He put a chubby arm out, reaching back, no doubt looking for Myrica, the only mother he had ever known. Then he started to cry.

"Oh, no, no; it is alright," Nootau tried to console him.

Just then, someone came crashing through the brush and called out, "No, wait, please! Please take me with you. Just for a while, to help him adjust!"

It was Myrica, and close behind her was another female. "Chief Kotori gave me permission to ask you. Please!"

Khon'Tor looked at the distraught young female. "I see only benefit in your request. You will be welcome. And it will give us an opportunity to start a friendship between our two peoples. We will slow our pace so as not to tire you. It is a while away. Do you need to bring anything with you for your own comfort?" He then looked at the other female.

"This is a friend, Awantia. She came with me in case I was able to go with you. She will return and tell our Chief that all is well."

"What of your own family?"

"I have no life-walker and no children, so I am free to do as I please and as the Chief allows."

The other female handed Myrica a small satchel, and Iella spoke again. "I am sure you will find our home pleasant enough. We know from our friendship with the Brothers nearby that our needs are very similar. After all, we are all provided for by the same Great Spirit."

"I will be fine," said Myrica. "Thank you."

As they walked, Iella and Myrica chatted. The first thing Myrica wanted to understand was how Iella communicated with Etera's creatures. Iella explained it was an ability that had simply developed and told of how she first saw evidence of it with the mother bear and her cubs when she and Nootau were out looking for fluorite. She added that she had been as surprised about it as others were but that possibly it had happened because she was the descendant of a line that contained many Healers.

Iella also told Myrica that Nootau was her mate and that Khon'Tor was a Leader of great reputation.

She told her about the Far High Hills and a little about what to expect and assured her that whenever Myrica was ready to return home, someone would make sure she was brought back safely.

"Ahanu is a sweet boy, as you will find out. He has a gentle disposition and laughs at everything. But he is lonely in a way. He is far too big to play with the children of his age. Much as it hurts, it is good that he is being returned to his own kind. Chief Kotori kept reminding me this day would come, and in meeting you, my fears about his future are alleviated."

As they walked into the entrance, Myrica looked up and around at the high ceiling, the rock walls, the tunnels at the back branching out in many directions. She would never have believed a cave system of this size could be so relatively close and that these people lived undiscovered.

She looked at the three who appeared to be waiting for them. An older woman and a younger one were standing with a man who was possibly the Chief. Everyone was so tall!

Whoever the older female was, Myrica immediately felt comforted by her presence. Then the male spoke, welcoming them.

Iella introduced Myrica, explaining her relationship with Ahanu and why she was there.

"I am Harak'Sar, Leader of the Far High Hills," said the male. "This is one of our revered Healers, Urilla Wuti. She is also the Overseer of our High Council, which we will have time to explain more about later. And this is my mate, Habil."

Urilla Wuti took Ahanu from Iella's arms. She seemed particularly interested in his long wavy black locks. Myrica saw something pass between her and Khon'Tor but had no idea what it was.

Habil stepped forward, "Let us take you to where you can stay while you visit us. We will send someone to show you around and also to bring you to the eating area at mealtimes."

Iella handed Ahanu back to her. "The evening meal is over, but I will bring you something to eat, and when you've finished, we can talk some more. I am sure you have many questions."

When Harak'Sar, Khon'Tor, and Urilla Wuti were alone, the Overseer mentioned U'Kail's dark, wavy hair and said, "No silver streak."

Khon'Tor said, "I noticed."

"There is no reason for you to reveal any part you may think you played in this, Khon'Tor," Harak'Sar said. "No good will come of it."

"He is right," agreed Urilla Wuti. "The offspring has enough bad history to bear without adding any more to it. I pray he can live a quiet life with Larara and her family, his past far from others' scrutiny."

"I would like to think that possible, but I see no way in which he can be protected from his past," Khon'Tor said.

"Acaraho was. Still is. He does not know the circumstances that brought him to be raised by Awan's family," Urilla Wuti said. "But if he ever learns of it, he will be able to make sense of it as an adult in a way he would not have been able to as an offspring. The same will be true of U'Kail.

"Larara's community is small," she continued. "I am sure she can garner agreement from everyone there to protect U'Kail from the tragedy of his parents' demise. It will be a challenge, no doubt, to tell him enough of the truth as not to lie, but not enough to make him blame himself for his parents' tragedy, as an offspring might do."

Larara arrived at the Far High Hills as soon as she could and was taken to Myrica, who was still caring for U'Kail.

Iella introduced the offspring's grandmother, who looked as if she could hardly contain herself. "Larara's daughter was Ahanu's mother. Though she knew him as U'Kail."

Myrica crouched down and set the offspring on the floor to play.

"I am so grateful you rescued him and gave him a home," Larara hastened to say. "I have dreamed of this day for so long. In my heart, I believed he was still alive, but my fears dragged me into dark places. May I? Oh, please—"

"Of course!" said Myrica.

Larara quickly got down on the floor a little way from U'Kail. He looked up from playing with the hide balls and sticks and watched her.

"He is so good-natured and gentle, and he loves animals. He has been a delight," Myrica said.

Larara scooted over a little closer and moved some of the balls around, making them hop as if they were rabbits. U'Kail finally laughed and smiled.

"I hope you can stay awhile, so he can get used to me. I do not want to traumatize him; after all, to him, you are his mother," Larara said.

"Perhaps if you spend time with us, and then we start reducing my contact with him and increasing yours, my finally leaving will not be so hard on him," Myrica suggested. "Do you have other family?"

Larara explained about her other offspring and that she had a mate who had moved to another community.

The next day, Harak'Sar sent word to Kurak'Kahn that U'Kail had been found.

Gatin'Rar of the Little River called Kurak'Kahn to him. "Word has come that Khon'Tor and some others found Linoi's son, and he is safe at the Far High Hills. Larara is with him. Do you wish to go and see him?"

"No. But thank you for telling me."

"Do you wish to send a reply back?"

"No, that part of my life is over. But I am glad for Larara's sake that the offspring has been found."

CHAPTER 3

Nadiwani and Adia were in the Healer's Quarters when Nadiwani glanced up and said, "You look pale. Are you alright?"

"Actually, I do not feel good."

"Come and sit down. What are you feeling like?"

"Sick to my stomach."

"What did you have to eat last night?"

"Nothing that should make me feel nauseated. Just mostly greens and some dried meat. The usual. Ooohhh," she moaned and doubled over.

"Is anyone else feeling this way? Acaraho? Is everything alright with An'Kru?"

"From what I know, the others are fine. Miss Vivian has An'Kru this morning. She just adores—" Suddenly, Adia ran over to the personal area and threw up.

"Is there any chance you could be—?"

Adia came out, wiping her mouth with a piece of

hide. "It seems too early after having An'Kru. But I suppose it is possible."

Adia knew that if she was seeded, Acaraho would welcome the news, but she was not sure how she would feel about it. She selfishly thought of how her years with An'Kru would be limited as it was, and another offspring would mean her time would be that much more divided. And not only An'Kru would be leaving, but also Nootau. She knew that was the last thing she should be dwelling on. Instead, she reminded herself yet again that she had to trust that when the time came, she would be shown the way to handle it.

"I am not going to say anything to Acaraho; time will tell if I am seeded or not."

"You, Acise, and Tehya, all seeded at the same time? And let us not forget that Pan said the six female Sassen Guardians are all seeded."

Adia mused, "Thinking of the seedings of the Guardians, there will be only six offspring. That does not leave many generations of combinations. I remember E'ranale saying that Guardians are almost immortal, so with their longevity, perhaps it does not matter if there are only six, as there has only been one Guardian at a time in the past, anyway."

"I guess all we need to complete the picture is for Iella also to be seeded!" said Nadiwani

"And Nimida," Adia added, and then the pang of guilt hit her again.

Nimida still did not know Adia was her birth

mother. All this time and each passing day compounded the damage of the secrecy. And the circumstances of how Adia was seeded and that Khon'Tor was her father? How would Nimida handle that? Adia feared it was too much to ask anyone to accept, and no matter how she explained it, Nimida would be crushed by the deception. Of all that Adia had been through, despite her rationale and wanting to protect Nimida, sending her daughter away was her deepest, most unrelenting sorrow. And it grieved her that her daughter would be the one to pay dearly for it.

Acise had not had any further problems, though she was doing as little as possible. Oh'Dar waited on her devotedly, though it came time that he felt he needed to return to Kthama to check on his grandparents.

"Go, I will be fine, I promise you. My mother and Ithua are here," Acise assured him.

Miss Vivian and Ben were thrilled to hear that Oh'Dar was coming back. They had started to feel as if the High Rocks was now their home. Oh'Dar's re-creating a bit of their world in their living quarters had gone a long way in that regard. They both often thought of Oh'Dar's great kindness as they sank into the wonderful soft sheets and mattress he had brought for them. The clock that had marked the time, sitting on the sidebar at Shadow Ridge, now ticked and chimed for them here as it had done there.

"Where is Acise? Did she not come with you?" Miss Vivian said, embracing Oh'Dar. "She will have your child by summer, but I hope we can see her before then."

"I know; I understand. I will stay with you for a few days, and after that, Grandmother, are you up to continuing with the school without me? I would like to get back to Acise before too long."

"Of course. You need to be with her at this time."

Snana and Honovi had been diligently looking after Acise. Having Ithua's presence and advice was comforting to her family, as it was hard to remain objective. They were all glad to see Oh'Dar return to their village, and Chief Is'Taqa asked to speak with him privately when he had spent some time with his life-walker.

"Pajackok and others have been diligent about watching to make sure that the two Waschini who were here have not entered the area again," the Chief said once they were alone.

"I wish I could promise they will never return."

"No man can promise the actions of another, but it is the one called Tucker who is of concern."

"I agree," said Oh'Dar. "I would not drop my guard.

Storis, the man who came looking for my grandparents, is not a bad fellow. But the other one— I have nothing but bad feelings about him. He as much as threatened to tell the authorities that I was sheltered here as a child. I doubt we have seen or heard the last of him."

"I fear that Waschini's intentions toward us; he was directly making threats," replied Chief Is'Taqa. "The People's High Council is a good thing because, more than ever before, we need to band with our other brothers."

Acaraho came in late to find Adia still awake, and An'Kru tucked peacefully in his nest, little hands balled into matching fists. He sat down by Adia as quietly as possible so as not to wake his son.

"I am sorry I am so late; there is so much to attend to. I heard that Notar and his people are settling in well. What an amazing last few days it has been. Are you alright?"

"I am. But I have news," Adia said. "I am seeded again."

Acaraho smiled, "That is wonderful." He looked more closely at her. "Are you not feeling well?"

"I am having some nausea as I did with Nimida and Nootau."

"When will our new offspring arrive?" Acaraho asked.

"Late in the summer, I believe. About the same time as Tehya's."

"Tell me why you do not seem overjoyed."

"I am happy we are having another offspring. It is just that— Oh, how do I say this without sounding like a monster—"

"You do not want to lose any time with An'Kru by having to tend to another offspring so soon after having him."

"Yes. Thank you. We will only have him for seven years. I know I have to keep working on making peace with it, that I cannot let my fears about the future steal the present, but it feels impossible."

"By the time Pan takes him to wherever, he will have many memories established. He will not forget you, no matter how long he is away."

"I know. Nor will he forget you, his father. But, lately, I am besieged with fears and regrets."

"It is a highly emotional time. Saraste'. Perhaps Nadiwani can help you? Or perhaps you should take a trip to the Far High Hills to spend some time with Urilla Wuti?"

"That is a good suggestion, but I would have to take An'Kru."

"I know that would cause a stir. Tehya would love to see you, and she has Arismae. It would be good for you to spend time with her, two mothers who are both seeded again."

"I have to realize An'Kru does not belong just to

you and me. I have to share him with everyone, so I will go to the Far High Hills; thank you, my love."

Then it was Adia's turn to search her mate's face. "You look strained. Is it all the additional responsibilities you have had to undertake, or are you still worried about Nootau?"

"It has been hard, I will admit. That he knows the truth has not changed our feelings for each other—at least it has not changed mine. But it cannot help but affect our relationship in other ways."

"What do you mean? He does not seem angry."

"No, he does not, but I am sure he is. I lied to him. I led him to believe I was his father. We have talked a bit, and he sees that Khon'Tor is not the same person who assaulted you. But there is a space between us now, one that I cannot name, and I do not know if it will ever change. It is not good or bad; it just is what it is."

Adia placed her hand on his cheek, "I know he loves you with an abiding love."

"I know that too. As I love him."

The Far High Hills was lit up with the news that the Healer, Adia, was coming and would be bringing An'Kru with her. Harak'Sar, his mate, Habil, and Urilla Wuti were waiting to greet them. Soon, they were joined by Khon'Tor and Nootau, both with their mates.

Tehya threw her arms around Adia, careful not to squish An'Kru. "I am so glad you have come. Everyone is so very excited, but we will make sure you are not deluged with admirers and questions."

"Thank you. I will make myself available as much as I can, though; I understand the curiosity about An'Kru."

Tehya escorted them to their temporary quarters. "I am glad you are here, but has something prompted your visit?"

Adia looked back to make sure they were alone, "I am seeded, and Acaraho thought I could use a break from my daily responsibilities."

"So we are both seeded! Oh, but Arismae is older than An'Kru. Do you have any reservations about being seeded so soon?"

"It feels like a lot to handle. But of course, the arrival of an offspring is always a blessing, and I know I will have all the help I need."

"Then it is losing time with An'Kru that concerns you? Any mother would understand," Tehya said.

"Only because the Guardian said she will take him from me when he reaches seven. And also, that Nootau said he will go with her to watch over An'Kru."

"I can see how that would put pressure on you. I do not have any sage advice. You already know that you cannot try to force more time into him than there is."

Adia laughed a little. "I suppose that is it. I am

trying to figure out how to squeeze seventeen years into seven. It is not possible, and I must find a way to deal with it, or it will create a frantic and stressful atmosphere for us all."

"Because of Nootau, Iella is also dealing with this revelation. Perhaps you should spend some time together while you are here."

"It seems as if I need to move here for a while." Adia laughed again, this time sounding more relaxed. "Your advice is much appreciated, and I will take it. Now tell me about Arismae and how she is doing."

"Oh, she is wonderful. And Khon'Tor adores her, and she adores him. I am so happy that the offspring I carry is a male, though. I think it will be good for Khon'Tor to have a son. Not to replace Akar'Tor— Oh, you know what I mean."

"I certainly do, and I agree."

"Did you hear that Iella found the lost offspring, U'Kail?"

"Yes, but not the details. Please tell me all about it!"

Tehya relayed the story. When she had finished, she said, "Something has happened to Khon'Tor; he is at peace now. I no longer sense the regret, the guilt, and the pain that has consumed him all the time we have been together. And another thing, odd really, the scars on his back from the jhorallax whipping have started to disappear, and the hair on his back is growing over. Soon he will no longer have to wear the cape to cover them."

Adia thought back to when Pan had left. She remembered the rush of energy that had shot through her and her subsequent exchange with Khon'Tor at the end of the High Council meeting.

"Pan told him to let go of the regrets of the past, and it seems he has truly done that. I am happy for him," Tehya said.

"I am, too, for all of you. And for Larara, who must be beside herself with joy at getting her daughter's son back."

Myrica was doing her best to help the offspring adjust. As the days went by, she started spending less time with him, letting Larara take over. But he still searched the room for her after she had left, and his eyes lit up when she returned.

"This is going to take longer than we thought," Myrica said.

"I know it is hard on you, having to give him up."

"I knew I could not keep him, Larara. Chief Kotori was right; he needs to be among his own people, so it is as it should be. I have no need to hurry back; we will do what is best for him."

CHAPTER 4

Newell Storis had moved into his new office in Wilde Edge. It did not take as long as he had anticipated, and he was relieved to be there, though Snide Tucker's threats were never far from his mind. He had arranged with the Webbs for Grace to start helping him in a few days; he just needed to get a little bit more organized on his own first, but he was so looking forward to seeing her every day. He had moved what he could from his office at Millgrove and had managed to bring his old desk and chair, a gift from his father when he started his law training. Now he unpacked the last few personal things he had, his favorite pen, a journal. He slid them into one of the top drawers along with the crude map he had made behind Tucker's back of the path to the Brothers' village.

There was a knock on the door, and Storis opened it to see Ned standing there.

"I came to invite you to dinner."

Storis accepted gratefully, and soon after, there was another knock. Presumably, Ned had forgotten to mention something.

But it was Snide Tucker. "I see you are finally here."

"Go away, Tucker; I'm busy, and our business with each other is done."

"It's just starting. I told you to find a way to keep me happy before I decide to go to the sheriff."

"I have learned a lot about you in the few short days I have been back. Your reputation has caught up with you. If I had known of it ahead of time, I would never have hired you—for anything."

"Compliments will get you nowhere. Now, when can I collect my first payment?"

"I am not paying you anything. If you continue doing this, I will bring action against you for blackmail."

"Fine with me, just a faster way to make it all public," Tucker said, now leaning against the door frame.

"I said get out," and Storis moved menacingly toward Tucker, who righted himself and stepped back.

Before the door could shut, Tucker tipped his weathered and grimy hat at the lawyer.

Storis was pleased to see the Webb house come into view. He knocked at the door and was greeted by Buster skidding around the corner, barking in delight. Storis reached down to pet him and then straightened up as the door opened.

"Well, hello, Newell. I see Ned delivered our invitation," said Mrs. Webb.

"Thank you. I could never miss any of your cooking."

She smiled. "Well, Grace is just as good a cook as I am."

"I am looking forward to having her work for me," Storis said.

"So is she."

They were soon seated at the dinner table, and conversation turned to Ned's apprenticeship with Mr. Clement.

"He said I will make a great animal doctor," Ned said.

"Will you move away from Wilde Edge, then?" asked Storis.

"Oh, no. I don't think so. Right now, the town doesn't need two animal doctors, but until he retires, I can still help Mr. Clement with his workload, to be sure."

"Ned helped treat one of the Morgan horses earlier," said Mr. Webb proudly.

Storis's face went blank. "What? The Morgan horses are still here?"

"Grayson was supposed to take them back with

him when he came to get the supplies he ordered, but he seemed upset about something and left quickly. We just assumed he had decided not to take them yet. I suppose we should have asked him about them; oh dear! I hope he won't think we were trying to keep them," she added.

"Oh, no, nothing of the kind, I am sure," Storis stammered. "No doubt he will be back for them at some time. I would not worry about it. He will be grateful you have taken such good care of them."

Storis set his napkin in his lap and tried to compose himself. Rebel and Shining Rose. The two Morgan horses were *still* here. Rebel was reported to have killed Miss Vivian and Ben, and there had been sketches of that horse put up along with the posters about the Morgan's funeral arrangements. He could easily be identified by anyone who knew a thing about the quality of the Shadow Ridge horses. With Tucker threatening to raise questions about the graves, Rebel's presence here would be damning.

"Which brings up something I need to talk with you about, Mr. Storis," said Mr. Webb.

"Please, call me Newell. We agreed to that, did we not?"

"Newell, then. That business associate of yours showed up here about a week ago while you were still in Millgrove."

"What did he come here for?" Storis could feel his heart starting to pound.

"The oddest thing; he asked for permission to court Grace."

"*What*?" Storis couldn't stop himself.

"I told him no, of course. He seemed unhappy about it and unhappy to hear that Grace would be working with you soon. I'm sorry now that I told him anything about it, but that came out before he asked about Grace," Mr. Webb explained.

Storis looked at Grace, who seemed undisturbed by all this.

"Maybe having you work for me is not such a good idea. I regret having anything to do with Snide Tucker, and my association with him now connects him to all of you."

"Oh, now, I don't know if that is necessary," said Mrs. Webb. "Grace is excited about working with you, aren't you, dear?"

"Oh, yes, Mr. Storis, I am not afraid of Snide Tucker if that is what you are concerned about."

"Ned can walk her into town and come back for her if you are concerned," suggested Mr. Webb. "We don't know the man, but surely he would not do anything to harm her? Is that what you're afraid of?"

"I really don't know," said Storis. "The more contact I have with him, the worse his nature reveals itself to be. I am not sure what I would put past him. I think we all need to stay as far away from him as possible."

"Well, enough of this distressing talk. Ned will accompany Grace, so now let's talk about something cheerful," said Nora, and she changed the subject to the upcoming warmer weather and their plans for a robust planting this year thanks to the Baxter boys, whom Grayson had hired to help.

When Storis returned to town, he went directly to the drinking establishment where he had first met Tucker.

"Where is he?"

Everyone turned to look at him.

"Who?" asked the barkeeper.

"Snide Tucker. He's always in here; where is he?"

"He hasn't been in today. For the past few days, actually."

"I overheard him say he was headed for Mill-grove," someone else said.

The Morgan farm. Tucker had left for Shadow Ridge.

Mrs. Thomas was told there was a man there to see her, and she had him escorted in. He told her his name was Zachariah Tucker.

"Ma'am, I heard you might be needing some workers here?"

She looked him up and down. Tall, a bit unkempt. Something about him unsettled her. "I do not know that we do, sir, I am sorry to say. You might try the Clemington farm up the way. They sometimes take in temporary help."

"Oh, are you sure you don't have anything, Ma'am? I am good with horses."

Her son had told her that he could use a few more hands. So against her better judgment, Mrs. Thomas sent him down to the stables and told him to ask for Mac.

"Your mother, Mrs. Thomas, sent me down here to see you. I'm looking for some work for a while. I'm a hard worker; I won't let you down. Name's Zachariah Tucker."

"We could use some more help. What can you do?"

"Whatever you want. Feed 'em, brush 'em down, muck the stables, break in the colts and fillies. Been around horses all my life."

"Doesn't pay much. Mostly room and board," Mac said.

"That's fine with me. Other than a little drinkin' money, room and board would be fine."

"Alright. Follow that path over there." Mac pointed. "That'll take you to the bunkroom. My brother, Daniel, he's down there. He'll show you where to put your things and tell you what you need to know."

Tucker took a good look around as he was walking down to the bunkhouse. It was an amazing piece of acreage. He could not tell how big the place was, but from the looks of the main house, the stables he had just left, and the pastures spreading as far as the eye could see, the former housekeeper, Mrs. Thomas, was now apparently very wealthy, just as the Morgans had been. It was exactly as he had suspected.

"Name's Zack Tucker. Lookin' for Daniel Thomas."

"I'm Dan Thomas. I assume you're here to hire on. Let me see your hands."

Tucker held them out, and the man turned them over several times.

"What you lookin' for?" Tucker asked.

"Calluses. Lots of people stop by here looking for work who have never worked a day in their life. Different if they're twelve years old, which you're obviously not. We'll give you two weeks to see if you work out, and then we'll decide whether to keep you on. Fair?"

Hopefully, two weeks would be enough time for Tucker to do what he had come to do. "Fair enough."

"Toss your stuff down and hop on the wagon. One of the boys here will take care of your horse, and I'll show you where the bunkhouse is later. We're repairing the fencing on the back eighty acres. You'll be expected to work alongside the others without my prodding you, so pay attention to where it is."

Tucker understood the cool treatment he was being given. Even newly rich people like the Thomases had to be careful who they let around. It then occurred to him that he was probably going to be watched closely and would have to bide his time a bit before putting his plan into action. He hoped two weeks would be enough.

At the dinner table, Mrs. Thomas asked her sons how the new man was doing.

"So far, so good, though he's older than we usually hire. Have to give it more time," Dan said. "He worked hard today, but most do at first. We'll see how long he lasts."

"Something about him didn't sit right with me, but I know you need the help," Mrs. Thomas said.

"We'll keep an eye on him," Mac assured her.

The stable hands were given one day off a week to take care of personal business. When Tucker had worked nearly a week, Mac told him that the following day would be his day off.

The next morning, Tucker ate with the other men before saddling up his hired horse and riding into Millgrove.

His first stop was the bank, where he inquired

about opening an account. The banker looked at him, thinking it odd that a working man such as this one appeared would be opening a bank account when most lived hand to mouth.

"How much would you want to deposit?" the banker asked.

"I'm just askin', not sayin' I'm ready yet. Is there a lawyer in town?"

"Used to be. Gentleman named Newell Storis. Just moved away—only a week or so ago, in fact. Pity; he was a great lawyer and a good man."

"Why did he leave?"

"Not really sure," the banker lied. "If you decide to do business, come on back. Bank hours are on the door."

Next, Tucker went to the General Store and tried to strike up a conversation with the man behind the counter there. He got about as far as he had with the banker. Apparently, Storis had generated a lot of loyalty, or else people in Millgrove just were not into gossip. At least not with a stranger.

A few days later, Mac and Dan went to Mrs. Thomas.

Mac spoke first. "I heard the new man, Tucker, has been asking questions around town about Newell Storis, for one. What his connection to Mrs. Morgan's old lawyer is, I can't imagine."

"Maybe we should let him go," Mrs. Thomas said.

"And today," Dan added, "Tucker was asking about the family gravesite. Said he saw it up on the hill and was just wondering. Problem is, you can't see it from anywhere he has been working. Something's up, and I don't like it."

"Then pay him, thank him for his service, and give him two days' bonus to get him on his way."

"We'll give him an escort off Shadow Ridge, too," Dan decided. "And tell him nicely not to come back."

Tucker was angry but managed to contain himself. He rode off into Millgrove and took a room at the local boarding house. Then he asked where the drinking establishment was. He realized it was where he should have gone in the first place. People had looser tongues in a place like that.

He slammed his coin down on the bar. "Shot of whiskey."

"So, you here looking for work?" the bartender conversationally asked as he set a glass down in front of Tucker.

"No, just passing through," Tucker said. "Say, isn't this the town where the Morgans live? The rich people with the horses?"

"Used to be; they died a few months ago. Sad story. Mrs. Morgan had just married old Ben Jenkins, who was hired by her husband when they first established Shadow Ridge. After Mr. Morgan died—a long time after, mind you—Mrs. Morgan took up with Ben. And not long after that, they were both killed in an accident. One of their prize horses kicked and trampled them both to death. Hit everyone really hard, even the town folks. Many of them are still grieving."

Tucker drained his glass. "I'll have another one." He figured as long as he was drinking, the bartender would keep talking. "So who took over the farm? Sons?"

"No. The Morgans had two sons, but one is in prison for murdering the other. After Mrs. Morgan and Ben were killed, there was only a grandson left. It's a tragic story, really. The Morgans were stand up folks. After the son was jailed, not an enemy in the world."

"So what happened to the farm?"

"Shadow Ridge? The grandson left it to the housekeeper—Mrs. Thomas is her name. Unusual, but I suppose it was her home for nearly all her adult life. She's looked after that house since she was young. Her sons help her run it now. Why're you so interested in them?"

"Oh, not really," Tucker said. "Just passin' time. Now tell me, where's the sheriff's office?"

A few weeks had passed. Whatever Tucker was up to, Storis knew it was no good. He was of half a mind to go after him but realized that, whatever Tucker was up to, he would find out soon enough. The lawyer had spoken with the local banker and had the assurance of money coming in soon, so he tried to keep his mind off Tucker, focusing on setting up his business. And Grace.

The more he was around her, the more he was drawn to her. One afternoon, while Grace was working, he went to the Webbs' house.

"Why, Newell, what a nice surprise. And in the middle of the day." Mrs.Webb wiped her hands on her apron. "Is Grace alright?"

Storis took his hat off and held it in front of him. "Yes, yes, she's fine; I didn't mean to concern you. Is your husband around? I would like to speak with him."

"Yes, of course, please sit down; I'll tell him. He's sitting on the back porch, resting his back."

After a while, Mr. Webb entered the sitting room, and standing up, Storis cleared his throat. Mrs. Webb left the men to their business.

"I am sorry to disturb your rest, Matthew. But there is something I would like to speak with you about while Grace is not around. The only way I could think to do it was while she is in town at the office."

"What can I do for you?" Mr. Webb asked.

Storis cleared his throat. "I know I'm older than you might want for your daughter and haven't yet fully established my business here, but I promise you it is just a matter of time as I already have at least one client arranged. I would like to ask your permission to court Grace, if you can see your way to it."

"I know Grace likes you. And I believe you are a good man and would do well by my daughter."

Mr. Webb sighed. "I admit your age bothers me a bit, and Grace is barely of age. But on the other hand, there are no other acceptable suitors around here. As long as you promise to provide for her if she outlives you, and if she agrees, then I will allow it."

"I am hoping she will accept me and that we will also one day have lots of children to watch over her after I am gone."

Matthew stood up and shook Storis's hand.

"I will do right by her, I promise. You'll see," the attorney assured him.

Mrs. Webb had been trying to overhear from the other room but was not able to make out the entire conversation.

When her husband later told her that Mr. Storis would be courting Grace, she clasped her hands together and smiled from ear to ear. "Oh, my!"

At quitting time, Ned picked up his sister as he had done faithfully every day on which she worked for

Storis. Instead of walking there to fetch her, this time he had the wagon as he had to bring some things back from town. He snapped the reins, and they were on their way, though it would be a short trip home.

"Your boss stopped by the house today; did you know that?" Ned said.

'No, when?"

"This afternoon. I saw him leaving as I was coming back into town."

"He left in the middle of the day and didn't say anything when he came back. I wonder what that was about," Grace mused.

"Could be nothing," Ned said. "Or—"

Grace playfully slapped him on the arm. "Stop it! If you know something, you have to tell me!"

"Oh, come on, sis. Don't you see how he looks at you? And how upset he was when Pa told him that Tucker had asked to court you. He's sweet on you. I wouldn't be surprised if Mr. Storis didn't ask to court you."

"Do you think so? Oh, Ned, don't get my hopes up!"

"Oh, I'm sorry. Maybe I shouldn't have said anything. We'll know soon enough." He urged the horses faster. "Hiya!"

Grace jumped off the wagon almost before it had come to a stop. She shoved the gate open and flew into the house. "Mama, Mama, Ned said Mr. Storis stopped by the house today!"

Nora put her arm around her very excited daughter and said, "Calm down, honey. Your father will tell you all about it at supper time. He is resting; let's try not to wake him."

Grace changed clothes and went out to do her evening stable chores, working diligently to try to keep her mind off the lawyer's visit and to manage her hopes.

Finally, they were all seated around the kitchen table, where Ned winked at Grace.

After her father said the blessing, she could hold back no longer. "Papa, I know Mr. Storis stopped by today. Please tell me."

"I suggest you start learnin' to call him Newell, honey. He asked if he could court you, and I said yes. That is, if you're agreeable to it."

Grace jumped up from her chair and flung her arms around her father's neck. "Oh, thank you. Thank you." She unwrapped herself from her father and embraced her mother, too. "I'm so happy, Mama! He's a good man. I know you believe that, or you wouldn't let him court me. But the more I am around him, the more I think of him. He reminds me of you, Papa. Honorable and fair."

"We are happy for you. Just take it slow, please," said her father.

"But Papa, he's not getting any younger," Grace quipped, and they all laughed together. Little Buster wagged his tail furiously from his place under the table.

No one was surprised to learn that Newell Storis, the new lawyer in town, was courting Grace Webb. Neither did anyone seem particularly bothered by the age difference. In his defense, the man looked much younger than his years, and those who had seen the couple together thought they suited each other. If there was talk about her working for him, it didn't make it back to the Webbs.

Grace sat next to Storis at the Webb dinner table a few nights later. She kept shyly looking at him. And when she did catch his eye, he smiled back. She had never felt awkward around him before, yet now it was somehow—different. She certainly didn't feel like his employee any longer. She was now a woman about to let herself fall the rest of the way in love with a man.

"There's a barn dance at the Baxters' this Saturday," Mrs. Webb said to her husband. "What do you say we all go; we could use some fun. With your back as it is, I wouldn't be expecting you to dance, but we could still all be together. Newell, too, of course."

"Sounds like fun. Does everyone want to go?" Mr. Webb asked.

"Yes, please," Grace said. "Ned, you want to go, don't you?" Her eyes pleaded with her brother.

Ned chuckled, "Of course. The Baxters have some handsome daughters, as I remember."

"Oh, my, now don't all my children go off and start their own families right away," Mrs. Webb exclaimed.

"So much for taking it slow," Mr. Webb said under his breath.

Grace was so excited about the dance that she couldn't sleep. She went through her dresses—there were only a few—and in the morning, asked her mother to help her pick out the best one.

On the day of the dance, she washed her hair, pinched her cheeks, and tried to quell her nerves as she waited for the rest of her family to finish getting ready. She had picked out her favorite, a simple dress made from rose-colored cloth, which everyone seemed to think complimented her fair coloring. She and her brother both had curly blonde hair, which suited her fine, but which Ned hated.

Soon they were loaded on the wagon together and heading over to the Baxters'. As they approached, even from a distance, they could hear the fiddles in the barn. The lights glowing inside and the sounds of the laughter amid the music raised everyone's spirits.

Once inside, Grace scanned the place, looking for Storis. Her heart fell when she couldn't find him.

Then she heard his voice say her name and twirled around. She practically bumped into the lawyer, who had come up behind her. She found herself looking up into his warm brown eyes.

"I'm sorry," he smiled, "I didn't mean to startle you."

"Oh, no, no, it's fine. I was just looking for you. My family is over there," and she pointed to a row of hay bales where her mother, father, and brother were seated.

"Do you want to dance?" Storis asked, offering her his hand.

"Why not?' she said and put her hand into his.

Within moments they were dancing with the others, sliding around the barn floor in a circle. Grace felt his strong frame supporting her, leading her gently yet expertly.

"I had no idea you enjoyed dancing," she said, loudly enough for him to hear over the music and laughter.

"I don't remember enjoying it so much, until now," he laughed.

"I want to ask you something, but I do not want to be forward," Grace said.

"It has not stopped you in the past," Storis smiled.

"I know," Grace smiled back. "But now things seem different, somehow."

"I understand. Please go on."

"Why have you never married? In all these years, I mean?"

"I know it seems strange for a man to be a bachelor this long, but I have always been consumed with my work. Long hours and dedication don't leave time to meet women. And the kind of woman I wanted just didn't seem to exist. Until now."

Grace had to shore up her strength not to melt into his arms in front of everyone.

"It's hot in here," she said as the music wound down.

"Really? I didn't notice."

"You're teasing me," she said.

"Because I love to see you smile. And yes, I am."

"Papa wants a long courtship," she whispered.

"I know. I'll do my best to hold out as long as I can," he answered.

Grace blushed and smiled all the more.

Her parents joined them. "What are you two laughing about so much over here?" Grace's mother asked. "Come and get something to drink." She glanced across the room. "Look at Ned with the Baxters' daughter, Alicia. Don't they make a fine couple?"

"One minute you're worrying about them leaving home, and the next, you're matchmaking. For heaven's sake, woman," Mr. Webb joked.

"I don't think Ned is in any rush to settle down, Mama," Grace said. "He's very serious about finishing his studies with Mr. Clement."

"I just look forward to the day when you are all settled, happy, safe, secure. That's all."

Grace gave her mother a kiss on the cheek. "I know, Mama. We all know that."

The evening wore to an end, and people started drifting away. Storis said goodnight to the Webbs. "I hope you all have an enjoyable Sunday. I will see you on Monday at work, Grace."

"You're welcome to Sunday dinner, of course," offered Mrs. Webb.

"Thank you, but unfortunately, I have business to conduct that will tie me up the whole day."

Grace tried to hide her disappointment and wondered what he could be doing on a Sunday that would keep him busy all day.

CHAPTER 5

Following the Guardian's instructions, Nootau began working with Urilla Wuti even more earnestly. Whatever his role would be with An'Kru and with Khon'Tor in ushering in the Age of Light, he wanted to be ready. Iella was still struggling with his announcement that he would be leaving with An'Kru and the six Guardians when Pan came to take them away.

Nootau and Iella had not been paired long enough for her to be worried about not being seeded, but because the others were, she did have a pang of concern.

"Saraste', pressure is not going to help anything," Nootau tried to console her. "I know you do not want me to leave with An'Kru, and perhaps you are feeling a need to start having our offspring right away so I can build memories with them, in case I—"

"Oh, no. Do not even say it. Never suggest you might not come back. As it is, it is all I can handle to accept your leaving. Who knows how long you might be gone. I pray that the confrontation, whatever that is, will happen here and not wherever she is taking you."

"Pan said that as An'Kru grows, he will draw more from the vortex, and that pull is what would alert the rebel Sarnonn to his existence. So from that, I assume he will be using the power of the vortex to fight them. I explained how the twelve Sarnonn Guardians were created when the Sarnonn opened Kthama Minor, and the outpouring of the vortex charged what we are now calling the generator stones. The twelve Sarnonn were standing in front of those stones, so I believe it is all tied together."

Iella's eyes were downcast.

"Please," said Nootau. "Talk to your aunt. Ask her to help you with this."

Urilla Wuti knew what was bothering Iella before she even spoke. The Healer had seen and felt Iella's reaction at the High Council meeting when Nootau announced he would leave with Pan and the others. They would both have to trust the Order of Functions with the one they loved.

"If you keep focusing on it," she advised Iella, "it

will steal your happiness in the present. And there is nothing you can do about it, you know that."

"You are right; it is consuming me. I do not know how to let go of it."

"You are focusing on a future that is only in your thoughts. You are scaring yourself with your— musings. Nootau leaving with Pan is not necessarily a bad thing, but you are making it so with your thoughts. Do you think the Guardian is not capable of keeping your mate safe?"

Iella looked up to meet Urilla Wuti's gaze. "Thank you. I will think about it. You are right; I am scaring myself with my fear of losing Nootau."

"Every relationship we have in this realm ends at some point. Either through our own death or that of our Saraste'. Do not waste your time with him now by anticipating the day when you will no longer walk Etera together. You do not know when that will be. And take comfort that whatever happens, you will be together in the hereafter."

"The hereafter?"

"That is a Waschini word I learned from Oh'Dar. They seem to be seeping into my conversations lately."

"Is the hereafter the same as when we return to the Great Spirit?" Iella asked.

"Yes. The same concept, but different sounds. You have been given an amazing ability. What you did in finding U'Kail changed everything for Larara. Do not lose sight of your own path by worrying about what might never happen. The Guardian said the abilities of all the Healers would be augmented, and I will need your help in assisting the other Healers to discover what their new abilities are as they manifest."

That evening when they were alone, Nootau said to Iella, "You look more relaxed. Did you speak with your aunt?"

"Yes. And, as usual, she had wise advice. I feel better, more grounded. How is your work with her going?"

"Well, I think. We are working on my ability to enter the Dream State. I met my mother there once. It may have been a fluke, but I hope not."

"I doubt it was a fluke; the Guardian said you have greatness in you. I am sure that is part of what, deep within you, is yearning to be born."

"Urilla Wuti told me that she and my mother once thought the Corridor would be the conduit to making Urilla Wuti's vision of long-distance communication between our people possible. Now she thinks it is the Dream World where that will happen."

"I have never been to the Corridor," Iella said wistfully.

"Neither have I. Perhaps someday Urilla Wuti will take you there. In the meantime, what we are both doing is very important work."

"Yes, no pressure, though," Iella said, and they both laughed.

Adia was enjoying her visit at the Far High Hills, though she was swamped with people wanting to see An'Kru and hold him. She had to limit this, as he needed to rest, and she, too, could not bear up under the constant attention.

Lying in bed one night, she started thinking about meeting Nootau in the Dream World. Just as she had, he had discovered the ability to enter the Dream World without any preamble. She remembered how, one night, she found herself in Acaraho's quarters and thereafter had learned how to enter that realm at will. As she replayed in her mind each visit to him, an idea suddenly popped into her head. *I have to tell Urilla Wuti about this.*

The next day, when Adia had finished telling Urilla Wuti about her flash of insight, the older Healer was equally intrigued.

"That is ingenious. I think you may have discovered how the Mothoc bred with the Brothers. At least, part of it."

"The rest is not that hard to figure out."

Urilla Wuti thought a moment. "Yes, you are right. There are more questions, of course, and we will probably never know all the details that went into accomplishing it, but this may well be a solution for us. We just need the cooperation of some Waschini."

"Oh, yes," Adia said. "Well, that could be a problem."

"But we are further along than ever before, and that is a great blessing! It would be easier to test out your theory with one of the People and a Sarnonn—as with Kalli, Haan's daughter by Hakani. There are no others of her kind. Getting the cooperation of the Waschini seems impossible, and we cannot do this Without Their Consent, as it appears the Ancients must have done."

"We need to talk to Acaraho, Haan, and the researchers about it before we seriously consider anything."

Each time Acaraho looked at Nootau, the pain hit him like a blow to the chest. This offspring he had loved since the day he was born now knew that they did not share the same bloodline and that his life until now had been built on a lie.

It was Acaraho who had stood outside waiting for news of his birth. It was Acaraho who had provided for him, taught him how to hunt, how to locate and follow the magnetic lines that ran deep within Etera. There were many nights they had lain outside with Oh'Dar, tracing the patterns of the stars moving overhead across the night sky. In every way that mattered, except one, Nootau was his son.

Though they had not talked about it since, he held fast to Nootau's words to him in the Great Chamber, *I am and always will be your son. No power on Etera or anywhere in creation can ever change that.*

Acaraho missed Nootau, Adia, and An'Kru. He had made plans to visit them at the Far High Hills before too long and see if Adia was ready to return home.

The next High Council meeting was several months away. When they met again, Acaraho was hoping to learn if the Waschini harassment of the Brothers was increasing. He was very concerned for their welfare. The Guardian had said that they were the teachers the white people needed so they could learn how to live in harmony with the Great Spirit. He could not see how the Waschini would ever listen, though, considering how they were already treating the Brothers.

In addition, the People and the Sarnonn, working with the Brothers, were somehow key to saving Etera from the negativity being ushered in by the Waschini and the rebel Mothoc. Their futures were tied together, just as their past had been.

In the meantime, Acaraho was focused on looking after Adia and An'Kru, and restoring routine life to Kthama. Miss Vivian had taken over the schooling, and Ben continued to work with the researchers on understanding the Wall of Records.

One day, when the most advanced male Whitespeak student, Dilmm, was with Ben and able to translate, Acaraho asked the Waschini how the work was going.

"It is slow as there is so much information there, but there are definitely patterns. We are at the point now, though, where it is difficult to piece the pictures together with the gap in recording that occurred once the place was closed off by the sealing of Kht'shWea so many eons ago."

"Those records are on the walls of the community just up the river from us," Acaraho explained.

"I thought that was a small cave system."

"It is, the living area. But there is a long tunnel, too small to be used for living space, which was dedicated to keeping the pairing records from them up to now."

"It must be very long; that is quite a few generations to keep track of."

"I have never seen it, but I hear it is. Would you like to visit it?"

"Absolutely. But Bidzel and Yuma'qia should also come."

Acaraho made arrangements, and soon Ben, Bidzel, and Yuma'qia were being welcomed by Lor'Kahn, Kurak'Kahn's brother, who was acting as Leader. Acaraho had also brought Dilmm along to translate.

Lor'Kahn led them down a long tunnel, which was dark and very narrow for the People to negotiate. Fortunately, Ben was not claustrophobic as the walls brushed the shoulders of those with him, and they had to turn sideways in some places in order to pass through. Finally, it opened up into a slightly larger area that was surprisingly well lit for its placement. Ahead, the tunnel seemed to go on indefinitely. Ben looked up to see ventilation tunnels, but there was still barely enough light for him to discern the markings, which covered nearly every bit of the available space.

They stood and studied the walls for a moment. Then Bidzel explained the sequence in which the markings were laid out.

"I am not sure I will be of much help," said Ben. "I can barely see in here."

"We could bring in fluorite or torches," Lor'Kahn offered.

"Not sure about torches; they use a lot of breathing air," Ben said, "even with the ventilation shafts overhead."

"Probably true," said Yuma'qia. "It is a confined

space, and we have never had the need to test them out in here, either."

"How is your research going?" asked Lor'Kahn.

"Slowly," said Bidzel. "We occasionally have a breakthrough, but have we found any answers to the inbreeding problem facing us? No, we have not yet."

"I can make some drawings of the last generation recorded in the Wall of Records," suggested Ben. "You can bring them back here and compare them to where these start out. Maybe that will help us connect the two."

The four returned to the High Rocks and gave their report to Acaraho. At the end, Bidzel told him that they needed the Sarnonn's pairing information, which now also included Notar's group."

"That presents a problem," Acaraho said. "As you will remember, the Sarnonn did not keep to the ways of Moc'Tor and Straf'Tor. Haan said their breeding has been indiscriminate, though we do not know about Notar's group. And whatever records they may have kept are most likely carved on the walls of their old communities."

Ben shook his head. "I do not mean to be pessimistic, but it is starting to feel as if it may be impossible to put this puzzle together."

"If that is so," Acaraho said, "and I can understand your saying that, then we must find another means by which to keep the blood of the People and the Sarnonn on Etera."

Ben was glad to be out of the dark, narrow tunnels and back home with Miss Vivian. Each night they sank into their warm, soft mattress and discussed the day's events. He shared with her his concerns over ever being able to piece together a plan to safely move forward the breeding program for the People and the Sarnonn.

"What we need is a miracle," confessed Ben.

The next morning, he climbed the soaring scaffolding in the Wall of Records with one of Miss Vivian's precious quills and some equally precious blank paper to copy the figures for Bidzel and Yuma'qia to take back to the Far High Hills. He squinted to try to see a little further up as he wanted to start at the top and work his way down.

He put one of his feet up on a support railing to hoist himself higher. He looked up, and moving too quickly, had a sudden attack of dizziness. He heard shouting below as he lost his balance and slipped from the platform.

One of his legs caught in a railing, which stopped his fall to the rock floor below, but the sickening snap that filled the chamber meant his leg had been broken.

Yuma'qia and Bidzel both rushed over to Ben,

who was conscious but clearly in pain, suspended by one of his legs which was bent in an unnatural position. Blood dripped from a deep gash down his thigh, where it had made contact with the wooden railing. Carefully, they freed him and lowered him to the sandy floor.

Bidzel called out for help, and within moments there was a group waiting to deliver aid. Haan came in a moment later and knelt down next to Ben. Someone had set out immediately for Kthama to tell Acaraho that Ben had fallen, was bleeding, and had broken his leg.

Ben groaned and tried to clutch his leg, but that made the pain worse. It felt like a long time before Acaraho and Nadiwani showed up. Nadiwani had a straight, flat branch with her and a long swath of hide.

Haan reached down and carefully supported Ben so Nadiwani could move his leg into a more natural angle. Ben's cries of pain echoed in the cavernous chamber. Once his leg was reset, Nadiwani used the branch to support it, and placing the soft material over the wound, secured it by wrapping the long piece of hide around his leg. When she was done, Nadiwani sent Mapiya ahead to find Miss Vivian and asked Haan to carry Ben back to the Healer's Quarters at Kthama.

Mapiya found Miss Vivian in the schoolroom with the offspring and some of the adults who were learning Whitespeak.

"Miss Vivian, school is going to have to end early today. Nadiwani sent me to fetch you."

"What's wrong?" Miss Vivian asked, her voice full of alarm.

"Your mate slipped off the platform in the Wall of Records, and his leg is broken. Haan is bringing him to the Healer's Quarters. Nadiwani is treating him, and Acaraho is sending someone to tell Oh'Dar."

Nadiwani had cleaned and re-wrapped Ben's leg until it was as stable as anyone could make it. She let out a sigh of relief when Oh'Dar arrived; he would be a comfort to Ben and would be able to speak with him more eloquently than the rough Whitespeak anyone else was capable of.

She stepped back while Oh'Dar also took a look at Ben's leg.

"We are lucky it wasn't worse," Oh'Dar told his grandfather. "If you'd tumbled all the way down, you could have been killed, but we still have to worry about infection. And for future reference, no more crawling on the scaffolding, please. No matter how important you think it is, it is not worth getting hurt —or worse."

Ben clasped Oh'Dar's hand. "Will I be able to walk again? Nadiwani thinks it is possible."

Oh'Dar looked over at his grandmother, who was sitting on the edge of a small boulder and trying not to cry.

"I don't know any more than Nadiwani does. It is too soon to tell. As she explained, from the way it is swelling, your knee was also damaged. Luckily there is still snow on the ground; we can apply some to keep the swelling down, but the knee isn't a simple lever like the elbow; it is far more complicated. It will be a while before you can even put weight on it. And you may have a concussion. You will need to be watched closely for any sign of complications."

He continued, "Nadiwani and I will try to stabilize your leg by wrapping it as tight as we dare to give it some support, but that gash is worrisome. She will be treating it very capably, and I will stay here for a while until I am confident you understand your limitations."

Miss Vivian said, "Does he have to stay here? Can he come back to our room with me?"

"He can, but you will need help."

Because of Ben's age, Oh'Dar knew it could take a great deal more time than usual to heal. He was torn between being there with his grandparents and being at the village with Acise. However, it was still some time before Acise would deliver, and right now, his grandparents needed him. Though the offspring and many of the adults were learning Waschini, being the only other of their kind at Kthama, he knew his presence comforted them.

"You need to get on with your life, son," Ben said, propped up in bed one evening. "We will be fine here."

"I am sure you would be, but I feel better being here with you, just another day or so. I can't help but worry about you when I am away. Are you still glad you came?"

Miss Vivian looked at Ben before answering, "I am. Oh, there are things I miss, of course. The delightful smells in the house from Mrs. Thomas's cooking. The warm breeze wafting through the open windows at night, fluttering the lace curtains. And butter!" She laughed.

Oh'Dar stopped for a moment and looked at his grandmother. Without her former diet rich in bread and butter and home-cooked treats, she had lost weight. Ben had always been trim from the physical demands of his job.

"I know it is hard for you to get outside in the winter. The paths are somewhat difficult, and the snow and ice make them dangerous," Oh'Dar commiserated. "But warm weather is just around the corner."

"And soon, there will be a grandbaby to love!" Miss Vivian added. "I am looking forward to spring

—I hope I will be able to help the children with the spring planting. I love the smell of the damp soil, and I want to experience the pleasure of pushing seeds down into the rich ground."

She sat on the bed next to Ben. "The children here are so delightful. So inquisitive, so full of wonder, so respectful. They are clearly loved, and they are always offering to help us whenever they can, bringing us second helpings or carrying things for us. Frankly, I feel like a celebrity!"

"And you, Ben?" Oh'Dar asked.

"I admit I miss working with the horses, and I miss the camaraderie of the farmhands. We had a great crew. The nights laughing around the campfire. Playing cards in the bunker, slapping that winning hand down on the table!"

Oh'Dar was starting to feel that perhaps Ben now regretted coming.

Then Ben added, "But there are exquisite pleasures here too. Don't get me wrong. Living a slower life that is not focused on tomorrow's plans, settling in at night with your grandmother, here in the bed you brought us. Being allowed into this incredible existence, a life we could never have dreamed of. Living among these beautiful souls, who are so closely wedded in service to all life."

"And most of all, being closer to you, Grayson," Miss Vivian added. She got up and came over to stand in front of Oh'Dar. She placed her hand on the side of his face. "All the gains outweigh any of the losses. We knew our life would be different when we decided to come with you. We have no regrets."

Oh'Dar was relieved. But in his heart, he also knew that their sacrifices had been great. And he knew all too well the loneliness of being the only Waschini among the People, and his heart ached that there was nothing he could do to ease that loneliness, the innate longing to be among one's own kind.

Knowing that everything had been done that could be for Ben, Acaraho decided it was time to do some visiting himself and check on Adia and An'Kru.

He was given a warm welcome by Harak'Sar and Urilla Wuti.

"We are so glad to have you here, Adik'Tar," said the Leader of the Deep Valley. "Your mate and your son have been quite the attraction. I suspect she is ready to return home as popularity can be quite exhausting."

"I am sure. How is Khon'Tor doing?" Acaraho asked.

"He and Tehya are fine, and hopefully, now things will settle down. Tehya's parents are overjoyed at her being seeded again. And it is a new chance for Khon'Tor to have the son he deserves after the tragic experience with Akar'Tor."

Pain went through Acaraho's core; he knew that Akar'Tor was not the only offspring Khon'Tor had.

There was Nootau, and most likely, the abandoned offspring, U'Kail, now called Ahanu, was also his. But these truths would benefit no one and hurt many. Some wrongs could never be righted, and in those cases, the truth had to remain in the shadows.

"Khon'Tor seems different," Harak'Sar said. "Content. Settled. He is training my son, Brondin'Sar."

"Your son will benefit greatly from Khon'Tor's wisdom and knowledge."

Harak'Sar then led Acaraho through the tunnels to Adia, who rushed into her mate's arms.

"Oh, what a wonderful surprise."

Acaraho wrapped her in his strong embrace and relished the feeling of her in his arms.

"An'Kru is with Tehya for the day, so Urilla Wuti, Iella, and I could get some work done together," Adia said. "I was just about to go and find them."

"I do not wish to interrupt. I want to talk to Khon'Tor, so if you are working, I shall search him out. Are you almost ready to come home, though?"

"Yes. In the morning, if that suits you."

"Good, I would like to get back sooner than later. There was an accident; Ben fell from the scaffolding in the Wall of Records."

Adia let out a gasp.

"He broke his leg, and his knee is damaged too. He also has a nasty gash, so it will take him some time to recover. But it could have been so much worse. Oh'Dar was staying to keep them company for a few days."

Adia was glad to be home. She went immediately to Ben and Miss Vivian to check on them. After admiring Nadiwani's work, she stayed and chatted awhile before retrieving An'Kru from Nadiwani, who had taken watching over him from Miss Vivian since Ben needed her care. He was the happiest little offspring and smiled and gurgled at everyone.

But Adia still marveled at how he attracted the forest creatures to him every time they were outside. Not only the squirrels, ground chippers, and rabbits, but also the birds of the air and even the fish in the waters. They all kept a respectable distance, so it did not really present a problem, but it was an oddity. Adia attributed it all to the powerful life force that An'Kru embodied, which Pan said would grow as he got older. While they were away, she had realized that An'Kru's abilities were similar to Iella's. The creatures he attracted were small, just as he was, and Adia wondered if as he grew, bigger creatures would join them. She also wondered if, in the future, An'Kru would be able to communicate with them as Iella did.

Longing to see the beauty of the Great River, she bundled An'Kru up and took him down to sit by the shallows.

"I love you so much," Adia whispered to him as she cuddled him and nuzzled his neck. "I will be the best mother I can to you, just as I was with the others; each offspring is a gift from the Great Spirit. I do not know what is in store for you, but without a second thought, I would gladly give my life to protect you."

Nadiwani came down to the riverside in search of Adia. "Ah, so I see the assembly has been called already," she said, looking at the creatures gathered not far away from Adia and An'Kru.

"Yes," Adia laughed. "It is quite wondrous, really. I am intrigued; what if he attracts larger animals as he matures?"

"It certainly would make hunting easier," Nadiwani said, at which Adia's mouth dropped open. "I am joking!"

"I need your opinion, please," the Helper continued. "What do you think of Awan?"

Adia smiled. "I thought I saw something between you lately. In my experience, he has always been an upstanding figure, and Acaraho would agree."

"I imagine so, as Acaraho made him High Protector. But I wonder why he has never paired. Possibly the duties of his position? Even the First Guard is taxed with responsibilities."

"He is still young enough to pair. And so are you," Adia smiled.

Nadiwani's cheeks were suddenly burning. "I

admit, there is something between us. I cannot decide whether to pursue it or not."

"You never believed you could be paired, but since the High Council allows it, you have to get your mind wrapped around the idea. I know it is a possibility you have put out of your mind all this time."

"It is not because of a motivation to have offspring but to have, as the Brothers call it, a life-walker. Someone to share the dark hours of the night with. The highs and lows."

"You know he and Acaraho were raised together by Awan's parents. They are alike in many ways, so I would not rule him out."

"I certainly know how to approach him after watching you and Acaraho all those years. You were nearly shameless."

"Yes, I know," Adia laughed. "And now Nootau has discovered the Dream World and is curious about what his father and I did there. At some point, if he continues to visit that realm, he may figure it out."

Nadiwani's tone turned serious. "Have Acaraho and Nootau spoken since—"

"Since Nootau revealed he knows Acaraho is not his blood father? No. I pray it does not change their relationship. I suppose it must, in some ways, but their love for each other is strong enough, I believe, to keep any distance from creeping between them. And what still always amazes me is the forgiveness of the community. Other than a select few who know what Khon'Tor did, everyone thinks that Acaraho seeded Nootau. They forgave me my perceived transgression as a Healer and still do."

Nadiwani did not mention the unspoken question hanging in the air. *What about Nimida? If she learned the truth, would she be able to forgive those involved?*

CHAPTER 6

Storis knew he was jumping the gun, but he could not help himself. He had spent the Sunday asking if there were any homesteads up for sale. It would be unusual as most families lived on their farms and passed them down through the generations. However, he was not so much looking for a farm as a sturdy two-story house for him and Grace to live in once they were married.

He had some money saved up from his work with Miss Vivian, and he was also confident that word would soon spread, and before too long, he would have several local customers, starting with the bank.

He pulled up to the house the banker had told him about. It had belonged to the banker's niece, who had gone to live with her children after her husband passed. It had sat vacant for a while, so would need some work.

Storis negotiated the overgrown path and the two

steps to the porch. He slid the key into the lock and walked in.

It was a pretty place. There was quite a bit of natural light, and it had a generously sized kitchen with a large stone hearth. Quite a few cast-iron pots and pans still hung from the ceiling on rough iron hooks. Ashes remaining from the last fire were a reminder that once the house had been a real home, filled with joy and laughter. The stairs creaked as he climbed them, a sound others might have minded but that he found welcome and homey. There were three bedrooms upstairs. By many people's standards, this was a house for well-to-do people, but then it had been in the banker's family.

Storis finished looking around inside and went out back to inspect the garden area. He was pleased to see there was a barn of sorts, more a shed. But it was big enough for Grace to keep whatever animals she wanted. He smiled to himself, thinking how pleased she would be if he could surprise her with this.

He saddled back up, and on the way back to town, his heart was filled with hope and happy anticipation for the future. If they could make a deal, he would arrange with the banker for the house to be refurbished to his specifications as soon as possible so that when he felt it was time to take Grace to see it, its original charm would be restored. After speaking with the banker, he would go to the General Store and place an order for some items he would need right away.

Monday came soon enough, and as Storis put the key in the lock to his office, he was interrupted by a voice behind him.

"Mr. Storis," a man's voice said.

The lawyer turned back to see the local sheriff. "Yes, Sheriff, how may I help you?"

"I need you to come with me, please."

"Of course." Storis turned the key back in the lock, securing his office. He knew Grace would be by in an hour or so, and she had her own key to get in if need be. But he was concerned she would worry that he had not already opened up.

"What is this about, Sheriff?" Storis asked.

Sheriff Moore kept walking. "This way, please."

When they were seated in the sheriff's office, he said to Storis, "Do you know a man named Zachariah Tucker?"

"I know a man calls himself Snide Tucker; is that the same fellow?"

"Most likely. A bit of a drifter. Heard you hired him to do some tracking a while back," the sheriff continued.

"I did. But I intend to do no more business with him. I found him, if you will excuse me, a bit of a suspect character."

"Yes, well, Mr. Tucker has made some serious allegations against you. I am aware of Mr. Tucker's reputation, so I did some checking of my own. Everything about you comes up legitimate. So I was not inclined to take Tucker seriously, but unfortunately, he went to the sheriff's office in Millgrove. Now, I know Sheriff Boone, and he told me he knows you and you are an upstanding citizen. But the constable was visiting, and as much as Boone would have liked to let the matter go, the constable was not so willing."

Storis was frowning deeply by now, "Let what go?"

"You were the Morgan's attorney, correct? Grayson Stone Morgan the Second and his wife Vivian Morgan, who later married Ben Jenkins. Out at the Morgan farm, Shadow Ridge?"

"Why, yes. I have just moved my business from Millgrove, as a matter of fact."

"You were at the funeral of Mrs. Vivian Morgan Jenkins and Mr. Ben Jenkins, I presume?"

"Yes. I was there to show my respects, and I had some papers to deliver to Miss Vivian's grandson, Grayson Stone Morgan the Third."

"So that was all there was, a funeral?"

"Yes. Up at the family grave on the Morgan property. If you don't mind, why all the questions?" Storis was starting to get a knot in his stomach.

"Just a few more; did you see the body of either Mrs. Morgan Jenkins or Mr. Ben Jenkins?"

"Oh, my heavens, no. I am sure no one did."

"Do you not think that is odd, Mr. Storis?"

"No, not at all, considering they were reportedly trampled to death. Not everyone likes to see their loved ones disfigured and mangled, Sheriff. Now, I do need to ask you what this is about."

The sheriff pushed his chair back and sat up straight. "Mr. Tucker claims there are no bodies buried in the caskets. He claims that Mrs. Morgan Jenkins and Mr. Jenkins are still alive. In fact, he claims that the grandson, Grayson Stone Morgan the Third, planned the whole thing."

"Are you saying there are some kinds of charges pending against Mr. Morgan? I have to stop this conversation here, Sheriff. Grayson Stone Morgan the Third is my client, and due to attorney-client privilege, I cannot speak with you about any charges of wrongdoing on his part."

"It is just a preliminary investigation at this point."

Storis got up as calmly as he could, wished the sheriff good day, and walked out the door. He put his hat on and straightened it, then pulled his overcoat down tight and headed back to his office. He was grateful no one was there to see his hand shaking as he once more put the key in the lock.

Grace arrived and apologized that she was late. Ned had forgotten some notes he needed to go over with

Mr. Clement, so they turned back. She chattered away while she was stacking some files on top of the desk and then stopped when she realized something was wrong.

"Here I am going on and on while something is bothering you."

"Snide Tucker seems to be causing trouble. I am sure it will all work out. It's just on my mind, that's all."

"Is there anything I can do to help?"

"Just stay away from Tucker. Don't go anywhere without Ned or your father with you. Or me."

He paused. "I think I might need to take a trip. It will take me about a week to get there and another to get back."

"Where must you go?" she asked.

"I think I should find Grayson Morgan and tell him about Tucker in case anyone shows up looking for him."

"You mean at the locals' village, the one you hired Tucker to take you to? Can you find it without him?"

"Yes. I made a map on the way there and added more information on the way back. I have it here in my top drawer. It was pretty detailed. I have to try, so I'll leave tomorrow morning. Please stay here now and keep the door locked; I am going to arrange for some supplies and hire a wagon. This time of year, it is too far to go without extra feed and water for the horse."

The next morning, when he got to his office, a man he could only assume was the county constable was waiting outside with Sheriff Moore.

"What can I do for you, gentlemen?"

"I'm Constable Riggs, and I have a few questions for you, Mr. Storis."

Storis rattled the key in the lock and managed to turn it, then pushed his weight against the door to get it open. "It sometimes sticks." Having entered, he tossed the key down on his desk.

"I know Sheriff Moore here spoke with you about Zachariah Tucker's allegations," the sheriff said. "I have come directly from Shadow Ridge, where we opened the graves. There are no bodies in the caskets; they were weighed down with bags of sand, just as Mr. Tucker alleged."

"Tucker said the caskets contained bags of sand? How would he know that?" Storis asked.

"No, Tucker said he didn't think any bodies were in the caskets. At least not those of Mrs. Morgan Jenkins and Mr. Jenkins. And he was right," the constable said. "He didn't say anything about bags of sand. That is just what we found."

The constable walked over and looked at Storis's law certificate on the wall. "Another interesting thing Tucker said. He said the horse that supposedly trampled them to death is at the Webbs' house, right here in Wilde Edge. Named Rebel, apparently. A striking animal. Not one you can miss." He turned to face Storis. "The family of the same Grace Webb whom I understand you happen to be courting. Would you know anything about that, Mr. Storis?"

"If you have something to say, say it, or leave."

"So you are denying seeing the Morgan horse at Mr. Webb's?" the constable added.

Storis stood silent.

"Very well, Mr. Storis, you are under arrest pending investigation into the whereabouts of Mrs. Vivian Morgan Jenkins and Mr. Ben Jenkins. Since you are a professional man, I will let you report to the Wilde Edge jailhouse on your own recognizance. Just be sure to be there by the end of the day. I suggest you do not try to leave town instead."

Storis remained silent. Saying anything would not be in his best interests. He had to warn Grayson, but now there was no way to do so.

"On what basis?" he finally asked. "On the conjecture of a man of Snide Tucker's caliber? This is preposterous."

"Questionable character or not, Snide Tucker was right. There were no bodies in the graves. So the question is, just where are Mrs. Morgan Jenkins and Mr. Jenkins? Someone went to the trouble of creating a huge ruse. And we need to know who was in on it and why. Tomorrow we are heading out to the village where Tucker said he saw Grayson Morgan. We are going to get to the bottom of this, I promise you that."

When Grace arrived, Storis explained that Ben and Miss Vivian had faked their deaths in order to live with Grayson without people trying to trace them. He told her that the authorities had opened their graves and found only bags of sand and that now there would be an investigation into the truth of what had happened to them.

He also told her that he was to be arrested on suspicion that he was somehow involved. "Now, go home and tell your parents that I will not be by. I have to turn myself in this afternoon.

"But I don't understand. They are alive, so why are you being arrested? My mother and I—our whole family—saw Miss Vivian and her husband, Ben. And so did Dr. Miller, who treated Miss Vivian for pneumonia! I don't understand."

"I can't tell you any more than what I have said, or it will create problems later. Please just stay home and be safe. Don't worry about the office here; I will lock it up tonight when I leave, and it will stay closed until this is settled."

Until then, there had been no physical contact between them, but emotions were running high. Storis reached out and gently drew Grace into his embrace. "It will all work out, I promise. Please don't worry." Then he kissed the top of her head and took her to find Ned to take her home.

Grace called out to her mother and father the moment her feet touched the walkway.

What is it?" Mrs. Webb came running out of the house, wiping her hands on her apron. "Calm down and tell me what's wrong."

"Where's Papa? I need to talk to both of you!"

"You go inside, and I'll fetch your father. Ned, you go inside, too."

Soon they were gathered together in the kitchen. "Now slow down and tell us what has you so upset," Mr. Webb said.

Grace explained that the sheriff was arresting Storis for something to do with the Morgans because, apparently, people thought they had died, though she didn't understand what they thought Newell's involvement was.

"I don't understand any of that, but we saw Miss Vivian here," Mrs. Webb said. "And Ben Jenkins. They were fine. All they need to do is ask us, and we can tell them that. Maybe we should go talk to the sheriff."

"Newell said for us to stay out of it and wait for things to work themselves out," replied Grace. "It's that Snide Tucker causing problems."

"No doubt because I wouldn't let him court you," said Mr. Webb. "Man like that should be ashamed of himself, expecting any right-minded father to let him around his daughter."

"It has something to do with the horses in the barn, too," Grace said.

"Odd you should mention that," said Mr. Webb, turning to his wife. "You mentioned something about them still being here, do you remember? Because Grayson hadn't taken them back with him as he had planned. And when you said that, Newell looked very startled."

"I'm worried," Grace said. "I don't believe for a moment he is involved in anything wrong, and I don't trust Snide Tucker."

Acise had continued to rest, and so far, there had been no more problems. Oh'Dar would be returning soon, which encouraged her, and she had slowly started returning to her normal activities. Her sister Snana was often at her side, talking about the new baby to come and tossing around names. Acise wouldn't say whether she hoped it was a boy or a girl, just as long as it was healthy, though she did say she hoped the baby would have Oh'Dar's blue eyes.

Honovi saw it differently. The last thing they needed was a blue-eyed child running around the village, especially with the hostile climate that was starting to form against the Brothers on the part of the Waschini.

Her young son, Noshoba, seemed unconcerned at the idea of a baby, but some of the younger girls were excited and played at making tiny moccasins for the little one out of leftover scraps of hide and fabric.

The winter snows were still coming in. It had been a harsh winter, worse than most. Everyone was enjoying the morning family fires when Pajackok and some other riders cantered in, bringing their horses into the center of the village.

"Waschini are coming. It looks as if they are headed here," Pajackok called out.

Chief Is'Taqa told him to send the women and children inside and gather whatever braves were close by. "I will tell Honovi to watch from our shelter in case she is needed."

Three riders approached and were intercepted by Pajackok and several other braves. The Waschini men gestured that they intended to enter the village, so Pajackok and the others turned their horses and escorted them in.

The village appeared empty by the time the three men arrived. Two dismounted and gave their reins to the third to hold before walking over to where Chief Is'Taqa was standing.

The Chief and Ithua recognized the man as the sheriff who had come long ago looking for Oh'Dar. The years had passed, and the sheriff was older, but he was definitely the same person.

Not understanding them, in silence, Chief Is'Taqa let them talk. Finally, he heard a few words he understood. Grayson Stone Morgan. They were looking for Oh'Dar, as he had suspected.

Watching from a distance, Pajackok had also figured out why they were there. He quietly slipped into the brush and up one of the paths to where he knew the People's watchers were invisibly stationed. Then, loud enough for the nearest watcher to hear, he said, "Please tell Oh'Dar that the Waschini are here!" They had very likely already realized and spread the word, but Pajackok wanted to be sure. He knew there was no way Oh'Dar could get there immediately, but their Waschini ally needed to know what was happening.

There were two men with the Chief. Honovi would never forget the name of the first; Sheriff Boone, who was the Millgrove sheriff, had been to the village before, long ago, when he was leading the search for Oh'Dar. She had been so afraid he would find some evidence that the baby had been there—if only briefly—and even now, her heartbeat stumbled at the thought.

He said something to her life-walker, but the Chief remained silent. From the way the sheriff frustratedly glanced around, turning a full circle, she wondered if he was looking for her to act as translator. The Chief must have a reason not to summon her, so she remained in the shadows at the entrance to their shelter.

The second man carried himself with arrogance, and his mouth was cruel. Honovi watched in concern as he left the others and wandered off on his own. He prowled around the far perimeter and disappeared in the direction where the horses and ponies were kept. It would be obvious to anyone from Millgrove that some of the horses there were from the Morgan stock.

Then, out of the blue, she heard the wheezy sound of a harmonica inexpertly played.

The man swiftly reappeared. "Who made that noise?" he demanded. "Come on out!"

Her young son, Noshoba, appeared from behind some bushes.

Careless in her horror, she was about to run to him, but Snana was there in a flash and took his hand, leading him away from the angry official.

In relief, Honovi sagged against Acise, who had joined her. It must be something Oh'Dar had given him. What a terrible time for Noshoba to play it. She clutched her daughter's hand.

The mean-looking man then walked briskly back to the Chief. His voice was raised, and she could now hear him clearly.

"I am Constable Riggs, and I am a very, very important person. I am in charge of all the land you live on, and I demand that you stop playing games. Those are Morgan horses, and that boy there," he pointed at Noshoba, "has a harmonica. Now, I want to know; where is Grayson Morgan?"

Honovi didn't know what to do. Is'Taqa had not yet motioned for her to come out. For some reason, he still did not want them to be able to speak to each other—or was he hoping to hide her existence from this new official? She clenched her fists and prayed that the Waschini would not take out their irritation on him.

The constable raised his voice further, "Where is Grayson Morgan? I know you know who he is. Snide Tucker and Newell Storis were here not too long ago, and Storis met with him. Don't play dumb with me."

Chief Is'Taqa turned and beckoned Honovi to come out. He must realize that the silence was no longer helpful.

Constable Riggs pointed at Honovi as she started to walk toward them. His focus was now on her, and he spoke as if she could not understand him.

"That woman is part white," he said and glanced at the sheriff.

"Yes," Sheriff Boone said. "Her name is—Honor? No, Hon—Honovi? Her mother married a white man, and after he died, they returned here."

"Are there others being held captive here?" the constable asked.

A chill went through Honovi. Involuntarily, she glanced at Snana, who also understood Whitespeak, and saw that she, too, was disturbed by the comment, shoving Noshoba behind her as if to make him invisible.

"Not held captive. This woman lives here. This is her life. She is not being held against her will," the sheriff said. He was frowning slightly; did he also think the constable was being too harsh?

"It's not right. How many are there? I demand to know."

Mildly, Sheriff Boone said, "If you are asking who here is part white, as far as I know, only this woman, and of course, if she has children—"

By then, Honovi had reached them, and the Chief spoke to her.

"The Chief asks why you have come to our land," she translated.

"We are looking for Grayson Morgan. We need to talk to him. And don't lie to me; he or someone else has been here, or that boy would not have a harmonica."

The sheriff turned to the man who must be his senior. "We know Grayson Morgan was here when the lawyer, Storis, visited a short while ago."

As Honovi translated what they had said, she had a sudden feeling that Sheriff Boone did not have much time for the constable, senior or not.

Constable Riggs peered around her. "Is that your daughter? Tell her to come out here," he ordered.

Honovi looked back to see Acise now standing outside the shelter. *No, my daughter!* She then glanced at her life-walker, who said nothing.

"I said, tell her to come out here."

Chief Is'Taqa beckoned, and timidly, Acise approached them.

The sheriff glanced at her swollen belly and quickly looked up.

"Does she have a husband?" the constable asked, openly staring at her belly.

"He is not here," Honovi answered.

"This isn't right, half white women living here. Breeding with them and producing more mixed children."

The constable tore into Sheriff Boone, "And you haven't done anything about this?"

"They are here willingly. It is causing no harm."

"I'm not sure the governor would agree, but I'll let it go. For now."

The Chief looked up, and following his gaze, Honovi saw that Oh'Dar had appeared at the edge of the woodland.

Fortunately, Oh'Dar was already almost at the village when the watcher intercepted him with Pajackok's message.

The two Waschini turned around as he went striding toward them.

"Who is that?" the constable asked Honovi.

"Who are you?" demanded Oh'Dar as he reached them.

The constable looked him up and down as if taking in his hide tunic and hide foot coverings, the blade at his waist, its sheath obviously made after the tradition of the Brothers. Then he stared into Oh'Dar's blue eyes.

"You're not one of them," he blurted out. "You're the Morgan lad."

"I am Grayson Stone Morgan the Third. I live among them, and I am one of them in every way that matters. What is your business here?"

"I am Constable Riggs, and this is Sheriff Boone, and that is his deputy. We are looking for you."

Oh'Dar waited for them to reveal more. He recognized Sheriff Boone but had never met the other man.

"Actually," the sheriff said, "We are looking for your grandparents." He introduced the constable. "Where are they?"

"What makes you think they are here?"

"Do you know a man named Snide Tucker?" the constable asked.

"He was here a while back with my grandparents' attorney, Newell Storis."

"Yes. And he said you brought Ben Jenkins here to meet him. Is that true?"

"What is the problem?"

"The problem is," the constable continued, "if your grandparents are alive, as Tucker alleges, someone went to a lot of trouble to fake their deaths, and we want to know why."

Oh'Dar let out a long breath. "My grandparents wanted to leave the life they knew. They were bored. They also wanted to spend more time with me. As a result, they decided to come and live here."

"That sounds a bit preposterous now, doesn't it. Mrs. Morgan Jenkins had a great deal of wealth. Where is it?"

"Mrs. Thomas, who was my grandmother's long-term housekeeper and friend, now owns Shadow Ridge. And a fair amount of the financial reserves."

"Where is the rest of it?"

"Under my control," Oh'Dar answered.

The sheriff stepped in. "Look, all we need is to see your grandmother and Mr. Ben Jenkins and talk to them. They had a comfortable life at Shadow Ridge, and you can understand it is odd that, at this point in their lives, they would leave everything your family worked for and disappear. But if that is the truth, we will drop our investigation. Seems a shame to fool so many people, though. Why didn't they just say they were leaving and wanted to be left alone?"

"My Uncle Louis was a threat to them. And even if they told people they were leaving, others would try to find them. They knew that. Just as you are here looking for them. They want their privacy," Oh'Dar said.

"But you were there when I arrested Louis at the funeral," the sheriff said. "You spotted him first and then kept him from running off."

"Yes, but they didn't know he would be recaptured. And besides, people make alliances in prison. He may have friends willing to do a favor for him, carry out revenge against his mother on his behalf. You can understand that."

"Just take us to them, and we will be on our way, case closed," the sheriff said.

"I can't take you to them."

"You can't take us to them?" the sheriff repeated.

"No, I can't."

"So you admit they are not living here in this village?"

Oh'Dar was thinking as fast as he could. "When their lawyer Mr. Storis showed up here with Tucker, he talked to Ben Jenkins. You just told me that. So what is the problem?"

"Yes, he said you brought Mr. Jenkins here. But not your grandmother. We need to hear from them that they are well and not being held against their will. If it was all a ruse that they were in on, though it seems quite extreme, then it is easily settled. If they are not here at the moment, it must be simple to fetch them."

The constable had listened quietly while the sheriff was asking questions, but now he appeared to have heard enough. "Listen, Mr. Morgan. You bring your grandparents back here immediately, now, or we're going to arrest you for suspected murder. How does that sound? In fact, to make sure you don't just disappear, the sheriff and I will go with you to wherever they are."

"Why would I be arrested for suspected murder? They came willingly. You can ask the Webbs in Wilde Edge. We stayed at their house for a few days on the way here."

"Let's say everything about this ridiculous story is true," the constable answered. "They wanted a different life. They wanted to disappear. They came willingly. Others saw them alive not too long ago. That is all fine. But we still need to know they're alive now. Take us to them if they are now living elsewhere."

"No," Oh'Dar said.

The constable glanced at the sheriff. "No. Just like that." He drew his pistol, cocked it, and pointed it at Oh'Dar.

Honovi and Acise both flinched, and Acise grabbed her mother's arm as Oh'Dar glanced across at them.

"You are under arrest for suspicion of the murder of Mrs. Vivian Morgan Jenkins and Mr. Ben Jenkins. You are coming with us back to Wilde Edge."

Acise scooted forward and grabbed Oh'Dar's hand, hard. "No, please," she said in English. "Do not take him; he has done nothing wrong."

The constable turned to Acise, "Since you can obviously understand me, what business is this of yours, might I ask?"

"He is my life-walker, my husband."

"So it is his child you carry?" the constable asked.

Acise glanced over at Oh'Dar, and in vain, he tried to look reassuring.

"We are done for now," the constable barked. "Get your ride, Mr. Morgan; you are coming with us."

Honovi was translating, and Acaraho, Adia, and Awan were also present.

"Where have they taken him?" Adia asked.

"Hard to say," Ben replied. He was sitting on the bed with his broken leg propped up. "Could be all the way back to Millgrove near Shadow Ridge. Or it could be to Wilde Edge, where Mrs. Webb lives and where our attorney said he was moving to. They will hold him until there is a trial."

"A trial is like a High Council hearing, then?" Adia asked.

"A group of people will hear statements from witnesses and will decide if a crime has been committed. Then, if he is found guilty, the judge, who acts as I imagine your Overseer does, will decide on the punishment," Ben explained.

"What are we to do?" Adia glanced at Acaraho and then looked at Ben once more.

"Clearly, we cannot ourselves intervene. But, somehow, they have to be told that you are both alive and well and there was no crime committed," Acaraho said.

"I need to go to Wilde Edge and find them and tell them we are alright," Ben said.

"How, Ben?" Miss Vivian asked. "You can't make it on your own and especially not now with a broken leg. We take longer to heal at our age, and your knee is also damaged; if you don't give it time to mend properly, you could be crippled for life.

"But I feel so helpless, and you cannot make that trip again!"

Adia tried to console them. "We have to pray for help, for guidance. We are not alone; somehow, an answer will come."

Miss Vivian wiped tears from her face. "My beloved Grayson. All he has done is try to take care of us, and now that horrible man, Tucker, is making trouble just out of what—spite? Jealousy?"

"I got sight of the man at the Brothers' village," said her husband, "and he looks to be a shady character for sure. Who knows what his motive is, but whatever it is, it cannot be honorable."

CHAPTER 7

At the Wilde Edge drinking establishment, Snide Tucker was nursing a shot of whisky. He had set his plan in motion and was now relishing his daydreams about what would come next. He'd get great satisfaction from seeing Storis and that Grayson Morgan brought down. Rich people—didn't know what it was like to work properly a day in their lives. Only one loose end to tie up, now, and that was with Miss Grace Webb.

"Oh. It's you," she stammered, looking up into the leering eyes of Snide Tucker. "What do you want? I was just locking up. My brother will be here any minute."

"He's been delayed," Tucker said. He reached out and took Grace's arm, pinching her in his tight grasp. He strong-armed her down the steps and around the side of the building.

"What are you doing? Let me go!"

"I've been waiting a long time for you to show up here again," he sneered.

Tucker pressed her up against the building and groped at the front of her dress, leaning in to try to kiss her at the same time. She turned her head to the side and struggled. "Stop it. Stop it, please!" she said as she tried to push his hand away.

"Your daddy thinks I ain't good enough for you. Well, we'll see about that right now," Tucker hissed, the whiskey pungent on his breath.

Tucker wrestled Grace to the ground, though she fought as much as she could. She started to yell for help, but he clamped a grimy hand over her mouth just in time to stop her. Only a muffled sound came out, and Grace heard him laughing as he started pulling up her skirts with his other hand.

She thrashed around, trying to get away from him. Suddenly he was lifted off her. Then she saw that Ned had Snide by the back of his shirt. He shoved Tucker to the ground a good distance from Grace, and the man slid further back in the mud before struggling up and coming at Ned, who slammed his fist into Tucker's face and knocked him down again.

"You stay away from her, you hear me! You come near her again, and I'll kill you!"

Tucker stayed down this time, and Grace ran to stand behind her brother. Her hair and clothing were smeared with mud.

Hearing the commotion, a group of people had started running over.

"What's going on?" the barkeeper asked. He looked at Tucker and then back at Ned and Grace.

"He— He tried to attack me," Grace said. "My brother saved me." She wiped wet hair away from her face with the back of her hand and tried her best to smooth down her muddy skirts.

Several of the men surrounded Tucker, dragged him to his feet, and held him fast.

Ned turned to the banker, "Would you please have Sheriff Moore arrest this piece of trash who attacked my sister. I need to get her home and take care of her."

Ned took Grace home and explained to their parents what had happened.

Their father was beside himself with anger and wanted to go after Tucker himself. "He'd better stay away from all of us, that's all I can say. And I'll look for the first opportunity to tell him to his face."

"Grace, honey, I am sure this shook you up. Why don't you go clean up and lie down, and I will be up in a minute with your dinner," Mrs. Webb said.

"I'm alright, Mama. But this is just one more example of Tucker's bad character. Oh, why hasn't anyone come to talk to us about all this?" Grace asked. "We could tell them we saw both Ben and

Miss Vivian with Grayson, and they were just fine. Nobody killed anybody. And Snide Tucker is a drifter; why would anyone listen to him anyway?"

"It doesn't matter that he's a drifter," said Mrs. Webb. "The law has at least to look into charges this serious. They must have found something, or they wouldn't be pursuing it. The question is, what?"

Mrs. Thomas and her family were gathered around the dinner table. Mac, as the oldest son, gave thanks before they started passing the bowls and dishes around.

"You've been awfully quiet lately, Tom," Mrs. Thomas said to her other son. "Is everything alright with you and the family? I haven't seen Emily and the children up here lately."

"No, she is busy sewing some new clothes for them, more suitable for the summers here. She just loves being in the place you used to live before you moved into the big house. She was kinda lost, rambling around in here."

"What's on your mind? I can tell something is bothering you."

Dan laid his napkin down by his plate and let out a long sight. "I didn't want to have to tell you this because I knew it would upset you. I was hoping nothing would come of it, and you might never have to know—"

"Please, spit it out, son; you're worrying me."

"Not too long after we let that Zachary Tucker go, the constable and some men came by asking about the gravesites of Miss Vivian and Ben Jenkins. I had to show them where they were. They said they were going to dig up the graves as Tucker told them there were no bodies in the caskets."

"What?" Mrs. Thomas said. "Oh, no. Tell me they didn't—"

"Well, I wish I could, but they did. I didn't want to look, that's for sure. But darn it all if the coffins weren't empty. I mean, there were no bodies in them. Just sacks filled with sand to weigh them down."

Mrs. Thomas froze her expression and made sure she didn't look over at Mac. She didn't want Dan to know she and Mac had been in on it.

"Why didn't they come and talk to me?" she asked.

"They said something about having questions for you later. Just needed to know if it was going to go any further; no need to get you involved if the bodies were in there," Dan said.

"This is upsetting to me," she said. "I think I need to lie down for a while."

"Go ahead, Ma, we'll clean up here and put all the food away," said Mac.

"I'm sorry to upset you. I didn't want to tell you, but since it looks like something will come of this, I didn't want you to be surprised if they showed back up to talk to you."

Mrs. Thomas laid a hand on her son's shoulder as she walked by, "No, you did the right thing. I appreciate it. Whatever happens, we'll deal with it as it comes."

She went up to her room, the same room that had been Miss Vivian's, and lay down. Then, as she often did, believing he could hear her, she said aloud to her late husband, who had passed years ago, "Oh, Jebediah. What is going to happen now?"

Storis woke up in his cell when he heard the front door open and slam shut. Men's voices were talking out in the office.

There were sounds of a chair being scraped along the floor. "Sit down and stay here," someone said.

"Name?" the voice of Sheriff Moore asked.

"You know who I am," another voice answered.

Storis's heart stopped.

"I have to ask you officially. Name?"

"Snide Tucker. Zachariah Tucker to you."

Tucker was in the sheriff's office? What had he done that had gotten him brought here?

"I'm going to have to hold you for a few days," said Sheriff Moore.

"I didn't hurt her," Tucker said.

"Don't bother telling me that. Enough witnesses

saw her state and how shook up she was, and they're telling a different story."

"Women. They tease you, and then when you try to give them what they're asking for, they cry bloody murder," Tucker said.

Storis was pressed hard against the cell bars, trying to hear every word.

"You might get away with saying that about some of the women in the establishments you frequent, but no one is going to believe for one minute that Grace Webb was asking for anything," the sheriff answered.

Storis started shouting at hearing Grace's name. "Sheriff! What is going on?" He started raking his metal water cup up and down on the bars.

"What's going on in there?" the sheriff hollered. "Quiet down!"

"Well, I do believe that's a friend of mine," Tucker sniggered. "That you, Storis? They finally got you put where you belong, huh?"

Storis heard the click of handcuffs being closed.

"You sit still," growled the sheriff.

When Sheriff Moore came into sight, Storis pelted him with questions. "Grace Webb. What happened?"

"Snide Tucker decided to steal a kiss—or two—from the lady. Maybe a little more if her brother Ned hadn't stopped him. Lucky for Miss Webb that he was there."

Storis's eyes narrowed, and his jaw tightened. "If he harmed her, I swear—"

"She's fine. Just covered in mud and shook up. Her brother took her home. Looks like you'll have company for a few days."

The man uncuffed Tucker and put him a few cells away from Storis. "You two don't get into it now," he warned them both before leaving the cell room. "Nothing good would come of that."

After the sheriff left, Storis had a few things to say to Snide Tucker. "You will pay for this. For all of this," he finished.

"I don't see how, since I'm in for a night or so and you're here for the long haul. While you were busy courting Miss Webb, I was doing a little investigating at the Morgan farm. Went to the local sheriff and told them that they ought to look at who or what's in the graves since it ain't Miz Morgan and that fellow she married."

Storis's blood ran cold.

"That Millgrove sheriff didn't seem too interested, but lucky for you, the constable was there, and he took it seriously. Turns out nothing in the coffins but bags of sand. You wouldn't know anything about that, would you?"

Storis knew Tucker was trying to torment him, so he didn't want to give the satisfaction of a response. But he did need to find out everything he could.

"You're trying to ruin people's lives, and for what?" Storis said.

"For what? That's easy for someone like you to say, someone who got schoolin' and has his own law office. People like the Morgans who're rolling in it. But what about the rest of us? Those who didn't get off so easy? I would have kept my mouth shut if you didn't value your precious money more than your freedom—or your future with Miss Webb. So now you have to live with it."

"That is not true; if I had started paying you, it would never have stopped. You would have black-mailed me forever."

"Well, maybe so. But you'd have your freedom and a pretty little wife and some kiddies. Now you ain't gonna have any of that, are you? The only future you're looking at is the end of your lawyer career."

Tucker sat down on the cot and took off his boots. Before lying down, he took one last shot at Storis. "Me, I'll be outta here soon. And then I'll finish what I started with your lady friend. Mhhhhh, that kiss sure tasted good. Wonder what the rest of her—"

"Shut up, you worthless—"

The sheriff opened the door to the cell room, "Stop talking and settle down in there."

"He's threatening to go after Miss Webb again when he gets out," Storis said.

"Mr. Tucker, I suggest you stop making threats before you make things any worse for yourself. You're already in enough trouble. Now I'm turning out the lights, so bed down for the night."

The next morning, having spent a while reflecting on the situation, Grace went to her father. "Papa, please go to the sheriff and tell him that you saw Ben Jenkins and Miss Vivian here with Grayson, both alive and well. Take Mama with you; maybe we can get the charges dropped before things go any further."

Mr. Webb agreed. "I think you're right, honey. There's no sense in waiting. Your ma and I will go into town later this morning and talk to Sheriff Moore. You stay home today and rest. Tucker's in jail, so he can't hurt you."

"I want to go with you; I want to talk to Newell."

"I know you want to talk to Newell, but Tucker is probably in the jail cell next to him, so it would not be wise. And they likely wouldn't let you see him, anyhow."

Later that morning, Mr. and Mrs. Webb took the wagon and drove into town to talk to Sheriff Moore. The rain had let up, and though the streets were still slick, they talked to him outside the office so as not to risk Tucker finding out that they were there.

Mr. Webb explained. "We saw Ben Jenkins and Miss Vivian. So did Dr. Miller. They were passing through with her grandson, Grayson Morgan. They were going with him of their own free will. This is about nothing but a bad man's spite."

"I have known you for many years, and I trust you, so if you say you saw them alive and they were willingly going with Mrs. Morgan Jenkins's grandson, then I believe you. Whatever the truth is, it will all come out in the trial, and if needed, you'll get your chance to tell your story again then. In the meantime, try to keep your minds off it because there's nothing you can do about it. It has to play itself out."

"What will happen now?" Mrs. Webb asked.

"No doubt someone from Millgrove is on their way to find Grayson Morgan and see his grandmother and her husband. If they're not there, he'll be brought back for trial. They would most likely lock him up at the Millgrove jailhouse until they can find a judge and jury to hear the case."

"What about Mr. Storis?"

"Everything depends on whether Mrs. Morgan Jenkins and Mr. Jenkins surface. If they do, and they convince the judge that this was all done with their consent, then whatever their reasoning was for this elaborate ruse, the matter will be dropped. If not, then there will be suspicion of murder, and Mr. Storis will also be tried, based on Mr. Tucker's testimony that he was involved in whatever happened to the grandparents."

"We both know Grayson Morgan; there is no way he would have done anything to hurt his grandparents. This will all get straightened out as soon as they find him; I have no doubt about it," Mr. Webb said.

"I hope you're right. As for Mr. Tucker, he will get some jail time for accosting your daughter. And if it turns out that he knowingly made false allegations of misdoing, he can be charged with that too," Sheriff Moore explained.

"This is a nightmare," Nora said. "And my poor Grace is right in the middle of it."

"Hopefully, everything will be back to normal before too long, Mrs. Webb, and she and Mr. Storis can get on with their courtship."

At the Far High Hills, Urilla Wuti continued to work with Nootau on strengthening his connection to the Great Spirit. She knew his direct knowledge was a special gift and that he had been able to enter the Dream World at least once. She focused on teaching him the techniques she had taught his mother to enter the Dream World at will.

In earlier years, Urilla Wuti had thought perhaps the Corridor would be the way the Healers would be able to communicate over long distances. She had taught some of them how to enter it at will, planning for the time when she believed it would be needed. But now, she believed she had to teach the other Healers how to enter the Dream World instead. It was not the other-worldly realm of the Corridor; it was just like being on Etera, except with the presence of only those who could enter it themselves. Whatever was coming, Urilla Wuti knew this would be an advantageous tool.

"So far, I have not been able to re-enter the Dream World, even with your help, so what do we do now?" Nootau asked.

"Just keep practicing. The High Council meeting is coming up, and I hope to start teaching the other Healers how to do this, but it would be good for you to have a breakthrough before we join them."

"It is possible it was just a once-off; I do not think I am a Healer, Urilla Wuti. I may never be able to do it at will."

"Perhaps you are not a Healer in the sense we have always understood it. But you clearly have some abilities, and you have been visited by Pan on more than one occasion. Regardless, do not worry about it; whatever your role is to be, the gifts you need will be provided in time. Now, let us try once more."

Just as Nootau had been practicing his gift, so Iella had been practicing hers. Her experience when they went to find U'Kail had fired up her enthusiasm for her new ability. In the privacy of the deep forests around the Far High Hills, she continued to work on communicating with Etera's creatures.

She learned that she could connect with any

creatures, both large and small. From the proudest stag to the tiniest insect crawling on a nearby leaf, they all responded to her in their own way. The only creature she had not tried to interact with was a Sarius Snake. She knew some they had been seen at the beautiful secluded area where Nootau had wanted to take her, where he was attacked by the jealous former High Protector, Thorak. But she was afraid and dared not try until she had her emotions under control in case her fear could distort her abilities. Iella was humbled at being granted such an incredible gift.

Pan had said the abilities of all the Healers would be enhanced, and their development accelerated. Like Urilla Wuti, Iella was looking forward to connecting with the other Healers at the next High Council meeting.

Iella had been thrilled by every opportunity she was able to spend with An'Kru. She wondered if, as he grew, he would develop the same gift for connecting with Etera's creatures. He already attracted them to him wherever he was, and she was able to connect with them when they came to him. She could feel the love passing between An'Kru and the creatures. The difference was that Iella had to create the link intentionally, yet with An'Kru, it was just there.

Iella was also happy that Tehya was seeded. Knowing Nootau would be leaving in seven years only increased her own desire to have offspring as soon as possible. Though they had only been paired for a very short time, Iella anxiously waited for each cycle to see if she was seeded. She remembered the contagion that had swept through their community years ago. Many of the males died, and others were left sterile. She tried not to worry that Nootau might have been affected and that perhaps they would never have offspring of their own.

Her conversation with Urilla Wuti had calmed some of her fears about his leaving, but it did not change the fact that she would miss him terribly and that it would be agonizing not to know where he was. She wanted their offspring to have as much time with their father before it happened.

CHAPTER 8

Oh'Dar was brought into the sheriff's office at Wilde Edge and told to sit down. He had remained silent nearly all the way, knowing that anything he said would later be used against him if possible. He felt grimy from the trip and knew he looked nothing like Grayson Stone Morgan the Third. He had no Waschini clothes, and he knew the less he looked like a Waschini, the more it would hurt him.

"May I clean up and get some different clothes?" he asked.

"Cleaning up, yes. As for different clothes, yes, at some point," Sheriff Moore answered.

"The Webbs might have something I could wear. And Storm needs to be stabled somewhere. He is not easy to handle, Sheriff; he would be best off with the Webbs."

"Once I get you settled in, I will send a deputy to

ask them about your horse and some clothing for you."

Sheriff Moore walked Oh'Dar back to the holding area. Storis and Snide Tucker both jumped to their feet in their respective cells when Oh'Dar was brought in.

Oh'Dar's eyes darted about, noting both Tucker and Storis in their separate cells. He had a feeling he knew why Storis was there but wasn't sure about Tucker. "What's he here for?" he asked.

"He tried to force himself on the Webb girl."

"Grace Webb?" Oh'Dar said with alarm. "Please tell me she wasn't hurt."

"Shook up but no permanent damage," the sheriff replied.

"It seems inappropriate to have my accuser in the cell a few doors down. I will need a lawyer and privacy," Oh'Dar said, looking at Storis.

"Yes, well, seeing your lawyer is also under suspicion, you'll need another one," the sheriff said. "I'll find you someone, but it may take a while. As far as the trial is concerned, I suspect it will be held in Millgrove as it's a larger town."

Storis said, "I am not sure that Millgrove is a fair venue. Most everyone knew the Morgans, and any jury will be prejudiced against us from the start."

It was a valid point. And there were witnesses to be called at both locations. But nothing could move forward until a judge had been appointed. It was likely to be the largest trial in some time as the Morgans were well known and well connected. Even finding an impartial judge around Millgrove might be a challenge.

The sheriff sent someone to locate the Webbs and have them find clothes for Oh'Dar and make arrangements for Storm.

Despite Tucker's being in the same jail, Grace was adamant that she wanted to see both Oh'Dar and Storis.

After Oh'Dar had changed into Ned's clothes, Grace and her mother came in at the back. The sheriff stood between them and Tucker's cell, keeping an eye on him and admonishing him to keep his mouth shut.

Storis looked over in Tucker's direction. "Sheriff, this is highly irregular. Snide Tucker is a witness for the prosecution, and he will overhear our conversation."

"There is nowhere else to put him. We can talk in the office, but he will still overhear you. None of you can be tried until we get a judge. So I either have to move both of you or Tucker to Millgrove, which is the closest alternative."

Looking worried, Grace kept her eyes focused on Oh'Dar and Storis.

"Why has it gone this far, Grayson?" Mrs. Webb

asked. "All they needed was to talk to your grand-parents.

"It isn't that simple," Oh'Dar said.

"Why isn't it?" asked Grace.

"It just isn't; that's all I can say," Oh'Dar answered.

"Oh, Grayson. Newell, talk to him," Mrs. Webb continued. "Make him understand that if he doesn't produce his grandparents, he is likely going to hang for their murders. We'll testify that we saw them both alive not that long ago, but it's very probably going to take more than that."

"What Mrs. Webb says is true, Grayson. If you don't prove they are still alive, they are going to assume you murdered them for their money and made up this ruse that they wanted a new life. We know you, and it still doesn't add up. It certainly isn't going to add up to a group of strangers, the jurors."

"Or the judge," Mrs. Webb added.

"I have no doubt it will be someone who knew the Morgans," said Storis. "Finding a judge there who did not would be nearly impossible."

When Mrs. Webb and Grace got home, they called a family meeting to tell Mr. Webb and Ned the rest of what they had learned.

"I don't understand why Grayson didn't just take the constable to his grandparents," Ned commented.

"He said it isn't that simple," Grace answered.

"It had better get that simple, or most likely he, and probably your beau, are going to be found complicit," Mr. Webb said.

"Can they do that without any bodies? It isn't fair; we know they're alive!" Grace said.

"Life isn't fair, and the law is tricky. They can make a case that looks very suspicious, and then despite Grayson's explanations otherwise, the only thing to convince a jury will be proof that the grandparents are alive and well."

Grace pursed her lips. "Then we have to make it simple. We have to find the grandparents and bring them here. Despite what Grayson says."

"How can we do that? We don't even know where they are," Ned said.

"And besides, it is too long a trip," said his mother. "Your father isn't well enough to go with you. No, it isn't safe."

"There's a map; Newell made a map when Tucker took him. I know where it is, too. Ned and I can take the wagon, the map, and some supplies and fetch them," Grace said.

Mr. Webb frowned. "No, it's too dangerous."

"We have to, Mama," replied Grace. "We have to try. Newell and Grayson are innocent. I am sure Grayson is worried about their health and the trip. But the cold weather is gone, and all we would have to deal with is any more of the spring rains. But if we leave now, we can take it slow and hopefully still make it back before the trial even starts.

And that will be the end of it. We don't have time to delay!"

"I know that in our place, Grayson would do it," Ned argued. "Look at what he has already done for us. We are all he has; how can we not help him now?"

Mr. and Mrs. Webb looked at each other, and each let out a long sigh.

"If you have your minds set on doing this," Mr. Webb spoke up, "let's think it through and be as careful as we can. It's a long trip, and not everything has emerged yet. And you had better try to remember what was on that wagon when Tucker and Newell set off."

"I can figure that out," Ned said. "Water and grain for the horses, just in case. Blankets, supplies for us."

"We can't tell Oh'Dar or Newell what you are doing," Mr. Webb pointed out.

"I know," Grace said wistfully. "Though I wish we could, to give them some hope. But it would only upset Grayson. I hate to go against his wishes, but Miss Vivian and Ben would never forgive us if they knew we stood by and did nothing. And neither would we. I just wish we knew who the judge was going to be."

Mr. Webb spoke up, "I know who it is. They were talking about it down at the livery this morning. The Judge's name is Matthias Walker."

Only a few days later, everything was set up, and with Storis's map in her pocket, Grace and her brother set out to find the locals' village. Hopefully, to bring Miss Vivian and Ben back with them.

Since Sheriff Moore had no other place to put him, Snide Tucker was on his way to the jail at Millgrove when the sheriff brought in a man to meet with Oh'Dar and Storis. He was Mr. Edward Cowell, a lawyer from Appleton.

"That's quite far away," said Storis.

"Can't be helped. Appleton is the nearest town other than Millgrove," the sheriff answered.

The lawyer, a wiry man with a thin face, pulled up a stool so he could sit closer to the bars. "I understand the charges against you both. They are quite serious, but I also understand there are witnesses here who can attest that they saw the Morgans alive and well not that long ago. Is that true?"

"Yes. Dr. Miller and all four of the Webb family," said Storis. "And I met Ben Jenkins at the locals' village."

"The graves contained only bags of sand. And there is the matter of the Morgan wealth. I have to say that unless the court sees your grandparents, Mr. Morgan, you are at serious risk of being found guilty of their murders."

He sighed. "To tell you the truth, I can't understand why you didn't let the constable meet them back at the locals' village. If they are alive, as you say they are, that would have ended it then and there."

"I have my reasons," Oh'Dar said.

"Whatever your reasons are, no matter how rock solid *you* think they are, they are not good enough."

Then he turned to Storis. "You're a lawyer; explain it to him. It's either produce the grandparents or hang."

Storis said nothing.

"Do you know where they are?" the lawyer asked Storis.

"I know where I met them. As I said, I met Ben Jenkins not that long ago. He was alive and well; I can attest to that."

"But not Mrs. Morgan Jenkins?"

"No. She was not well enough to come."

"This was at the local village. So if you say she was not well enough to come, that means they were not staying at the local village. So that's the problem. If they are alive, and if you both tell me they are, then as your attorney, I have to believe you."

He turned to Oh'Dar, "What is the big secret you're protecting, Mr. Morgan?"

When Oh'Dar said nothing, Cowell made another attempt. "I can't help you if you don't tell me what is going on."

"That's enough," Oh'Dar abruptly said and stood up. He walked to the back of the cell.

Storis went over to him. "Is that the problem? It must be, because you couldn't immediately fetch Ben when I first came looking for you. So they're living in another village. What's the big deal, Grayson? Yes, I know that the locals are being harassed, more and more, it seems. But is hiding the existence of another village worth dying for?"

"I can't explain it, I can't, so that is the end of it. I am sorry you got involved in it, and I will testify that you had no knowledge of this at any point. I will do my best to prove your innocence."

"You are not thinking clearly, Grayson. If I were able to represent you, I would advise you to take the authorities to your grandparents. If they are at another village, it is just a matter of time before they're discovered. And the constable could send out his own search parties to find the village if he wanted to."

"That can't be allowed to happen. I will confess to their murders before I would let that happen."

"What are you saying?"

"That if my death is what it takes to end this, so they can continue on and live the rest of their lives in peace, that is what will happen."

Storis threw up his arms and returned to Mr. Cowell. "I will be glad to talk to you about my part in this as I need you to defend me. It is fairly straightforward. I wasn't in on any ruse; I discovered it when I delivered some papers to the Webbs, and they told me Mrs. Morgan Jenkins and her husband had just passed through there with her grandson. It will depend on the judge and jurors believing me. But I can't testify against Grayson, as he is my client." Then Storis added, looking back at Oh'Dar, "And there is nothing to testify against him about, anyway. Even if I hadn't seen Ben Jenkins, I wouldn't for a minute believe he killed his grandparents."

No matter what happened, Oh'Dar knew he could not reveal the whereabouts of Ben and his grandmother because the People must never be discovered. He had overheard the sheriff and his deputies talking about the growing inclination in political circles toward taking the Brothers' land. To Oh'Dar, the Brothers and the Waschini were pretty much the same physically, but the Waschini in positions of power seemed to have no qualms about robbing them of their way of life. What more would they do to the People if they discovered them? Or the Sarnonn. There had been rumors of the Sarnonn's existence, but what if they had absolute proof of that? An entire organized society of people so unlike them. Oh'Dar had no doubt the Waschini would do everything they could to destroy both the People and the Sarnonn.

CHAPTER 9

The trial of Grayson Stone Morgan the Third was becoming the talk of the town. Nearly everyone within any reasonable distance of Millgrove knew the story of the murder of the second Grayson Stone Morgan and his wife, Rachel, and the disappearance of their infant son. They also knew that the son had turned up alive and that his uncle, the older brother, Louis, had been found guilty of orchestrating the murder of the young couple.

When Miss Vivian and her new husband were killed by one of her prize horses, everyone in the county had been shocked. That Mrs. Morgan Jenkins's grandson was to be tried for their murder had set every ear ablaze, listening for any shred of new information.

Because of the visibility, the governor had gotten

involved and moved quickly to find a judge to begin jury selection. Storis had been right about one thing; there was no judge who did not know something about the Morgans. The first Grayson Morgan had been a benefactor to many in the territory. In the end, the governor chose the best-respected judge of them all with the longest-standing career, Matthias Walker. And because he could not be assured of finding an impartial jury, the judge decided to hold the trial in Wilde Edge, where they would be tried together so neither could pin the blame on the other, and in the process, risk a hung jury.

The prosecutor, Mr. Ash, could barely contain his excitement over such an open-and-shut case. The publicity made it sweeter, as from what he already knew, a guilty verdict was all but assured. Bringing the murderer of Mrs. Morgan Jenkins and her husband to justice would no doubt only enhance his reputation and might well be the making of his career. He might even be appointed as a judge one day. He was practically licking his lips at the thought of prosecuting Grayson Morgan.

Judge Walker presided over the jury selection. The prosecutor knew that a speedy trial was in his best interests for a conviction, so he didn't belabor the selection. On the off chance that Grayson Morgan was telling the truth, Mr. Ash didn't want

him to change his mind and produce the grandparents.

Day one of the trial was close at hand, and
neither Oh'Dar nor Storis had much hope of coming
out of it without being found guilty.

Grace and Ned were on their way to the Brothers' village. Both had studied Storis's map and
found it to be detailed enough that they were
confident they could find it. They could already
feel the undercurrents of the warmer weather
taking hold, which was a comfort to them,
considering they were planning on bringing
Grayson's elderly grandparents back with them.
They had taken great care to plan for comfort on
the way back, having plenty of supplies, cush-
ioned mats, and light blankets stored in the
back.

The farm horses were strong and sturdy and up
to the task of pulling the wagon and supplies. Now
all they needed was continued good weather, and
within days, they would be in the local village
explaining why they needed to see Grayson's grandparents.

"How will they understand us?" Ned wondered.

Grace was sitting next to him on the front bench.
"Newell said there was a woman there who
translated."

Ned gave the reins a snap and urged the team onward.

As was customary, all rose as the judge entered the room that was being used as the court. The wood floors creaked as they stood. He took his place behind a long heavy wooden table at the front and placed an ornately carved wooden gavel at his right hand. He looked over at the prosecutor sitting at a table on his right and then at the Public Defender who was seated on the left with the defendants, Grayson Stone Morgan the Third and Newell James Storis. Behind them, more people than usual filled the room. The trial was creating a great deal of interest in the small town.

The judge rapped his mallet. "This trial will now come to order. The charges against the first defendant, Grayson Stone Morgan the Third, are kidnapping, murder, and conspiracy to commit murder. The charges against the second defendant, Newell James Storis, are accessory to a crime and obstruction of justice. Attorneys, you may proceed."

The prosecutor made his opening remarks, stating that Grayson Morgan had created a ruse to lure his grandparents away from their comfortable life in order for him to steal their fortune. The defense attorney, Mr. Cowell, explained that it was all a misunderstanding based on circumstantial evidence and that he would show that Grayson Morgan the Third had only made his grandparents' wishes come true, to live out the rest of their lives in privacy. He then said that Newell Storis had not participated in any way in the ruse surrounding the deaths of Mrs. Vivian Morgan Jenkins and Mr. Ben Jenkins and that both should be found innocent."

Mr. Ash began. "I call Mrs. Ermadine Thomas to the stand." After she was sworn in, the prosecutor asked, "Would you state your relationship to Mrs. Vivian Morgan Jenkins?"

Mrs. Thomas looked the prosecutor over. He was a stout man with a pinched face, and she thought his eyes looked shifty. She immediately didn't trust him. "I was her housekeeper for the past several decades. But I was more than that; I was also her friend."

"Did you inherit anything when Mrs. Morgan Jenkins was allegedly killed?"

"No."

"You are under oath, Mrs. Thomas. Is it not true that you inherited a great deal of wealth as well as the horse farm known as Shadow Ridge?"

"I did not inherit it. It was a gift from Miss Vivian's grandson."

A sour look immediately passed over the prosecutor's face. "And what were the conditions upon which he gave you such a generous gift?"

"There were no conditions."

"Did you know that there were no bodies in the caskets that were buried at the family grave?"

"Yes."

A gasp filled the courtroom, and the judge called for order.

"So you were in on the ruse all along?"

Mr. Cowell jumped up. "I object, Your Honor; that is prejudicial."

"Sustained. Restate your question or withdraw it, Mr. Ash."

"Were you aware that Mrs. Vivian Morgan Jenkins and Mr. Ben Jenkins were not really killed by the horse named Rebel and were, in fact, alive at the time of their so-called internment?"

"Yes."

"And so the gift from Grayson Morgan was more like hush money than a generous gift, correct?'

"Objection!"

"I withdraw the question. Mrs. Thomas, how much younger are you than Mrs. Vivian Morgan Jenkins, may I ask?"

"About ten years."

"So, had Mrs. Morgan Jenkins lived out her natural life span, Shadow Ridge would have been yours far later and for a shorter period, would it not?"

"I suppose so, yes."

"Well, yes, because you might not even have lived to inherit Shadow Ridge, isn't that so? But now you are enjoying wealth that few housekeepers, if any, experience, and much sooner."

"Your Honor," Mr. Cowell objected, "is there a question here, or are these closing remarks?"

"Sustained," the judge said. "The jury will disregard the prosecutor's last remarks."

"No more questions for this witness at this time. Your Honor."

The judge asked Mr. Cowell if he wished to cross-examine Mrs. Thomas. The lawyer said he did not at that time, and the judge told Mrs. Thomas she could step down, but must remain in town in case she was called back.

But before Mrs. Thomas left the stand, she glared at the prosecutor and said, "Shame on you. Grayson Morgan is a good man. Miss Vivian wanted a different life. I didn't want her to leave, but it was what she wanted!" Mrs. Thomas blurted out. "This is nothing more than grandstanding to further your career, and we all know it!"

"Your Honor!" the prosecutor called out.

"Mrs. Thomas, any more remarks like that and you will be held in contempt of court."

Mrs. Thomas picked up her bag and left, glaring at the prosecutor on her way out.

"The prosecution calls Newell Storis to the stand."

"Mr. Storis, what was your relationship to Mrs. Vivian Morgan Jenkins?"

"I was her attorney as well as the attorney to her late husband, Grayson Stone Morgan the First."

"As her attorney, did Mrs. Morgan Jenkiins not have papers drawn up to leave Shadow Ridge and a portion of her estate to Mrs. Thomas?"

"Yes."

"And were those papers ever executed?"

"No."

"And why not?"

"Because she was reported to have been killed, along with her husband, Ben Jenkins, before she signed them."

"And what happened next?"

"Her existing will stood. Her grandson, Grayson Stone Morgan the Third, inherited her entire estate. The day I passed the papers to him, he asked me to draw up a transfer of Shadow Ridge and a large portion of the Morgan estate to Mrs. Thomas."

"But not all of it, correct?"

"Not all."

"What happened to the rest of it?"

"Grayson kept a portion of the Morgan wealth."

"What percentage would you say?"

"Perhaps half."

The judge looked at the defense. "Counsel, please approach the bench. Mr. Cowell, do you wish to object to this line of questioning?"

"I don't see why, Your Honor. He is making a case for the generosity of Mr. Grayson Morgan. I am sure the jurors can understand he did not have to do any of that."

"Alright, then."

The prosecutor turned back to Storis. "To your knowledge, was Mrs. Morgan Jenkins in good health?"

"Objection. How would he know?"

"Your Honor, Mr. Storis has testified that he was the Morgan's attorney for some time. The Morgans had a wide array of business dealings, even after the Senior Morgan's death. It is reasonable to believe that she would have disclosed any serious health problems to her attorney."

"I'll allow it, but be careful, Mr. Ash." The judge leaned toward Storis, "You may answer the question."

"Yes, she was. If there had been something wrong, she would have confided in me."

"So she conceivably had many years yet to live. A long time for an ambitious man waiting to inherit a fortune," the prosecutor said, turning to look directly at Oh'Dar.

"Objection, Your Honor!"

"Sustained."

"Where is your current business located, Mr. Storis?"

"In Wilde Edge."

"You moved your business there from Millgrove not long ago, is that correct?"

"Yes."

"Would you tell the court and jury why you moved your long-established business to the small town of Wilde Edge?"

"The Morgans were my largest client, and without them, it was difficult to stay open. So I moved it."

"And what was the reasoning for moving to such a small town? Do you have any clients there?"

"Not yet officially; I just opened my office."

"Is there anyone you know in Wilde Edge whom you would consider to have any association with the Morgans?"

"Yes."

"And who are they?"

"The Webb family."

"The Webb family. Explain your business dealings with the Webb family."

"Grayson Morgan had a trust established for Matthew Webb and his wife after Mr. Webb was seriously hurt in a fall and unable to provide for his family. And also for the Webbs' two children."

"There was a provision by Grayson Morgan for the Webb children?"

Storis stirred in his seat. "Yes, there was. As part of the trust, Grace and Ned Webb were each also provided a stipend, but which they cannot access until they are twenty-five years of age."

"What is the monetary level of the stipend?"

"It is enough to cover their basic living expenses, adjusted for future inflation."

"Let the record show that, indeed, Grayson Stone Morgan the Third provided a stipend for each of the Webb children. An amount that would be considered even by future standards to be a substantial amount. Now, a few more questions. Are you now the attorney for Grayson Morgan?"

"Yes."

"Is there any romantic relationship between you and any of the Webb family members?"

"I am courting the Webbs' daughter, Grace."

"So is it safe to say you followed the Morgan money to Wilde Edge? Alright, yes, Your Honor. I withdraw the statement."

"The jury will ignore the last statement by the prosecutor. Do you wish to ask any more questions of this witness?"

"Not at this time."

Mr. Cowell declined to cross-examine Storis as he didn't want to show his hand until he called Storis to the stand.

"I call Grayson Stone Morgan the Third," the prosecutor said.

Oh'Dar stood and walked calmly to the stand. He was wearing the elegant clothing that Mrs. Webb had bought him out of the money he arranged for her use. After being sworn in, he looked at the jury, being sure to make eye contact with each one.

"You are the legal grandson of Mrs. Vivian Morgan Jenkins, are you not?"

"I am."

"Is it your testimony that your grandmother and her husband, Mr. Ben Jenkins, went with you willingly, leaving their wealthy life of ease to live among the locals who raised you?"

"Yes."

"And why would they do this?"

"They wanted a different life."

"And where are they now?"

"They are alive and well."

"They are living with you at the locals' village?"

"No."

"Then where are they?"

"Elsewhere."

"Are you aware that you are on trial for a serious crime? And that this could all be resolved if you would just allow the law to see your grandparents? Did not Sheriff Boone and Constable Riggs travel to the village to talk to you about this before you were arrested?"

"Yes."

"Why did you not take them to your grandparents and avoid a trial—if they are alive and well as you say."

"Because it is not what they wanted. They left so they could live a different life in peace. That is what they wanted."

"Wanted?" The prosecutor stressed the past tense of Oh'Dar's wording.

"Want. It is what they wanted, and they have never changed their position on that."

"You realize that if found guilty of the murder of Mrs. Vivian Morgan Jenkins and Mr. Ben Jenkins, you could hang?"

"Yes," Oh'Dar stated calmly.

"And that this could all be resolved by producing evidence of their wellbeing?"

"Yes."

"So your grandparents are not living in the local village, and you won't say where they are. Isn't it more likely that you lured them away with some story about who knows what, and then before they could change their minds, killed them? And that they are dead and buried somewhere because you didn't want to wait for them to die to get your hands on their money?"

"Objection, Your Honor!"

"I withdraw the question. No more questions for this witness, Your Honor."

The room had been totally quiet the whole time of the testimony, and the faces of the jurors had been deadpan until just then.

Mr. Cowell rose to re-direct. "Mr. Morgan, did you lure Mrs. Vivian Morgan Jenkins and Mr. Ben Jenkins away with the intent to collect control of the Morgan estate?"

"No," Oh'Dar answered.

"Did you murder Mrs. Vivian Morgan Jenkins and Mr. Ben Jenkins?"

"No. I did not."

"Was Newell Storis in on the ruse to fake the death of Mrs. Vivian Morgan Jenkins and Mr. Ben Jenkins?"

"No, he was not."

Mr. Cowell shot a solid stare over at the prosecutor, Mr. Ash. "That is all, Mr. Morgan. You may step down."

The judge stated, "We will adjourn for the day. Jurors, you are not to speak to anyone about what you have heard here."

Storis watched Oh'Dar return to sit next to him. Neither man spoke.

Storis had done a good job of making the map, and with clear weather on their side, Ned and Grace had made good time. They had been traveling for almost the anticipated five days. Though it felt strange being so far away from home, they passed the time talking about their futures.

"When this is over, I think Newell is going to ask me to marry him," Grace said.

"I think you're right. Despite the aspersions being cast against his character, I believe he is a good man."

"He is. But I wonder what will happen to Snide Tucker. I hope he will stay away," Grace said.

"I also hope he will."

"What about you?"

"I don't see anything changing. I will finish my studies with Mr. Clement and take over his business when he retires."

"That is a long way off," Grace said.

"Well, he said I can work as his assistant. I don't want to leave our parents. Or you. Besides, I hope to be an uncle someday!"

Grace smiled and laid her head against her brother's shoulder. "Though I hate the circumstances, this is one of the most exciting things I have ever done. We hardly ever leave Wilde Edge, and it seems like we should be getting close to the village."

"I expect they will intercept us before we get there. This is not really a route to anywhere, so I doubt they see many travelers. Let's hope the woman who translates is the first one they take us to."

"Once Miss Vivian and Ben understand how important it is, I know they will come back with us. Then this will all be over and behind us."

Little did they know that day one of the trial had already started.

The next morning, Ned arose to the sight of riders lined up on a nearby hill, backlit by the rising sun. "Grace, wake up. We have company."

Grace rubbed her eyes and sat up, quickly pushing back the blankets and throwing on an overcoat. "I hope it's the people we are looking for," she said as she shielded her eyes with her hand, trying to see them more clearly.

"Looks like about five. I don't know if we should signal to them or what would be best."

"We should be friendly. They will either be welcoming or not, and we may as well find out sooner as later."

"You're so brave. Have I ever told you that?" Ned said.

"Bravery is often born out of desperation, I think."

They stepped around from the back of the wagon and into clear sight and waved at the riders. For a moment, nothing happened, then the horses slowly started toward them. Grace reached out for her brother's hand and held it tight.

She remembered how Storis had explained who he was looking for, and when they got closer, she did the same. She waited until they were near enough, and then she said, "Grayson Stone Morgan," and pointed to the blue sky overhead and then to her eyes.

The lead man looked at his companions and said

something to them before dismounting and walking over to the siblings.

"Oh'Dar," he said.

"Grayson Stone Morgan," Ned repeated. "We are friends of Grayson Morgan. Can you take us to your village? Your Chief?" Ned hoped some of his words would make sense.

The man nodded and motioned to them to get their wagon ready to go. Ned and Grace hurried to gather up their things and ready the horses, and then they were on their way, two of the riders in front of them and three bringing up the rear.

"We're into it now," Grace said to her brother.

"No turning back. But I don't think there is anything to be afraid of. Grayson said they were good people. After all, they raised him."

The village fell into commotion when they saw Pajackok bringing two Waschini in a wagon. Someone ran to get Honovi, who came over immediately and stood next to Chief Is'Taqa.

"A couple, a young couple," she said.

"More and more Waschini. Coming directly here, too," Chief Is'Taqa said. "No doubt this has something to do with Oh'Dar. But he is not here."

Ned stopped the wagon and climbed down. "Hello! Can anyone understand me? We were told there is a woman among you who can speak with us."

Honovi looked at her life-walker, and he nodded.

"I am Honovi, wife of Chief Is'Taqa. What is your business here?"

"We are friends of Grayson Morgan. We are here to see his grandparents, Miss Vivian and Ben Jenkins. We were told they are living here with you," Ned said.

Honovi translated for the Chief, and at his bidding, asked, "Why do you wish to speak with them?"

"Grayson has been arrested and is being held for their murder. We need them to come back with us to prove that they are still alive. If they don't come back with us, they are going to find him guilty, and they will kill him."

Honovi looked at her life-walker and translated.

Just then, Acise came out of their shelter, hands against her belly. "What is going on?" she asked her mother.

"They said they are friends of Oh'Dar's. They want to talk to the grandparents. They said that Oh'Dar's grandparents have to go back with them or else Oh'Dar will be killed—"

Acise's hand flew to her mouth. "But the grandparents can't travel. Momma, you know they can't travel."

"I know," Honovi said. "Miss Vivian is too old for that type of journey. And Ben's leg is badly broken, from what I know. They would never survive the trip. And Oh'Dar would never forgive us for allowing it."

Acise covered her face with her hands. Her beloved, her life-walker, might not live to see their child born. And she would have to travel the rest of her path without him.

"Can they at least come here and meet with these two?" Honovi said out loud.

"Even that is too risky. The paths to the High Rocks are slick with the spring run-off. But perhaps there is another route we could take them to Oh'Dar's grandparents without giving anything away."

Feeling that Grayson Morgan's testimony had sealed the case for him and no longer caring about Newell Storis, the prosecutor rested. The judge then turned the trial over to the defense, who called Mrs. Thomas to the stand.

"Mrs. Thomas, how well do you know Grayson Morgan the Third?"

"Very well. He lived at Shadow Ridge off and on for several years."

"Did you ever witness any hostility between him or his grandparents?"

"Absolutely not. He always treated them with love, kindness, and respect."

"You went along with the ruse to fake their deaths. Why was that?"

"It was what Miss Vivian said she wanted. I was sad at the thought that they would leave. I was close to her and to Ben, too. But she said their lives had become humdrum, and they wanted to spend their last years with her grandson and his children. They said they knew that their new life would be different. Primitive, but it was what they wanted."

"And why the big ruse? Why didn't they just tell people that it is what they wanted?"

"They were afraid that their son Louis would try to find them if they told people they were leaving. And also that others would. They wanted privacy, and they felt the only way to get it was to have people believe they had been killed."

"But they were not killed, were they?"

"No. We made the story up. And Rebel, the horse who was accused of stomping them to death, was hidden at my house, where Ben and Miss Vivian were staying until after the funeral."

"Why did Grayson Morgan leave you Shadow Ridge and a portion of the Morgan wealth?"

"He knew it was what his grandmother wanted. And he is a good man."

"Was it a payoff for your silence?"

"Oh, no. Not at all. I never once considered it that. Nor was anything like that ever said."

"Did you hire a man named Zachariah Tucker for a period of time?"

"Yes. But we didn't keep him on. He was acting suspiciously. We paid him extra days and let him go."

"By suspiciously, what do you mean?"

"We would find him in areas of the property where he had no business. He was asking questions in town about Miss Vivian and Shadow Ridge. He asked about the Morgan family gravesite, in particular."

"Objection, Your Honor, Mr. Tucker is not on trial here," the prosecutor said.

"Your Honor, this leads to credibility. I will show its relevance shortly."

"See that you do, Mr. Cowell."

"One last question, do you in any way believe that Grayson Morgan meant his grandparents any harm?"

"No. Never. He loved them deeply." Then Mrs. Thomas looked over at Oh'Dar, "He still does. And they still love him."

"Objection. Conjecture on the witnesses' part that Mrs. Morgan Jenkins and her husband are still alive."

"Sustained. Jurors, disregard Mrs. Thomas's last statement."

"That is all for this witness, Your Honor."

"Cross-examine, Mr. Ash?"

The prosecutor declined to cross-examine Mrs. Thomas. She was a convincing witness and was only shoring up Grayson Morgan's honor.

"I call Newell Storis to the stand."

Storis pushed his chair back, looked at Oh'Dar, and took the witness stand.

"Were you aware that the deaths of Mrs. Vivian Morgan Jenkins and Mr. Ben Jenkins were staged?"

"No. Not at the time of their funeral."

"When did you learn that they were still alive?"

"When I delivered some papers to the Webbs, and it came out in conversation that they had just passed through with Mr. Grayson Morgan the Third."

"Anything else?"

"On learning that, I hired a tracker named Snide Tucker to find Grayson Morgan. He took me to the local village where Grayson Morgan had reportedly been living."

"And did you find him there?"

"Yes."

"What about the grandparents?"

"I talked with Ben Jenkins myself. Mrs. Morgan Jenkins was not up to traveling to meet with me."

"When you met with Ben Jenkins, was he under duress of any kind?"

"No. He was calm and friendly. We had known each other for a long time. It was clear to me that he was not being held there against his will. I was convinced, and still am, that this is what they wanted, just as has been testified to by Mrs. Thomas and Grayson Morgan."

"What happened after you returned?"

"I tried to go on with my life, but Zachary Tucker

threatened me. He said if I did not pay him out of the Morgan wealth to keep quiet, he would go to the authorities and tell them that the graves did not contain the bodies of Grayson Morgan's grandparents and that I was in on their murders."

"And did you pay Mr. Tucker?"

"No. That would have been illegal and unethical. But if I had, we wouldn't be sitting here."

The courtroom, which had been quiet until then, broke out in murmurs. The judge pounded his gavel and called for order.

"A few last questions, Mr. Storis. For the record, you stated that you were not in any way involved in staging the deaths of Mrs. Vivian Morgan Jenkins and Mr. Ben Jenkins. At the time that you did become aware of it, was your silence bought by Grayson Morgan?"

"No. Absolutely not. I was silent out of loyalty to Miss Vivian and Ben. It is their life; they are entitled to live it out as they wish."

"No more questions for this witness at this time, Your Honor."

"Your chance to cross-examine Mr. Ash."

"I do not wish to cross-examine Mr. Storis, Your Honor."

The prosecutor no longer cared about Newell Storis. He believed in the attorney's innocence, and after hearing Storis testify that Tucker had tried to blackmail him, he didn't want any more testimony going down that path. The conviction of Grayson

Morgan was the prize, and he was not going to be waylaid going after a little fish such as Storis. As far as the jurors were concerned, the prosecutor knew he had human avarice on his side. Nothing pleased the not-so-well-off as seeing the wealthy brought down.

"Call your next witness, Mr. Cowell."

"I would like to call Grace Webb to the stand, Your Honor, but she is not available. So at this time, I will call Constable Riggs."

The judge looked around the courtroom. "Constable Riggs is not here, either. Someone, please try to locate him. Gentlemen, approach the bench."

"It's your responsibility to have your witnesses here, Mr. Cowell."

"Constable Riggs was supposed to be here. He said he would be. As for Grace Webb, I didn't know she would also be absent."

The court clerk came forward to deliver a message to the judge. "Your Honor, Constable Riggs has been called over to Braxton county on a family emergency. It will be almost a week before we can get him back here."

"Do you have other witnesses to call, Mr. Cowell? The constable will not be available for some time."

"His testimony is crucial to my case, Your Honor. It will show that this accusation against my client came out of the vindictiveness and bad character of Zachariah Tucker, triggered by Mr. Storis's refusal to concede to being blackmailed."

"Do you not have any other witnesses to call while we locate the constable and Grace Webb?"

"Not at the moment, no."

The judge called the court back to order. "There will be five days' recess while we await the return of a key witness for the defense. Jurors, you are dismissed with the same instruction that you speak with no one about what you have witnessed here."

Acaraho and Adia listened carefully to Honovi. She had explained what she had learned of the two Waschini who had come to the village looking for Oh'Dar's grandparents, that they were friends of his and members of the family who had first cared for Oh'Dar. How, in Etera, they had found the village was beyond everyone's understanding, but Honovi was convinced that this was the best chance to prove that Ben and Miss Vivian were still alive, and thereby free Oh'Dar. She then explained the solution that she and Chief Is'Taqa had thought of.

Adia kept tight control over herself. This was her son, the Outsider offspring she had raised nearly from his birth, and without a miracle, he would be put to death for a crime he had not committed. As she listened, she was silently praying that somehow the plan might be workable.

Miss Vivian had been almost inconsolable after learning about Oh'Dar's arrest. Ben, though also upset, had done his best to help her believe that something would intervene to save him. So their relief was tremendous on hearing that Grace and Ned Webb had traveled all the way to the Brothers' village from Wilde Edge and that Honovi had a plan. They listened carefully, and after hearing what was being proposed and realizing that Acaraho and Adia had agreed to it, they agreed to it too.

It was a risk, but all were confident that, no matter what, Grace and Ned would keep the secret of Miss Vivian and Ben's situation. They all wanted Oh'Dar's name cleared and for him to be safely returned home.

Grace and Ned agreed to be blindfolded. Pajackok checked the bindings carefully. Then, to make sure they could not see anything, he placed a second layer over their eyes.

"We are placing all our trust in you," Honovi told them. "If Grayson knew we were doing this, he would be very upset, but we all agree it is the only way to save his life. You have promised not to remove your blindfolds nor try to figure out where you are being taken."

"We have," Grace answered, "And I promise you I can't see a thing."

"Me neither," Ned said.

"The last thing is that you must wad up these tiny pieces of woven fabric and put them into your ears."

Honovi placed the pieces into their hands, and they dutifully twirled them into little balls and stuffed them in their ears.

"We are as ready as we can be," Honovi said to her life-walker.

Chief Is'Taqa raised his staff, and Pajackok and several other braves helped the two Waschini up onto horses, and then one sat behind each.

It was a tedious journey, but finally, they were at the entrance to Kthama and helped to dismount.

The High Protector Awan and First Guard Thetis were there to take them the rest of the way to the grandparents' living quarters. No words were spoken. Acaraho had cleared the rooms and tunnels along the way to ensure that the two Waschini could be escorted through without overhearing anything.

Grace heard a loud scraping and bumping sound, which made her jump. Then a gentle hand on her back urged her forward. After a few steps, the scraping sound returned, followed by a familiar voice that said, "You may take your blindfolds off now."

Grace pushed the band away from her eyes. "Miss Vivian!" she exclaimed and ran into her arms.

"You are alive. You are both alive, just as Grayson said!"

Ned was as quickly at Ben's side, shaking his hand.

"Oh, but where are we?" Grace said as she disengaged from Miss Vivian's embrace and looked around.

What an odd contrast. On the one hand, the room was filled with beautiful wooden furniture. Ben was lying on a large dark walnut bed, with Miss Vivian in an upholstered chair next to him. There was a large bureau and a chest of drawers. Resting on top of the bureau was a mantle clock, slowly ticking away. But the room itself had rock walls and a rock ceiling, like a cave. The only light came in from some type of opening overhead. Looking around, she saw a large wooden door, presumably where the scraping noise had originated.

"This is our home, now. As you can see, we are well cared for and in good health for our age." Then Ben winced. "Other than that I took a fall recently and broke my leg."

Grace walked over to the lace curtain hanging on one of the walls. She touched it gently and realized there was no window behind it. But it did give the appearance of a window.

"You live in a—a cave?" Grace asked.

"Please do not ask questions. I know you are curious. But the only reason we agreed to this was to clear Grayson's name. It is important that you do not learn any more about this place than the minimum you see here. And when you testify that you saw us, mention only that we are alive and well, and happy. You can explain that was one of the conditions on which we met with you. That, and that you only tell the truth, of course."

"Yes, as my wife says, we are here of our own accord," Ben added. "No one forced or coerced us to come. This is what we both wanted, and Grayson did everything in his power to make it happen. He must be cleared of any wrongdoing as he only did as we asked and now is being persecuted for it."

"He will be very upset that you were brought here," Miss Vivian said. "But make him understand we cannot sit by and let him be found guilty of our murders when nothing could be further from the truth. If we could have traveled there, we would have.

"Oh, it is so good to see you both; how I wish you could stay with us a while. But you need to get back as soon as you can."

"We can go back and testify now that we saw you both and what you told us," Ned said. "There are two of us who will swear under oath that you are both alive, well, and here of your own free will."

"Please tell us anything more you know about the

trial. Have they picked a judge? Has it started yet?" Miss Vivian asked.

"It hadn't started when we left Wilde Edge, but, yes, they did pick a judge, a man named Matthias Walker."

"They could not have made a better choice," exclaimed Miss Vivian. "Judge Walker is a fair and experienced judge. But without your testimony, I fear Grayson will be found guilty."

"Let's just hope it is enough," Grace said.

CHAPTER 10

The High Council meeting had been brought forward to accommodate the upcoming deliveries of Adia and Tehya. Adia was anxiously awaiting Urilla Wuti, Nootau, and Iella. She longed to hear how Nootau's training was going and if he had managed to enter the Dream World at will. She struggled to keep her mind off Oh'Dar, praying that the visit from the Webb offspring would be enough to win his freedom.

Though the gathering was still a couple of months away, the community was starting to prepare for the guests. The High Council meetings would now be attended by the People's Leaders, their Healers and Helpers, and the same from Haan's community. All Brothers who wanted to attend were also welcome from now on. It would take everyone working together to secure Etera's future.

Adia was also looking forward to the assembly of

the Healers that Urilla Wuti had planned. Only the tragedy of Oh'Dar's arrest tainted her anticipation. But by now, Oh'Dar's friends, Grace and Ned, were well on their way back to testify that Miss Vivian and Ben were alive and well.

Nadiwani interrupted her thoughts. "I am anxious to hear how Tehya's seeding is coming along."

Tehya and I will deliver not far from each other," Adia said.

"And Acise as well. How wonderful to have three new offspring added to our family circle! An'Kru will have plenty of friends to grow up with."

"Don't forget the Sarnonn Guardian females," Adia added.

"What an influx of offspring!"

"You said it a while back. Tehya, Acise, me, the six. It heralds something, I am sure."

"What do you think will happen when at the appointed time the twelve Sarnonn Guardians come together with An'Kru?"

"I assume it will be part of heralding in the Age of Light? Obviously, something will happen, but who knows what. Given that Pan is taking him away in seven years' time, it will not be until after he returns. I wonder how old he will be then," Adia said quietly.

"I am sorry I brought it up. I know it hangs heavily over your head. Maybe having another offspring will help."

"It will be wonderful to have another, but one cannot replace the other."

"I know. I was just trying to find something uplifting to say."

Adia looked at Nadiwani, "Thank you for being such a good friend."

Try as hard as she could, there was too much weighing Adia down. The upcoming birth of her second offspring with Acaraho, the High Council meeting, Acise and Oh'Dar's offspring, that Nootau knew Acaraho was not his father by bloodline and that Khon'Tor was. And Oh'Dar's imprisonment. Every time anyone spoke of Oh'Dar and Acise, it was as if a blade pierced her heart.

She needed some peace and quiet, so she sought out a place she had not visited in years.

Tucked far away in the back tunnels, through a small opening that most would never notice, the charming little cave that enclosed a small, shallow pool.

Adia's seeding was not far enough along that she didn't fit. Had it been further into warm weather, she would have eased her toes into the little eddy that trickled through to form the little pool of water. Instead, she leaned back against the smooth rock wall and breathed in the humid air.

Her thoughts traveled back to when she first

came to the High Rocks. How much her life had
changed. She had weathered many trials, but she
had also received many blessings and had witnessed
miracles. More than any other time, she needed to
reaffirm her faith in the blessings of the Great
Mother so she could raise An'Kru and her new
offspring in joy. The last thing she wanted for them
was the burden of an emotionally distracted mother.

Oh, but if Oh'Dar was not returned safe and
sound, how would she ever recover from that loss?
She had protected him from the moment she picked
him up out of that bundle of blankets he was in,
watched over and protected him all his growing-up
years. And now, she was powerless to save him. And
now he was so far away, out of reach of her embrace
or her help.

At the Far High Hills, it was time for Myrica to return
to her village, and Larara would soon be taking
Ahanu home to the small, unnamed community. She
was glad she had come as she now knew with
certainty that, living among his own kind, Ahanu
would be loved and protected for the rest of his life.
In addition, she would return to her own village with
much assurance for her Chief of the goodness and
kindness of the People.

Myrica had worked diligently with them both,
helping Ahanu shift his dependency from her to

Larara, and she hardly ever spent any time with him now. When they both entered the room, he now reached for Larara first. Because the boy thought his name was Ahanu, his grandmother had elected to keep calling him that. She told Myrica that this had somehow also helped her to let go of his tragic beginnings.

"I am sorry to see you go," Larara was saying. "Adik'Tar Khon'Tor would like to go with you and speak to your Chief."

Myrica picked up Ahanu and held him close one last time. "Most likely I will never see him again," she said quietly.

"I will tell him about you, I promise. Come, if you are ready, we will find Khon'Tor, and you can be on your way. I am sure many will be glad of your return."

Pakwa was out, fishing along the riverbank. The air was rich with the scent of thawed ground, and the migrating songbirds were returning. Myrica smiled from ear to ear when she saw him. A moment later, he heard her approach and looked up from his task.

"Myrica! You have come home!" He glanced at the tall figure standing a few steps away.

"One of the People has come back with me to talk with Chief Kotori." She introduced them, saying, "Remember, Adik'Tar Khon'Tor was here when they came in search of Ahanu." Pakwa raised his hand in greeting before gathering up his things.

Chief Kotori was pleased at Myrica's return. He welcomed Khon'Tor back, and then she told him and the others who had assembled that she had successfully handed Ahanu over to his grandmother. She assured them all that in their way of life, the People were peaceful and honored the Great Spirit.

Khon'Tor waited patiently for Myrica to finish answering the Chief's questions. The Chief then turned to him and said, "You have come to once again invite us to join your High Council of Leaders."

"Yes, Chief Kotori. Word continues to reach us of the Waschini's aggression against your people. We would like you to join us so we may offer you our protection and help if needed and wherever possible. Our People are many; communities of us are spread throughout the Brothers' territory. We can place watchers on your perimeters who can provide an earlier warning than your own people of any riders encroaching. Please consider our offer."

"I have considered it since you first made it."

"We have a council meeting coming up at the next full moon. I would be glad to return and escort you and whoever else you wish to attend. You will meet other Leaders of your people, some of whom you may know, perhaps others whom you may not. There is strength in unity."

"Return at the appointed time, and I will give you my answer then."

Lellaach and Thord had just finished meeting with the other Sassen Guardians. There was great joy between them at the knowledge that each of the females was seeded and well on their way to delivering. Though they had known each other all their lives, it had brought the six females closer as a group, knowing each would soon have an offling in her arms. While the females were rejoicing in their happiness, the males continued to meet with Pan for their training in the sanctity of the Corridor.

In contrast to the warm weather on Etera, the shimmering landscape of the Corridor was covered in snow and glistened with indescribable beauty. The air was crisp, fresher than anything any of them had experienced, and its delicious coolness filled their bodies with a vigor not even they had felt before. Pan gave them a moment to adjust once more to the intoxicating existence in the Corridor.

"The Ror'Eckrah is a powerful tool. You have experienced it on two occasions. The first was when the specter of Straf'Tor was manifested to thwart the Sassen attack on Kthama. The second was when Haan opened Kthama Minor, now Kht'shWea. It was that event that turned the granite boulders you placed in the meadow into the generator stones and each of you into Guardians. Through those stones, now crystals, you can access even greater power than a Guardian normally could without them."

"But we are not as powerful as you are," Thord said. "We are Sassen Guardians, not Mothoc. You are the last true Guardian."

"I am the last of the Mothoc Guardians. But you are Guardians in your own right, as is An'Kru, who is an Akassa, and who will possess abilities even greater than mine."

"How can that be, since he is not Mothoc? Are your powers not greater than ours due to the Mothoc blood in your veins?" Norir asked.

"It is true, as you say, that we have different concentrations of Mothoc blood. In that respect, yes, An'Kru has the least Mothoc blood flowing through him. But An'Kru is not just a Guardian; he is—something more."

"The Rah-hora kept us from the Akassa," said Norir, "lest they influence us to weaken our bloodline by using the Brothers' seed, as did the Fathers-Of-Us-All. And it was to protect them from our greater strength. So how does it not now matter that we are Sassen and An'Kru is Akassa."

"Just as you were transformed into Guardians by the power unleashed by the vortex when Haan opened Kht'shWea, the same energy affected An'Kru in his mother's belly. You were all changed in an instant, forever altered to the tiniest elements of your being. It was what had to happen, but it was far more dangerous than anyone realized—even Haan. Releasing that much of the creative force through the vortex under Kthama into a single part of Etera could have had devastating consequences."

Pan motioned around her. "The Corridor appears to be the same as Etera, yet everything is more vibrant here. More alive, even. The colors are deeper, the sounds sweeter—more melodic or more resonant. That is because the creative force is purer here. It is the same creative force that transformed you into Guardians. The same creative force that also transformed An'Kru into a Guardian."

"Though it is true that, as a Sassen, you carry more Mothoc blood than An'Kru, the concentration of the original Mothoc bloodline is not a crucial factor because of how you were all created."

"I am sorry, Guardian, I still do not understand," Norir said.

"If only your physical attributes were altered, then your offling would not be Guardians. No, the transformation took place in the deepest building blocks of your beings. Your souls, your memories, who you are, all were unaffected. But your entire structure was remade in the instant that the concentrated creative force was released by the Ror'Eckrah."

Pan looked around at the six faces, knowing they were doing their best to understand what she was telling them.

"Your seed was also altered. For these reasons, you are the purest Sassen ever to walk Etera. As if you are not a combination of the seed of the Mothoc and the Brothers but pure creations in your own right. And your offlings' bloodlines will be clear."

"Clear? What do you mean by that?" Thord wanted to explain this to his mate.

"The problems of the bloodline will not exist for your offling. They can pair with anyone. There will never be a threat of inbreeding as there are no deficiencies that could combine. So there will never be a threat to an end of the Guardians."

She waited while they took in her words.

"For a moment, let me return to the Mothoc blood and the split forced between the Sassen and the Akassa. The Sassen blood had to be kept undiluted so you would have the ability to form the Ror'Eckrah and open the vortex—not just to open Kthama Minor, but to create each of you. Had the Sassen blood been weaker, there would not have been enough of the Aezaitera available to Haan. So the Ror'Eckrah could not have been formed, and Kht'shWea could not have been opened. And none of you, or An'Kru, would exist."

Pan looked at blank faces.

"Though there is no sense of fatigue in the Corridor," Pan continued, "I can see that this is enough for today. I will return you to Etera's realm. Share this with your beloveds. Assure them that their offling can find mates among each other as they wish."

"Before you send us back, what of An'Kru?" asked Clah.

"An'Kru is also clear. He will be able to pair with anyone of his choosing. Whether he does or not, whether that is part of his destiny, I do not know."

"Does the Healer, Adia, know what you have told us?" Thord asked.

"No. But you may share it with her if you wish."

The six male Guardian were instantly returned to their bodies at Kht'shWea. They needed to rest, but as soon as they recovered, they would seek out their mates to share the mind-bending information Pan had just shared with them.

CHAPTER 11

The trial was on hold, waiting for the appearance of Constable Riggs, so Oh'Dar and Storis had been returned to their cells. Sheriff Boone let the Webbs send over special food and other items to provide some comfort. It was out of the ordinary, but he was willing to bend the rules while the constable was not around.

Oh'Dar was staring out of a tiny window in the cell wall.

"It is not going well," Storis said.

"It is not going well for me, but you will get off. Mr. Cowell has made a good case so far, leading to the conclusion that you were not involved in any of this and that it was Snide Tucker's intention only to cause trouble for you since you refused to let him blackmail you."

Oh'Dar peeled a small piece of loose wood from

the window frame and flicked it onto the floor. "As for me, I am resigned that they will find me guilty."

Storis said nothing.

Oh'Dar turned to face him. "The only way out is for me to produce my grandmother and Ben, and we both know I will never do that."

"We have come together this far, Grayson. When we get out of this, and I do mean *we*, will you tell me the rest of this story? Whatever this great secret is that you bear, it is surely too much for any man to carry alone."

Oh'Dar shrugged. "Perhaps. But I doubt there will be any opportunity for that. If there had been any way out, I would gladly have taken it. In a way, I just wish it were already over." He turned back to the window. "I'm sure you and Grace will have a wonderful life together."

After a moment of silence, he said, "I wonder if Sheriff Boone would give me some paper and a quill."

"Do you wish to draw up a will?" Storis asked.

"No, though that is a good point. I want to write letters to my mother and father and my grandparents and my beloved Acise. And perhaps a letter to my son or daughter, to be given to them someday when they are old enough to understand."

Storis's voice was low. "I am sure the sheriff would. It is a fair request."

"I want to tell my parents how much I love them for rescuing me and taking me in and giving me a life few could imagine. My mother protected me at every turn, always making my welfare the foundation of every decision she made. She suffered for me, and now, she will have to endure outliving me, which is something no parent should ever have to experience. As for my grandparents, well, they will also have to carry on without me. I wanted to be there for them, to help them live out the rest of their lives as easily as possible. I introduced them to a strange new world, and now I have to abandon them to it."

Oh'Dar let out a long breath. "Regret is a hard master. I don't remember who told me that once, but it is true. Yet, if I had to do it all over again, what would I change? I could not have asked for a more loving mother, a kinder or wiser father. My brother was always at my side, there to guide me and look after me. I married the woman of my dreams and gave her a child to remember me by. All in all, it has been a good life. A life of magic and mystery, really. I am just sorry it will end so much sooner than I expected."

Oh'Dar spun around. "I don't want to leave them, Storis. Can you understand that?"

"Yes, of course I can. What can I do to help, Grayson?"

"Just make sure they get the letters I write. Promise me that. The locals will give Grandmother and Ben and my parents their letters. And while we are at it, you are right; I should draw up a will. I need to do something with the Morgan wealth so it can continue to be used for good. My grandmother still has the right to control it, but given where they are, it would be difficult to do so. They had faith in you, as I do, so it would be fitting that you should manage the Morgan Trust after I am gone. I am worried for the village; I am worried for all the locals. And I won't be here to help protect them. Any of them."

"Grayson. It isn't over yet."

Oh'Dar turned again and stared out of the little jail cell window. "Yes, it is, Newell. And we both know it."

Oh'Dar did as he had said he would and used the time to create a will and write letters for Adia, Acaraho, Nootau, Ben, his grandmother, Acise, and his unborn child. He also wrote to Chief Is'Taqa, Honovi, and his friend, Tehya. That done, his soul found some peace, but he had a last favor to ask of Storis, something to be taken care of the moment the trial was ended and the lawyer was free.

Constable Riggs, free of his family obligation, was on his way back to Wilde Edge, and Sheriff Boone let Oh'Dar and Storis know that court would be in session the next morning.

That night, Oh'Dar did not sleep at all. It was his last night before the inevitable guilty verdict, and he wondered what it would feel like, having the rope set about his neck with someone behind him, tightening it. He imagined the moments ticking past, like the hands on his grandmother's beloved clock, the last seconds of his life passing, waiting until they dropped the door under his feet, and he left behind everything and everyone he loved.

"Order in the Court. Order in the Court," the clerk announced.

Judge Walker rapped his gavel. "This court is now in session. Mr. Cowell, call your next witness."

Constable Riggs took the stand.

"When did you first meet Zachary Tucker?"

"Mr. Tucker came to Sheriff Boone about a month ago and said he believed that the graves of Mrs. Morgan Jenkins and Mr. Jenkins were empty. That their deaths had been faked, and they were abducted against their will."

"Did he make any allegations about who was involved?"

"Yes. He said that Newell Storis, who was Mrs. Morgan Jenkins's attorney, had been involved in the ruse."

"And what happened thereafter?"

"I took some deputies and went to Shadow Ridge and had the graves opened."

"Do you usually take such drastic action on such statements?"

"No."

"Then why did you this time?"

"Because of the nature of the entire Morgan case. The murder of the oldest Morgan son and his wife, Rachel, and that no traces were ever found of their baby son, Grayson Stone Morgan the Third. That a stranger appeared later, claiming to be the same Grayson Stone Morgan the Third. A stranger who—in time—stood to inherit a great deal of wealth."

"Did you investigate Zachary Tucker before you took action based on his allegations?"

"No, but Sheriff Moore at Wilde Edge knew him."

"And how would you describe his character?"

Mr. Ash jumped up. "Objection; you are asking the witness to draw a conclusion."

"I am asking the witness to state an opinion. He is entitled to his opinion of Mr. Tucker. Considering what is at stake, a man's life, it has relevance, Your Honor."

"Objection overruled. Answer the question, Constable."

"I am not going to argue that Zachary Tucker is a man of good standing. I admit that he is not."

"And the accused, Newell Storis? What do you know of him?"

"He was the Morgans' long-standing attorney."

"Has Mr. Storis committed any crimes, to your knowledge?"

"Only this one."

The judge didn't wait for Mr. Cowell to object; he scowled at the constable himself. "Mr. Riggs, you will refrain from any further remarks of that type. Do you understand?"

"Let me restate my answer. No, Mr. Storis has not been involved in any questionable activity to my knowledge. Or, not according to the records."

"Is it fair to say this entire case was opened on a claim by Zachary Tucker that the family gravesite at Shadow Ridge did not contain the bodies of Mrs. Vivian Morgan Jenkins or Mr. Benjamin Jenkins?"

"Yes."

"Were you aware that Zachary Tucker tried to blackmail Mr. Storis, threatening to go to the authorities with this story if he was not paid to keep quiet?"

"Objection, hearsay. Whether Mr. Tucker blackmailed Mr. Storis has not been established, only that Mr. Storis testified to that effect."

"Let me ask my question another way. Constable, do you have any concrete proof that Mr. Storis was in any way involved in the fabrication of the deaths of Mrs. Vivian Morgan Jenkins and her husband, Mr. Ben Jenkins?"

"No."

"No further questions, Your Honor."

"Do you wish to cross-examine, Mr. Ash?"

"No, Your Honor."

Oh'Dar watched the constable leave the witness stand. He stopped to memorize the moment. He had

nothing more to say in his own defense, and he knew
that within moments Mr. Cowell would rest in his
defense of Newell Storis. He had done a good job,
and Oh'Dar was convinced that Storis would be
cleared of wrongdoing. As for his own fate, Oh'Dar
didn't blame Mr. Cowell. After all, he had given the
attorney nothing to work with.

"Mr. Cowell, do you have any more witnesses to
call?"

"No, Your Honor, the defense rests."

"In that case, gentlemen, we can move to closing
remarks."

The prosecutor buttoned his coat as he stood up
and walked to where he could face the jury.

"Gentlemen, you have heard the testimony of
many witnesses in defense of Mr. Newell Storis and
of Grayson Stone Morgan the Third. It is now up to
you to determine the truth of this matter. On the less
grievous side of this tragic story, you must decide
whether Newell Storis was involved in the initial
cover-up of the falsified deaths of Mrs. Vivian
Morgan Jenkins and Mr. Ben Jenkins. If you believe
he was, then you are to find him guilty. As for
Grayson Stone Morgan the Third, his involvement is
far more serious. You have heard his own testimony,
his refusal to produce the grandparents whom he
claims are alive and well, even to reveal where it is he
says they are living, or to take anyone there.

"Beyond all understanding, Grayson Morgan has
given you no reason whatsoever to believe that his

grandparents are alive and well. Only his word. The word of a man who profited greatly by their falsified deaths. A man who inherited a vast fortune that no one else in this room will ever enjoy. Mr. Morgan would have inherited his grandmother's estate in time. But he was impatient. And there was always a chance she could change her mind. So instead, he took matters into his own hands to convince them to come with him and orchestrate this fantastic ruse, the end result of which was that the Morgan estate passed into his hands while he was still a young man."

With dramatic flair, the prosecutor walked back and forth in front of the jury stand, then turned to look at Oh'Dar.

"The entire history of the Morgan family is heartbreaking. Not only did Mrs. Morgan Jenkins survive the death of her first husband and then those of her firstborn son and his wife, but a thorough search for her only grandson turned up nothing. Further heartbreak ensued when Mrs. Morgan Jenkins learned that her older son, Louis, was behind the murder her younger son and his wife and that the infant grandson had also been a target, all designed so that Louis Morgan alone would inherit the Morgan fortune. How ironic that Louis Morgan's plan to dispose of his brother and his brother's family ended up putting Grayson Stone Morgan the Third in the very same position Louis coveted. Being the sole beneficiary of the Morgan estate.

"But it wasn't enough, was it? Mr. Morgan is just as twisted and greedy as his uncle Louis. Luring his gullible grandmother and her second husband away with a tale of a mysterious new life, getting them to agree to fake their deaths, only to murder them far from home. And so they are not even interred at Shadow Ridge as they should rightfully have been. Their bodies were no doubt heartlessly disposed of somewhere in some wilderness and left to rot, never to be found."

Suddenly, the doors to the courtroom were flung open, and in walked Grace and Ned Webb. The judge looked up as they hurried down the aisle and approached the bench.

"Please, Your Honor. Please, stop everything. You must let us testify," said Ned.

"Your Honor," Mr. Ash exclaimed. "Whatever it is they have to say, it is too late. We are already in closing remarks."

"Please, Your Honor," Grace pleaded. "You must hear what we have to say; it is about Miss Vivian and Ben!"

Mr. Cowell stood up and quickly walked over. "What is your objection to their testifying, Mr. Ash? What is the rush? Surely you wish for justice to be served. True justice. If these two have something to share that might change the outcome of this trial, what is your objection?"

The judge eyed the prosecutor, waiting for an answer. Judge Walker had just about had enough of

Mr. Ash and how he was very obviously intending the outcome of this trial to enhance his reputation and further his political ambitions.

"I— I—"

"Never mind, Mr. Ash. I will allow it. Please swear in these two young people," the judge ordered.

Mr. Cowell did not know what was going on, but he could see that Grace and Ned Webb felt they had something important to share, something they felt would help his client.

Mr. Cowell looked first at Ned then at Grace. It was a risk, having no idea what they might say, but at this point, his case was lost. They couldn't make matters any worse. He elected first to call Ned to the stand.

"You are the son of Mr. and Mrs. Matthew Webb, is that correct?"

"Yes."

"The courtroom and jurors are aware from other testimony of the relationship of Mr. Ned Webb and his sister, Miss Grace Webb, to Grayson Morgan, so with the court's permission, I will not go over those details again."

"Proceed."

"Please tell us why you just now entered the courtroom in such a state of obvious agitation?"

"My sister Grace and I, we just got back and came as quickly as we could. We talked to Miss Vivian and Ben. They are both alive and well. Well, not totally well. Ben has a broken leg, but it's healing. The point is, they are not dead. We both talked to them at length."

A murmur spread through the courtroom, but a glare from the judge quickly quietened everyone down.

"Why did they not come back with you?"

"Just as Grayson said, they aren't able to travel this far. Miss Vivian certainly couldn't make that trip again. And Ben broke his leg in a fall and twisted his knee. Neither of them could come, but they said they would have if they could."

"Is there any doubt in your mind that they were truly Mrs. Vivian Morgan Jenkins and Mr. Ben Jenkins?"

"Oh, absolutely not. I know them. They spent several days with us when they were traveling through with Grayson. Anyone who met them would never forget them."

"No more questions for this witness, Your Honor."

Mr. Ash declined to cross-examine, and Grace took the stand.

Mr. Cowell greeted her and said, "You have just heard your brother's testimony that he spoke with Mrs. Morgan Jenkins and Mr. Jenkins. Is this your testimony as well?"

"Yes, it is. It was wonderful to see them. We spent an afternoon with them. They are alive, and no harm has come to them. They are in good spirits and send their love," and Grace looked directly at Oh'Dar, who was sitting perfectly still.

"I will ask you the same question; is there any doubt in your mind that it was indeed the true Mrs. Vivian Morgan Jenkins and Mr. Ben Jenkins whom you spoke with?"

"None at all. As my brother said, we know them. It was them."

"No more questions, Your Honor. Mrs. Vivian Morgan Jenkins and Mr. Ben Jenkins are alive and well."

Mr. Ash stood up. "I would like to cross-examine this witness."

He stepped over to the witness stand. "You are Grace Webb, is that correct?"

"Yes."

"Please state your relationship to the accused, Newell Storis."

"We are courting. I expect you could call him my beau."

"And just where did this conversation with Mrs. Morgan Jenkins and Mr. Jenkins take place?"

In spite of himself, Oh'Dar flinched.

"Objection, Your Honor. Irrelevant," said Mr. Cowell.

"It is not irrelevant. Where Mrs. Morgan Jenkins and Mr. Jenkins are is entirely relevant because the state of their health and wellbeing is critical to the case against Grayson Morgan."

The judge said to Grace, "Describe where they were when you met with them."

"Ben Jenkins was sitting on a bed, a beautiful bed with a high headboard and a footboard. His leg was bandaged because it was injured in a fall. Miss Vivian was seated next to him in a rose-colored brocade chair. I remember there was a lace curtain. It was a really lovely setting."

"Thank you, Miss Webb," the judge said.

The prosecutor continued, "What is your relationship to the man accused of their murder, Grayson Stone Morgan the Third."

"He is a friend of the family. We took him in when we found him first wandering through Wilde Edge a few years ago."

"Is there any financial relationship between you and him?"

"No."

"No? And yet earlier testimony showed that a generous stipend was set aside by Grayson Morgan for both you and your brother."

Grace looked perplexed.

Oh'Dar leaned over to Mr. Cowell and whispered something in his ear.

The defense attorney stood up. "Your Honor, neither Ned nor Grace Webb were made aware there was a fund set up in their names. In Grace's case, Mr. Morgan thought it was best not disclosed until she was of age to receive it so as not to attract unsavory suitors."

"And so the only ones who knew that there was a stipend set up for Grace Webb was her beau, Mr. Storis," the prosecutor said.

"Is there a question here, Your Honor?" Mr. Cowell objected.

"Your question, Mr. Ash," the judge said.

"You described the room you met them with, but that is all. So is it your position Miss Webb, that you refuse to tell us the whereabouts of Grayson Morgan's grandparents, just as he does, yet you, too, expect us to take your word that they are alive?"

"Miss Vivian said you would do this," Grace said.

"What?" Mr. Ash was caught off guard. "She told you *what*?"

"She said that you would try to make it look as if we made it up just to save Grayson. So she gave us this."

All eyes were on Grace Webb as she reached down and pulled several sheets of folded paper from her pocket.

The judge leaned over and asked Grace what it was she had.

"This is a note from Miss Vivian. Well, a letter, actually. She said not to lose it and not to show it to anyone until I was sitting on the witness stand and then to hand it directly to you, Your Honor."

Grace held the papers up to the judge. They were bound together by a piece of pink ribbon.

"Objection! I have not had time to examine this piece of evidence."

"Overruled, Mr. Ash. Neither has the defense. Miss Webb, where has this been, exactly?"

"Miss Vivian wrote it out. My brother and I sat and watched her. Then she folded it up and told me to do just as I have said and make sure the next person to touch it was you."

"Have you read it?"

"No, Your Honor. She didn't say I could. I kept it folded and tied up just as it was when I handed it to you. She asked that it be read aloud."

Mr. Ash spoke up. "Before the letter is read, Your Honor, I would like to confirm that it is Mrs. Morgan Jenkins's handwriting."

"She said you would say that, too, and that you would not accept anyone's saying it was her handwriting because anyone who could testify that it was would have a stake in it being so. She said to just read it aloud, that the contents would speak for themselves."

"In light of the highly volatile nature of this trial, I will read the letter aloud," Judge Walker said. He carefully untied the ribbon and opened the packet of papers.

I, Vivian Elizabeth Morgan Jenkins, in concert with my husband, Benjamin Bartholomew Jenkins, write this letter to the court to clear up any misunderstanding about the facts of our continued existence. I am giving this letter to Grace Webb to be personally delivered by her to the court. Ned and Grace Webb told us that the Honorable Matthias Walker would be hearing this case. If that is not correct, then please stop reading this instant, and find Judge Walker. He alone can prove the validity of this letter, but it is imperative that he be present before the next portion is made known.

The judge stopped and said before returning to reading, "Before I continue, let the record show that I am the judge, Matthias Walker, named in this letter."

Both Ben and I are alive and happy with our choices. We left Shadow Ridge willingly, though we are sorry for the grief we caused by the way in which we did so. It was not our intention to hurt anyone, only to prevent others, out of curiosity, from trying to find us. My grandson, Grayson Stone Morgan the Third, went along with our wishes, though now we understand he is being tried on suspicion of our murder. I cannot state strongly enough that this is a travesty. Grayson Morgan has done nothing but take care of us, love us, and do everything in his power to make our lives easier. Please respect our wishes and let us have our privacy. Please return my grandson to me.

"Your Honor, please!" the prosecutor objected. "Anyone could have written that who knows even the slightest amount about this case."

"She said you would say that too," Grace interjected. The prosecutor shot her a dirty look.

"Keep reading, please, Your Honor. There's more."

The judge flipped to the second page. *Grace and Ned Webb sought us out in an attempt to prove that we are alive by bringing us back. But we are not well enough to travel. Knowing that seeing his letter, even with both of our signatures on the last page, might not be enough to prove its validity, I decided to include some information that would be known to only a very select few people, which would prove that it is I who am writing this.*

He paused and looked over at Grace, then at Ned, and finally at Oh'Dar.

Judge Walker, please take the last sheet of paper in this letter and lay it face down on your bench. I apologize for the theatrics of this demonstration, but since I cannot be there in person to prove I am alive, it is incumbent on me to prove beyond a shadow of a doubt that it is indeed I, Vivian Morgan Jenkins, who has written this letter. Now, find a separate piece of paper and quill before continuing.

The judge paused again as a court clerk handed him a piece of paper and a quill.

My father watched you first become a lawyer. He gave you the frame into which your degree is set. On the back of it, he wrote an inscription. He told me he watched you read it. Please write that now on the piece of paper, fold it and hand it to someone reputable in the courtroom. Then and only then, please continue reading.

As the letter directed, the judge scribbled something down. He then folded the paper in half and handed it to the clerk standing by. Then he returned to reading.

The inscription my father wrote reads, "A lie has many disguises, and evil well knows that time is not on its side, for the truth is sometimes slow to surface and needs patience and diligence for its light to be uncovered. Only those who truly seek the truth will wait for its appearance and tarry in their rush to judgment.

The judge then ordered the clerk to unfold the paper and read aloud what was written there. Though not exactly the same wording, there was no mistaking that it was the same message.

The courtroom burst out into a clamor of talking. The judge swiftly raised his gavel and brought it down. "Silence. Order in the Court. Let the record reflect that what is written in the letter is nearly word for word what I wrote."

Then he picked up the letter to finish reading it.

Judge Matthias Walker, my grandson has done nothing wrong. And neither has our attorney, Newell Storis. He had no prior knowledge of the ruse we put together, and he was not involved in any way. He only learned of it later, by mistake. Both of these men are fine and honorable.

I have known you for a long time. You and my husband grew up together. You climbed trees together in your parents' backyards, in particular a stately black walnut that was later split down the middle by lightning. If I am not mistaken, I remember my husband telling me your father carved the gavel resting on your bench out of that very tree. Please stop this travesty of injustice. As I asked before, do not try to find us. Let us live out the rest of our lives in peace. As for Grace and Newell, both Ben and I hope they find a lifetime of happiness together.

Judge Walker laid the letter on his desk. "It is

signed Vivian Elizabeth Morgan Jenkins and Benjamin Bartholomew Jenkins. I can attest that this is indeed Vivian Elizabeth Morgan Jenkins's handwriting."

He turned to Grace, "You may step down, Miss Webb."

Then the judge said, "Having read the letter handed me by the witness Grace Webb, I stipulate that this letter is indeed the work of Mrs. Morgan Jenkins. Based on the evidence presented in this letter and the testimony of witnesses, it has been made clear beyond a shadow of a doubt that neither Grayson Stone Morgan the Third nor Newell Storis is guilty of any wrongdoing. Furthermore, it is ordered by this court that, in keeping with the wishes of Mrs. Morgan Jenkins, her privacy and that of her husband, Mr. Ben Jenkins, will be honored. Anyone seeking to discover their whereabouts will be found in contempt of court.

"This case is dismissed, the accused are free to go, and the jurors are excused."

At the smack of the gavel, Grace flew over to Oh'Dar and Mr. Storis. She hugged Oh'Dar first and then embraced Mr. Storis. Ned and his parents were also quickly there. Mr. Cowell gave them a few moments to express their joy and relief.

Prosecutor Ash gathered up his papers. Though his expectations of glory had been shattered as the judge's gavel hit the wooden block declaring Grayson Morgan innocent, he was in his heart a good man.

He went over to shake hands with Mr. Cowell. "I thought it was an open and shut case. But in the end, justice prevailed. I would never choose to lose, but in a case such as this one, where it becomes clear there truly was no wrongdoing, I am happy to do so."

Across the room, the constable was not showing such good sportsmanship. He was leaning against the courtroom wall, glaring at the victors. After a while, he pushed away and headed out. Oh'Dar stopped him as he reached the door. "You were just doing your job, Mr. Riggs. I realize that."

"It's Constable Riggs. Enjoy the moment, *Mr.* Morgan."

Meeting his eyes, Oh'Dar felt cold in the pit of his stomach. Constable Riggs was not going to let go.

Everyone reconvened at the Webbs' house, though Mr. Storis said he needed first to stop by his office and would be right along. Mrs. Thomas happily joined them as she was not leaving until the next day.

Exhausted from the stress of the past few weeks yet exhilarated from the victory, they needed to celebrate and start the healing process together. Buster was waiting excitedly at the door for them, and as always, jumped directly into Oh'Dar's arms and smothered him with kisses. Mrs. Webb wanted to put on some dinner, but she also didn't want to leave the others and miss a thing. So they all crowded into the little kitchen to continue their conversation. It was only a few minutes before Storis showed up and joined them.

Finally, they were all seated around the kitchen table with a few chairs from the other room brought in and squeezed in. Oh'Dar set Buster down on the floor where he took his customary place under the table, rather prematurely hoping for crumbs to drop.

"If it hadn't been for you and Ned—" Oh'Dar said to Grace. "And also, we have you to thank, Nora and Matthew, for letting them go. What a courageous thing to do. However did you find the village?"

"Not trusting Tucker," said Storis, "and not wanting to be any more dependent on him than necessary, I secretly made a map on the way there and checked and enhanced it on the way back. He caught me doing it, but it didn't matter. I mentioned it to Grace before they arrested me because I was about to head there myself to find you, Grayson."

Oh'Dar wanted to ask Grace and Ned about their visit with his grandparents and how that was arranged but did not want it discussed out in the open.

"I don't want to live through anything like that again," Mrs. Webb said as she plunked down a bowl of potatoes. "Does anyone want to help peel?"

"If you like, Mrs. Webb, I would be glad to make biscuits," Mrs. Thomas volunteered.

"Oh, please, call me Nora. Yes, that would be

wonderful. Grayson has often talked about your biscuits."

Mr. Webb turned to Oh'Dar. "When will you be heading back, Grayson?"

"As soon as I can. I am sure everyone back home is worried sick, including my grandparents. I haven't been around to tell you, but my wife is expecting a baby."

"Oh, how wonderful!" Mrs. Webb exclaimed as others chimed in as well. "But, oh, to have had that on your mind as well. That you might never see your—"

"Please, no unhappy thoughts. Newell and I have our names cleared, and we are free to continue our lives," Oh'Dar said.

Storis glanced at Grace, who was seated next to him. "On that note, I have something to ask."

Nora stopped drawing the water for the potatoes, and Ned threw a fleeting look at his sister before breaking into a grin.

Grace's eyes widened as Storis pushed his chair out from the table and bent down on one knee. "Grace Webb, you are the most wonderful woman I have ever met. Your sweetness, your kindness, and your bravery are without match. Please do me the honor of becoming my wife."

All the strength Grace had mustered dissolved in an instant, and tears flooded her eyes. "Oh, Newell, yes. Yes. Yes!"

As Storis stood, Grace threw her arms around his neck, and in turn, he wrapped his arms around her.

"I love you so much," he whispered into her ear.

Then he turned to Mr. Webb. "I apologize; I should have asked your permission first."

"Under the circumstances, Newell, it is the perfect end to what we have all been through." Mr. Webb rose from his seat to pat Storis on the back and extended his hand, "Welcome. I have heard it is always good to have a lawyer in the family."

There was a chuckle around the room.

"Tomorrow, if you are up to it, I have a surprise for you," Storis said to Grace.

"Another surprise? This was not enough? I am not sure I can take any more," she laughed.

"I want to know what it is!" Ned exclaimed. "There is no such thing as too many good surprises."

"Do you have it here with you?" Mrs. Webb asked.

"No, it is somewhere else. We will have to go somewhere to see it."

"Perhaps we can all go?" Ned asked before realizing he was being forward. "Oh, I'm sorry, I shouldn't have asked."

"If Grace doesn't mind, it is not a problem that we all go. Grayson, are you in, too?"

Oh'Dar thought a moment. He had things he had to take care of, and as urgently as he felt the need to get back, he was here now. "Of course; I wouldn't miss it for the world. I cannot avoid taking another day to do some urgent errands and gather up some supplies for the return trip."

"Storm is ready for you; I've been taking good care of him. All of us have," Mr. Webb said.

"I was supposed to take Rebel and Shining Beauty back with me before, but there was too much on my mind." He let out a long sigh. "I am not sure I want to take them. We honestly have enough Morgan horses at the village for our purposes. I know my grandparents would not mind if I left them here with you."

Mr. Webb nodded. "Of course, as long as you need to."

"No, I mean, permanently. You could sell them; they would fetch a good amount, and Newell could help you. You deserve the money."

"That is very generous of you," Mr. Webb said. "They are of no use as workhorses, and of course, we would never use them as such."

"Rebel's name has now been cleared; he is no longer a man-killer. In fact, you might capitalize on his fame after the outcome of the trial gets out."

"They are both beautiful animals. A testament to Ben Jenkins's horse-breeding expertise," Ned said.

"Grace, Ned, I would like to talk to you both privately before I leave for home," Oh'Dar said.

Grace spoke first, and Ned echoed her. "Of course."

"When do you plan to be married?" Mrs. Webb asked.

"As soon as possible." Storis sat again and pulled Grace down to sit on his knee.

She blushed at the obvious display to which her father remarked, "It looks as if that would be a good idea."

"Judge Walker is probably still in the area," Oh'Dar suggested. "I know that would please my grandparents no end."

"I didn't know your grandmother knew him," said Mrs. Webb.

"It seems there are few prominent people my grandparents did not know. All the years of their goodwill toward others saved my life," Oh'Dar said.

"Grayson is right," chimed in Mrs. Thomas. "The Morgans were very well connected in high places."

"Miss Vivian is a genius to think all that through. She was so right; the testimonies of Ned and Grace would not have been enough," sighed Mr. Webb.

"You must give them our love, please, Grayson," Mrs. Webb added.

Then Storis said, "I can try to find Judge Walker in town tomorrow and ask him if he would marry us."

"Grace, then I have a surprise for you," Mrs. Webb said. She excused herself and returned with a beautiful dress made of a soft blush material.

"Oh, Mama!" Grace exclaimed.

Mr. Webb shook his head, "And how long have you been working on that, woman?"

"Oh, for a little while," Nora admitted. "I bought

the material out of some of the money Grayson gave us. I knew you wouldn't mind, Matthew."

"Of course I don't. Grace will look beautiful in it," Mr. Webb said. Then, with some apparent pain, he got up from the table and embraced his daughter. "I am so glad for you, honey, and I wish you a lifetime of happiness."

The next morning, Storis got up early and found Judge Walker at the Wilde Edge Inn.

"I am sorry to interrupt your privacy," Storis said.

"No problem, Mr. Storis, please sit down."

"I realize you are most likely in a hurry to leave, but I have a favor to ask."

Judge Walker took a sip of his coffee and then set it down. "What is it?"

"Grace Webb has accepted my proposal of marriage. We would greatly appreciate it if you would marry us."

"I see. Well, congratulations. But when did you want the ceremony conducted? These betrothals usually last some time."

"Not in this case. This entire nightmare has impressed upon us how short and fragile life is. We are ready to be married. Today, even. This afternoon?"

"I think I can squeeze that in. I can just as easily leave tomorrow."

"Thank you. May I return later to pick you up?"

"That would be fine."

Storis then went to his office, gathered some materials, and returned to pick up the Webbs.

By the time he got back, Ned already had the wagon and the horses hooked up. The rest of the family, including Oh'Dar, appeared to be waiting for his return. Storis didn't even get to knock; the door flew open the minute his foot hit the porch.

"We're ready!" Grace exclaimed, and Storis could see the rest of the family lined up behind her. "We just need to get our coats."

"Can Buster come?" Ned asked. "He's part of the family, too."

Grayson elected to ride Storm, and the others loaded into the wagon. As he alone knew where they were going, Storis took the reins, with Grace at his side on the front seat. Mr. Webb needed some help getting in, but soon he and Mrs. Webb, Ned, and Buster were loaded in the back.

"It's not that far," Storis said. He flicked the reins, and they were off.

The team pulled the wagon easily enough, their hooves kicking up little clumps of dirt behind them as they went on their way.

Winter had left. The first buds were appearing, and new bright green grasses were starting to peek out of the ground.

It wasn't long before they turned into a little road,

and Storis pulled the team over. Everyone looked around but could not figure out why they were there.

The attorney jumped off, came around, and lifted Grace down. "We're here; everybody out!"

"Where is here?" laughed Nora.

Grayson dismounted, and he and Ned helped Matthew out of the back.

"Here is home," Storis said, looking at his betrothed. "That is, Grace, if you want it to be." Then he gently turned her so she could see the beautiful little two-story cottage. It was painted a soft butter yellow with ivory lace covering the windows and a white picket fence surrounding the front yard.

"There's a decent-sized area in the back for a garden and a good-sized shed that could be used as a small barn and plenty of room for children to explore and appreciate nature."

"Oh, Newell!" Grace exclaimed with shining eyes. "It's perfect."

"Shall we go in?" he asked.

"Oh, yes, please."

"Judge Walker will be over later to marry us," he laughed.

"What!?" Mrs. Webb exclaimed. "Later? Later, as in, later today?"

"Yes. I hope that's alright," Storis said.

"Oh, my. Well, of course it is," she said. "We'll be ready somehow."

Storis opened the white picket gate for Grace to enter. They walked up to the porch and to the front door. Storis took the key from his pocket and opened the door for Grace to step inside.

She paused to look around. The floors were beautiful wide chestnut planks, and the walls were painted the same butter yellow as the outside, with white-painted trim and crown moldings. The delicate ivory lace curtains she had seen from the outside adorned every window. A large fieldstone fireplace was set on one of the side walls, and a stack of wood sat waiting on the hearth.

Grace took a few more steps in and entered the kitchen. Another stone fireplace, only this one had a hearth with enough room to cook many a meal for a large gathering. To the left was a wood cookstove, just like in her mother's kitchen.

"There are no dishes yet," said Storis, "but you can pick those out yourself. However, as you can see, there are already iron pots and kettles; they were left by the prior owner. And of course, we need furniture."

Grace ran her hand over the beautiful walnut mantle above the hearth.

"There are three bedrooms; one down here and two upstairs. It's larger than it looks, and I know it needs some more work."

"Oh, Newell, it's perfect. And we will create wonderful memories making it ours."

Grace turned back and called the rest of her

family in. Ned set Buster down, and he immediately took off exploring, his little nails clicking across the wooden floor.

Oh'Dar said, "As my wedding gift to you, I will set up an account at the General Store for you to furnish your house."

"Oh, no, Grayson, that's too generous," Grace exclaimed.

"What good is wealth if you cannot use it to take care of your family and those you love?" he answered.

"I can't let you do that, Grayson," Storis said. "It is my job to provide for my family."

"Well then, you can pay me back in free lawyering," Oh'Dar said. "I have a feeling I will be in need of your services again."

"Alright, it's a deal then," Storis smiled, and they shook hands.

A peculiar look came over Grace's face.

"What is it?" Storis asked.

Grace looked around, then stood up on tippytoe and whispered to Storis, "We are going to be married this afternoon, but then where will we spend our first night together. At my parents?" She sounded horrified.

"Why, here, of course," he answered.

"But you said there is no furniture," she whispered again.

"Oh, I understand." He turned to the others, and

taking Grace's hand, asked everyone to excuse them a moment.

Storis led Grace out of the kitchen and through the living room to the back. He led her into the bedroom, and she found herself looking at a beautiful brand new oak bed. The headboard was simply carved with a matching footboard, while a soft cream quilt and matching pillowcases finished it off. On each side of the bed were nightstands with oil lamps that had pink roses painted on their shades.

Grace blushed and then turned and buried her face in the shoulder of her betrothed. When she stepped back, Storis took her hand and led her back to her family, neither of them saying a word.

"We had best be getting back to your place, I think," Storis said to Mrs. Webb. "I will be picking up Judge Walker in a few hours."

It was time. The Webbs and Oh'Dar were gathered in the Webbs' drawing-room. Grace was wearing the delicate dress her mother had made for her. She had pulled her hair back in an upsweep and wore her mother's pearl earrings, one of the few things Mrs. Webb owned of any value, a gift from Miss Vivian.

The door opened, and there stood Storis and the judge. They stomped the dust off their boots and came in. Mrs. Webb met them and took their coats before leading them into the room where everyone was waiting.

"Judge Walker, thank you so much for coming," Mr. Webb said. "We truly appreciate this and know you have your own business to attend to."

"My pleasure, Mr. Webb. I am glad I can do something to help you after the travesties through which this entire family has been put." Then he turned to Oh'Dar. "And especially you, Mr. Morgan."

Grace and Storis took their places in front of the judge.

"Friends and family, we are gathered here to witness the marriage of Newell Storis and Grace Webb. Mr. Storis, repeat after me. I, Newell James Storis, take thee, Grace Webb, to be my lawfully wedded wife. I pledge to be faithful only to thee and care and protect thee all the days of my life."

Newell repeated the vows, then the judge turned to Grace. "Repeat after me. I, Grace Webb, pledge to honor thee as my husband and be faithful to only thee. To care and minister to thee, to share my sorrows and my joys with thee all the days of my life."

Taking his cue from the judge, Storis then produced a gold ring and slipped it on Grace's extended finger.

"I now pronounce you man and wife."

Storis placed his hand gently on the side of Grace's face and gave her a soft, gentle kiss. The others broke into spontaneous applause and congratulated the new bride and groom.

Oh'Dar approached the judge. "Thank you, Judge Walker. May I give you a ride back to town, so you can be on your way."

"Yes, that would be good."

Oh'Dar decided to give Judge Walker some peace on the short trip back to town, so the two rode in silence. When they arrived at the hotel, however, Judge Walker turned to Oh'Dar.

"Your grandmother is an exceptional woman. Your grandfather and I were friends, and until that letter, I thought that there were only three people who knew that my father carved my gavel from that black walnut tree that he and I used to climb. My father, who carved it, and your great-grandfather, who was there when my father gave it to me. Somewhere along the way, your great-grandfather told your grandmother about it in great detail."

The judge paused a moment. "Even with as long as I have been sitting on the bench, I am still in awe of how the seemingly insignificant things in our lives can later have such impact."

He extended his hand to Oh'Dar. "I wish you the best, Grayson. Please give my regards to your grandmother and her new husband, Mr. Jenkins."

The rest of the day was spent back at the Webbs

in celebration over a hearty meal with lots of laughter and high spirits. As promised, Oh'Dar had returned in time to miss very little of it.

As twilight descended on Wilde Edge and with the meal consumed and everyone still sitting contentedly around the kitchen table, it was time for Newell and Grace to start their new life together.

Grace hugged everyone, including Buster.

"Will we see you tomorrow for dinner then?" she said

"Yes!" replied her mother.

Oh'Dar was very anxious to get back to Acise, but before he left, he needed to speak in private with Grace and Ned. Mrs. Webb had organized a dinner again for the next day, and he arranged to speak with them then. He would head home the day after—far later than he liked, but he still had some crucial errands to run, and they would likely take most of the day.

Storis had borrowed the Webbs' wagon, and after helping his bride in, turned it toward their new home. A warm spring breeze was passing, the perfect ending to a beautiful day.

When they arrived, Storis secured the team to the hitching post out front and helped Grace down. When they reached the front porch, he unlocked the door and swept Grace up into his arms. They were both laughing as he carried her across the threshold and set her down.

At the lawyer's request, Ned had slipped away and started a fire in the kitchen cookstove, so the little house was cozy and warm. Storis took Grace's light shawl and hung it on a row of pegs next to the front door, and gave her a moment to look around again.

"It will be a delight watching you transform this empty house into a home where we will spend many years loving each other and watching our children grow," Storis said. "Are you tired?"

"A little; it has been an exciting day."

"Let me make a fire in the fireplace, and we can sit there a while. Of course, it would be much nicer if we had a couch!" he joked.

Before too long, Storis had a roaring fire going that, in addition to warming it, lent a beautiful glow to the room, which was now darkening as the sun slowly set. He sat down next to Grace and pulled her over to lean against him.

"I am so happy," she said in a low voice.

"So am I."

"A nightmare has turned into a dream come true."

"Yes, we must always remember to be grateful for our blessings and take none of them for granted." Then Storis turned Grace's face to him and kissed her gently.

Snide Tucker was still locked up in the Millgrove jail, awaiting his punishment for accosting Grace Webb. He had not heard the outcome of the trial but savored his thoughts of Grayson Morgan hanging from the end of a thick rope and seeing Newell Storis discredited and stripped of his right to practice law.

Oh'Dar had asked Storis to take care of some business for him, and the next day was able to finish up what he needed to do in person. As soon as he had set up the account for the newlyweds, he bought a satchel at the general store, and into it he safely transferred the letters he had written. He was even more impatient to return to Acise and to get news to his parents and grandparents that he had been freed. He knew they might be fearing the worst, and he was worried about Acise's health.

While waiting for dinner to be ready, he asked Ned and Grace to join him outside.

"I am sure you have an idea why I wanted to speak with you both privately."

"You want to know how we got to speak to your grandparents. And where, no doubt," Grace said.

"Yes. Not that I intend to gloss over my gratitude for what you did."

"We understand," Ned replied. "I will let Grace tell it."

"We found the village and the woman there who could translate for us. Honovi was her name. There was quite a discussion, which we did not follow, of course, about how to get us to your grandparents since they are not living there. Of course, where they are living seems to be the secret of the century. Oh, sorry," Grace added, "I do not mean to make light of it."

"I know, Grace. And you are right, it is a big secret. And a terribly important one, for reasons I cannot explain."

"Oh, I understand. We were blindfolded, very well blindfolded, and led to them on the locals' ponies. We were finally escorted through some kind of tunnel, I think—at least, it sounded like that from the way our steps echoed back to us. Even though we had something stuffed in our ears, we could hear that. When we were allowed to take the blindfolds off, we were with your grandparents in a room made of rock or stone.

"It was a cozy room and nicely appointed— apparently your doing. Ben was on the bed and clearly recovering from an injured leg and knee. Your grandmother looked fine, though I have to say she has lost a considerable amount of weight."

"It is the different diet. Do go on," Oh'Dar said.

"We talked a while, and then Miss Vivian had the idea for the letter. It took her a while to compose, and when it was ready, we were taken back to the village. After a night's stay to rest up, we headed back."

"Your grandmother is very smart," Ned added.

"Do you understand why you cannot discuss the circumstances of meeting them?" Oh'Dar asked.

"Wherever they are living, it is nothing like we could have imagined. And they are certainly not staying at the village," Ned said. "But do not worry, Grayson. Both Grace and I will take what we know about your grandparents' situation to our graves."

"You cannot even tell Newell," Oh'Dar said to Grace.

Grace sighed. "I haven't, and I never will. He understands that."

"What a mystery, though, I have to say," Ned shared. "I am jealous of the real-life adventure they are no doubt living. It is hard not to let my imagination run away with me."

"You have no idea," Oh'Dar said, then immediately regretted it.

"Grayson," Ned added, "do you think at any time in my lifetime, you might confide to me, and Grace too, if you could, the truth of your past, of where you are going now? Of where your grandparents are living? I promise I would keep it to myself. It is just that a door has been opened the tiniest sliver, allowing us a glimpse of the greatest secret of our lifetimes and now to have the door slammed shut on it is very hard to live with."

"I know, Ned. Believe me, I know. I have had to live with that secret my whole life and keep it from everyone here and everyone else I come into contact with. It is a great burden, one I would never have wished to lay on the shoulders of either of you."

"I would welcome it. I promise you. I mean, what is lying ahead for me? A life as the local town animal doctor, marriage, children? I do not mean to diminish our lives here—but after having seen what we have, it all seems mundane in comparison to what my life could be."

"What are you saying, Ned?" Oh'Dar asked. "Are you saying you want to come back with me?"

"Well, maybe not today. But someday," Ned answered.

"Ned, you do not know what you are asking. Once you step through the doorway my grandparents did, it slams shut behind you. Forever. There is no coming back. Ever. My grandparents understood that."

"I can also understand that; honestly, I can," Ned said. "You have to believe me."

"I believe you mean it. But making that kind of life choice at my grandparents' age, having lived a full life already, is utterly different. You are a young man, and the chances are good that you might soon come to regret your decision."

Grace asked her brother, "You would leave us forever? Never to see us again?"

"You aren't saying I could never see Grace again, are you? I mean, if she came to the village as we did?"

"Ned, Grace, I can't deal with this right now. Please understand that the enormity of what you are asking is beyond your comprehension, and I need to get back before the birth of my child."

Oh'Dar looked at the disappointed faces. "I will return someday. Until then, Ned, think about what you are asking. Carefully consider it. I am not even sure I could get permission. We will talk about it another time, but until then, I am asking you again. Please keep this entire conversation between ourselves. It is critical that you do. I cannot impress upon you how much is at stake if you betray the trust that has been placed in you by everyone I love."

CHAPTER 12

S torm seemed to sense Oh'Dar's excitement at heading home. Oh'Dar had packed the travel satchels full, grateful that the spring thaw would give them plenty of access to water along the way. His primary concern was making sure there was enough for Storm to eat, but with all the new spring growth, he was not very worried. He knew every piece of the way back and was confident they would make it all in good health. There was so much on Oh'Dar's mind. He replayed the trial over and over, reflecting on the key moments of the testimony. He reflected on Grace and Ned's courage in finding Miss Vivian and Ben and on his grandmother's genius in writing the letter to the judge. He reflected on the providence of the Order of Functions that provided a judge whom his great-grandfather had known so well. The inscription on the back of the framed law certificate was such a simple thing, a traditional gesture—but one that had spared his great-grandson's life so many years later.

He thought happily of Grace and Storis and the life that would unfold for them. And Ned. Oh, yes, Ned. He saw the same passion in Ned's eyes that he had seen in Ben's. The longing to explore the unknown. But Ned did not understand what he was asking for. On the other hand, Oh'Dar had been about the same age as Ned when he left behind the only family he had known to venture into the unknown in search of his Waschini family. Were they so different? Both were quests for the truth, for knowledge of the unknown, even when the cost was high. But Oh'Dar had known he could return to the life he had left. To his mother, Adia, to his father, Acaraho. For Ned, it would be a one-way trip, and there would never be any going back. He did not believe that Ned understood what the reality of that would really mean.

Ned had his whole life ahead of him, just as Grace had. Ned could marry, settle down, stay and become an animal doctor, help with the Webb farm, be an uncle, and become a father in his own right. And, if he came to live among the People, where would he find a wife? Perhaps among the Brothers? After all, Oh'Dar had found Acise. Perhaps it was not so terribly far-fetched an idea, but Ned was far too young to make such a life-changing decision.

Oh'Dar also passed the time praying for everyone he loved. For his mother and his father, for Nootau in his new life with Iella, for Acise and their child. That was the hardest to think of. Acise knew Ned and Grace had taken back proof that his grandparents still lived, but no one back home knew the outcome yet. They were perhaps thinking that Oh'Dar was dead by now. He could not bear the grief that Acise might be going through. He knew how easily thoughts could turn to dreadful outcomes. And he also knew that stress could put her and their baby at risk. Acise was only a month or so away from delivering, and she'd had problems from early on.

Something else was on Oh'Dar's mind. The constable's last remark. The immediate problem may have been solved, but Oh'Dar was convinced Constable Riggs would find other ways to make trouble for him and those he loved.

At the Brothers' village, Honovi and Ithua were doing their best to keep Acise's spirits up. They had been encouraged by the appearance and actions of Grace and Ned Webb, but now they had to wait and pray.

Acise had no more issues with her pregnancy as such; all her problems were emotional. She was filled with fear that she would never see Oh'Dar again, and she was not eating or sleeping well. Honovi and Ithua were becoming concerned about the baby's development.

"You have to eat. Your baby needs you to eat," Honovi encouraged her daughter, and Ithua nodded her agreement.

Snana was also at Acise's side. "Please, we know you are worried, but you have to think of your baby."

"I am trying; honestly, I am," Acise said, tears again welling in her eyes. "I just want him home. I just want to know he is going to come home."

Honovi did not know what to say. No one could promise Acise that Oh'Dar would come back. She was hopeful that Grace and Ned's testimony would result in his being freed, but hope did not feel like enough right now.

Honovi smoothed the hair away from her daughter's face. "Please, rest. If you like, I will stay here with you. Or Snana will."

"No, you have chores to attend to. There is nothing any of us can do now but wait. And pray." Acise suddenly doubled over and grabbed her belly. "Ohhhhh," she exclaimed. She curled into a ball on her sleeping blanket. "It hurts."

"Describe what it feels like," Ithua said.

"Cramping. Hard cramps," Acise struggled to say.

Ithua exchanged a worried look with Honovi. The last thing this baby needed was to be born early.

It felt to Oh'Dar as if he had been traveling forever, though he had run Storm as hard as he dared. His entire body relaxed when the familiar mountains and hillsides around the Brothers' village came into view.

Children's voices filled the village and were carried into the shelter where Acise rested. "He's back," they cried, "Oh'Dar is back!"

Acise's heart leaped, and tears of relief rolled down her cheeks into the soft, colorful blanket below. She silently thanked the Great Spirit as a great deal of tension immediately left her body.

"Stay here!" Honovi said and ran outside. She could see the unmistakable Storm pounding toward the village and knew there was only one man who could be riding him. She ducked her head back into the shelter, "It's true; Oh'Dar is home. He is safe!"

Ithua placed her hand on Acise's forehead. "Do not get up. You know he will come directly here to see you. Please, do not move."

There was more commotion as children and adults alike surrounded Storm and Oh'Dar. Noshoba took the reins as Oh'Dar slid down off his majestic steed.

Honovi pulled him toward the shelter. "Acise needs to see you!" she said.

Oh'Dar ducked into the opening and knelt down carefully beside Acise, who was curled up on the sleeping mat. Ithua had stayed with her, knowing he would have questions about his life-walker's condition

"I'm home. I'm alive. The case was dismissed. Ned and Grace saved me by coming here." Looking at Ithua, he said, "Please tell me, what is wrong?"

"Acise has some cramping," Ithua said. "She has not been eating or sleeping properly; she has been under a lot of stress, as you can imagine."

"Any more spotting?" Oh'Dar asked.

"No, that cleared up long ago and did not come back. Hopefully, now that you are here, she will be able to relax, and her appetite will return."

"Saraste'," Oh'Dar said, using the People's endearment. "I love you so, and I am here now; everything worked out. Soon we will have our own little one. Please hang on. Please."

He lay down behind Acise and wrapped his arms around her. He repeatedly whispered how much he loved her.

He could feel her relax even more, and she let out a long sigh.

"Sleep if you can. I will not leave your side; I will be here when you wake, I promise."

As much as he wanted to see his mother and father and his grandparents, Oh'Dar kept his word. He did send an urgent message that he had returned and all was well, but that he needed to stay with Acise until her condition improved. He had helped her to eat more, and she was now sleeping soundly with him by her side. He left her only for the necessary few minutes he had to, but otherwise, either he was wrapped around behind her, or she was resting against him, whichever was most comfortable for her.

Ithua and Honovi kept a careful watch. Though they were relieved that Acise was eating and sleeping better, they both still had concerns for the baby's welfare.

It surprised no one when Adia showed up within a couple of days.

"Mother!" Oh'Dar exclaimed when he saw Adia crouching down so she could see through the shelter entrance.

"Shhh," she said, seeing Acise was asleep.

Oh'Dar extended his hand, beckoning her to come closer.

Now Adia could see for herself that Oh'Dar was home safe and sound. She noticed immediately that he and Acise had both lost weight. It was understandable, considering the stress they had been under. However, it was for Acise that Adia was worried; she should have gained weight, not lost it.

For the first time, Adia was seriously concerned about the offspring.

"I just had to see you," she said, "although I know you will come home when you can. Everyone is ecstatic. Oh, my son, I am so relieved!"

Oh'Dar squeezed Adia's hand, and keeping his voice low, he said, "I thought I was about to die. It was the worst time of my life." As he spoke, he couldn't stop glancing at his sleeping life-walker.

Adia knew he was as worried as she and the others were. Acise's baby was a month away from being born. They were so close to having their own offspring, the start of their family together. Adia prayed that having escaped one tragedy, they were not headed for a different one.

Each day that passed without Acise delivering the baby allowed the release of a tiny bit of tension. Under Oh'Dar's tender care, she improved her eating. It was too early to tell if she was gaining any weight, but they were confident that she at least was no longer losing any. She had been slight to begin with, and they knew her baby needed all the nutrition possible.

"Sit up," Honovi ordered as Oh'Dar watched from across the shelter.

"What is that?" Acise frowned.

"Quail eggs. Eat them."

Acise obeyed and swallowed the raw eggs one by one.

"And what's that?" she asked as Honovi offered her something else—though she was sure she knew.

"Eat them; they are your favorites."

Acise actually smiled at her mother's joke. Though unable to keep from making a face, she chewed up and swallowed the bitter green leaves. Some of the first to sprout in the spring, they provided an early food source for many of the animals as well as nectar for the bees. The children, especially, enjoyed seeing their bright yellow heads appearing. But the leaves were certainly not tasty. Oh'Dar had told her that the Waschini called them dandelions.

"Momma," Acise propped herself up on one elbow. "How long before I will deliver—I need to know how much longer I have to hold on."

"Until the next full moon."

"One just passed," she said. Then she wearily dropped back onto the blankets and quickly fell asleep.

All the fears Honovi had been pushing down came rushing up into her consciousness. All this time, she had admitted her fear that Acise might lose the child, but it had only now occurred to her that they might also lose Acise.

Honovi covered up her sleeping daughter, glanced at Oh'Dar, and stepped outside. Snana would stay with Acise if he needed a break. She pulled her light blanket around her shoulders and walked up into the forest.

The fresh smell of the fir trees filled the air. Beneath her feet, the thawed ground gave easily, leaving a wake of indentations in the rotting leaves.

The blue sky seemed to herald that all was well with Etera. But Honovi knew it was not, at least not in her world. As she walked, she prayed to the Great Spirit. She prayed harder than she ever had before. She prayed for Acise, for the unborn child. She prayed for protection for her people against an uncertain future. She had recently noticed that Ithua was growing frail with age, so she also prayed for the Medicine Woman's health. Then she resumed her prayers for Acise and Oh'Dar. The Great Spirit had brought her people through so much. *Please do not abandon us now.*

Honovi knew she should not let doubt creep into her soul, that no matter how hard, things were unfolding as they should. If she lost her daughter and her grandchild— It was out of her hands, and she would have to accept it. There was nothing more she, Ithua, or Oh'Dar could do for either of them. And if they survived, in her weakened state would Acise be able to feed the baby enough to keep it alive?

The shawl fell from her shoulders as she dropped to her knees and dug her fingers deep into the rich soil that carried the promise of a bountiful harvest later in the year. With her dark hair brushing the ground beneath her, Honovi allowed her tears to flow freely. She gathered all her will, her heart, and her soul into one point of focus, and with everything she had, she prayed yet again to be spared the tragedy she feared was waiting for them. Moments passed.

Finally, she raised her head. "It is in your hands now. But whatever I can do is still mine to do."

An eagle cried overhead as, pensive, she rose to return to the village.

As she rejoined the path, she looked down and saw a huge feather where there had not been one before. A beautiful, perfect eagle's feather. It had not been there when she arrived, though, in her despair, she could have missed it. Picking it up, she thanked the Great Spirit for the gift.

When she got back to the village, she told her life-walker she would not be back for a while.

Adia's first shocked thought was that Acise had lost the offspring, and Honovi had come to tell them. But then, as her own emotions subsided, she could sense that Honovi was worried but not devastated.

"I need your help. We need your help," Honovi said.

"Anything, whatever we can do."

"I need to plan for a wet nurse, and right now, there is no one in the village who can help. I do not think Acise is going to have enough milk to nurse her child, even if it survives, because she is so thin and so weak. And if she dies, then—"

Adia quickly thought through the names of the new mothers at the High Rocks. There were several, and there was no question that any of them would not have milk to spare. But if the offspring was small, would she be able to latch on, given the size difference?

She noticed the perfect Eagles feather that Honovi was carrying. "I see you have the quill; do you have an animal bladder?"

Honovi shook her head.

"I have the rest of what you need in the Healer's Quarters; come on."

On the way, Adia sent the first person she came across to ask one of the new mothers to please come to the Healer's Quarters as soon as she was able.

Honovi waited while Adia looked for what they needed to create a feeding system for Acise's newborn, using the Eagle's quill as a nipple. Finally, Adia spotted it and lifted down a newly hollowed-out gourd. What was different was that it had a tiny opening at the small end, something Nadiwani had been experimenting with as a more accurate pouring spout.

The end of the quill could be inserted into the gourd, and it would lengthen the spout. The Brothers had long ago discovered how to create their own system using a quill with a small animal bladder to hold the milk. In this particular case, the contrivance would be particularly helpful given the difference in size between the Brothers and the People.

Shortly, one of the new mothers arrived, her

offspring in her arms. Adia explained the situation while Honovi watched with hope in her heart.

Constable Riggs was furious. Like the prosecutor, Mr. Ash, he had banked on the Morgan trial to make a name for himself. One that would bring him notoriety and set the stage to catapult him into politics, maybe set him up to be the next governor. Unlike Mr. Ash, the constable was not at heart a good man. The trial had brought notoriety, yes, but not the type he wanted. Instead of talk of his tremendous victory in bringing to justice the murderer of Mrs. Morgan Jenkins and her husband, there was only talk of his persecution of one of the Morgan men. The one who had already survived his uncle's plans to murder him and had now had to endure the stress of an unjust trial.

Instead of Grayson Stone Morgan the Third coming out as the villain, he had come out a hero, willing to die to protect his grandparents' last wishes.

Sheriff Boone was resting his feet on his desk. "I didn't expect to see you back here for a while, Samuel."

Constable Riggs's look was poison. "Judge Walker gave me directions to tell Mrs. Ermadine Thomas that Grayson Morgan and Newell Storis were cleared of any wrongdoing."

Riggs looked around the empty office. "Where is Zachary Tucker? Has he been tried and sentenced already?

"No; as a matter of fact, he was let go."

"On account of what?"

"On account of a letter from attorney Storis, sent back with Mrs. Thomas on behalf of himself and his wife, the former Grace Webb." The sheriff put his feet down and handed a letter to the constable.

"They dropped the charges?"

"Read the letter."

The constable tossed the letter down on the sheriff's desk. "If it's all the same to you, I'm a little averse to letters lately. Just tell me why."

"They said that if Tucker would leave town, never go near any Thomas or Morgan property again and never contact any of the Thomas family members or the Webb family members, and stay away from Millgrove, Wilde Edge, and the local village, they would drop the charges."

When the constable said nothing, the sheriff continued. "Even sent money for him to buy his own horse, saddle, and supplies to leave the territory."

"Wealthy people are stupid. They had him by all rights."

"Not stupid at all. In fact, I think it was a brilliant move. They ended what would have been another bothersome trial, as a result of which he might have been put away for a while if the blackmail charges were proven—but not forever. As for his accosting of Grace Webb, again, minor charges and no time to speak of. This way, they ended this battle, and by helping him out, no doubt future battles to come."

"They may be rid of Tucker, but they aren't rid of me," the constable said.

"Let it go, Samuel," said Sheriff Boone. "As your kin, I'm warning you; it's over. In the end, justice prevailed because Grayson Morgan did not trick his grandparents into leaving. He did not lure them away and steal their fortune. And he did not murder them. There is no disputing it."

"Grayson Morgan humiliated me. Him and that Webb girl. And the lawyer too."

"You have to admit that the trial resulted in the proper outcome. The letter was not forged; it has too much detail in it for that. You were there when Judge Walker read it. Leave them in peace and focus on repairing your reputation; don't risk destroying whatever is left of it by continuing this vendetta against Grayson Morgan."

Now pacing back and forth, Constable Riggs ignored the Sheriff.

"I want to know where the grandparents are. They have to be somewhere close to that village because it didn't take that long for Morgan to show up. I think I know how to flush them out."

"Don't look at me. Not only is it out of my jurisdiction, but you are on the wrong side if you continue to persecute Grayson Morgan and his family. You need to drop this."

"I'll be on my way. Thanks for the update on Tucker, *Cousin*."

After a hasty journey, Constable Riggs was standing in Sheriff Moore's office back in Wilde Edge.

"I'm going to the local village, and I need you to come with me."

The sheriff stared at him. "For what reason? There are no further charges in any regard pending against Grayson Morgan."

"The governor put me in charge of identifying rich hunting lands which might be better utilized by, shall we say, someone other than the locals."

"And why do you need me to go with you? Why wouldn't you take Sheriff Boone?"

"It's complicated, but I need a witness. You must come with me, so you can affirm I didn't accost Mr. Morgan or any of his savage friends."

If Sheriff Moore had disliked Constable Riggs before, now he disliked him even more. But he did like the Morgans and the Webbs, and he knew evil when he saw it. And the locals were not savages; the only savage Sheriff Moore was acquainted with was standing in front of him.

"Well, you're going to have to give me a few days. My niece's birthday is coming up this weekend."

"Your niece's birthday? Good heavens, what are you, a schoolgirl?"

"You may not have any family, Mr.Riggs, but I do. If you want to go through life unattached and die alone, that's up to you, but family is important to me. We can leave Monday morning, and that's soon enough."

When Constable Riggs had left, the Sheriff paid a visit to Newell Storis.

Acise held her own, neither improving nor losing any further ground. Her family and Ithua counted each day, each mouthful, each moment she slept soundly, so the last thing any of them wanted was the commotion that ensued very early one morning.

Oh'Dar got up quickly to see what was going on. His anger rose when he saw Constable Riggs and Sheriff Moore talking to Chief Is'Taqa and Honovi. He trip-hopped, pulling on his leggings as he rushed to get out of the shelter and over to them.

Until then, he had never heard Chief Is'Taqa raise his voice.

"What is going on?" Honovi turned to Oh'Dar while Chief Is'Taqa stared long and hard into Constable Riggs's eyes.

"Tell your Chief here to calm down," Constable Riggs said to Oh'Dar. "No need to get all upset; I was just delivering some news. You can tell him the government needs this land, and the sooner they relocate elsewhere, the better for them. They'll find plenty of other land elsewhere. Make him understand that if my men and I have to come in and do it, it won't be pleasant. I'll be back in a while, and when I return, it'll be with a warrant to take this woman and her children with me. They don't belong here."

"And why are you here, Sheriff?" Oh'Dar asked.

"He asked me to come along, but it turns out I needed to anyway. Here, this is for you." Sheriff Moore handed Oh'Dar a packet.

Oh'Dar broke the seal that held the package shut, and took out a sheaf of papers. He briefly glanced at it, and when the Sheriff handed him a quill and ink, he signed the document on top and then stepped toward Riggs until he was close enough for the constable to feel his breath.

"Sheriff," Oh'Dar said as he looked directly into the constable's eyes. "Kindly tell Mr. Riggs to get the hell off my land."

"What?" The constable backed up and looked at the sheriff. "What are you talking about?"

"This," and Oh'Dar held up the papers. "For as far as an eagle can fly in a day in every direction, the land you are standing on now belongs to the Morgan Trust. You are on private property. And if you come back again, I'll have you arrested and prosecuted for trespassing."

"That's not possible!" Now red in the face, the constable looked at the Sheriff then back to Oh'Dar.

"You didn't have time. What—did you *warn* him somehow that we were coming?"

"The Sheriff didn't need to warn me of anything," Oh'Dar said. "My attorney started working on the purchase the day after the trial ended."

Just then, Ithua came running out of the shelter that belonged to Oh'Dar and Acise. "Honovi! Oh'Dar! The baby is coming."

Oh'Dar shoved the packet of papers inside his tunic and hurriedly turned to the Sheriff. "If he is not saddled up and on his way by the time I reach that shelter, arrest him."

Acise's water had broken. She was moaning, but not loudly; it was as if she didn't have the strength. Honovi got behind her and helped her sit up, trying to get her into a better birthing position. Snana was right there with a blanket to wrap the baby in.

The birth was over in no time, and the moment the baby was out, it was clear why. She was small. She was so small.

CHAPTER 13

Adia had been resting and sat up with a start. Oh, no. She knew immediately that Oh'Dar's offspring had been born and was in distress. She threw off the hide she had been resting under and ran out of the Leader's Quarters.

"Acaraho! Acaraho!" she called as she ran, her bare feet slapping against the stone floors of Kthama.

By the time Adia and Acaraho arrived with the wet nurse, half the village was already gathered around the shelter. Many were sitting peacefully, most were chanting softly. They looked up in awe as three of the People walked between them and stopped in front of the shelter's opening.

Adia spoke softly, and Honovi pulled the curtain back. She invited Adia to enter while the others remained outside.

Acise was barely sitting up, the newborn

wrapped and at her breast. "Is she able to feed her offspring?" Adia asked.

"Barely; oh, Adia, I am so happy you are here," Honovi gasped out. "It is a girl; come and see her."

Adia crawled carefully over to Acise and peered at the tiniest little bundle she had ever seen in her life. Her heart ran cold with fear at how small the offspring was. She gasped when Acise pulled back the blanket.

The tiny offspring had a thick mass of bright red hair, and when she opened her eyes, Adia gasped again. The same startling blue eyes she had seen when she first picked up and held Oh'Dar, were staring up at her.

"How can this be?"

Honovi said, "My father's mother had red hair, so it is in my family."

And Miss Vivian's red hair and blue eyes. The blue eyes of Oh'Dar's father and grandfather and Honovi's grandmother. Somehow all that had combined to produce this remarkably striking yet frighteningly fragile offspring.

"At least she is nursing. And she latched on right away. All in all, in spite of her small size, she is stronger than her mother is right now," Ithua explained.

"Where is Oh'Dar?" Adia asked.

"Right after the baby was born, and it was determined she was strong, though so tiny, Oh'Dar went with Pajackok and some others to make sure that the constable had left," Honovi said.

"The *who*?"

"I'll explain later. I barely understand it myself."

Adia then said to Acise, "I have brought a wet nurse with me. Her name is Agara. She has plenty of milk if you need her. We will make sure your offspring does not go hungry."

Acise tiredly nodded her thanks.

Then the flap was pulled aside again, and Oh'Dar looked in. "Mama, Father told me you were in here." He squeezed over to his mother's side and hugged her. "What do you think of her, Mama? Please tell me."

Weakly, Acise spoke. "Ithua and Momma say she is tinier than she should be, and I am so worried."

Adia could see the strain they were both under. She bent over the precious miracle and extended her smallest finger to see if the offspring would wrap her fingers around it. She did, and the Healer smiled.

"May I have a moment alone with Acise and the offspring?" she asked.

When everyone had carefully left the shelter, and they were alone, Adia turned back to mother and daughter.

She carefully stretched out her full length next to Acise, who was still holding the tiny bundle. Then, lying prone next to her, Adia placed one hand on the crown of Acise's head and the other on the tiny form, her hand completely covering the little body.

Acise let out a gasp as she felt a flood of love radiate from Adia's touch and spread through her. At the same time, the baby gurgled and squirmed, and Acise knew that her daughter was experiencing this same thing. It was like the warm air passing over an evening fire on a cold night, only this was not just warmth; it was love. It was the manifestation of love itself.

Acise felt strength returning to her. And hope. "I feel so much better. Whatever you just did—"

"I do not know what I just did, but it seems to be some kind of ability given to me by the Guardian Pan at the last High Council meeting. It feels to me like a warmth starting in my center and then spreading out through every part of my body and my consciousness. And then it seems to come out through my hands. I feel it well up within me and pass through. I believe that in some way, it brings, or helps, healing."

"I believe it does. I believe with all my heart and soul that you just saved my life and our daughter's."

"I thank you, Acise, but I can take no credit. But I am grateful to be allowed to serve as a channel for the Great Spirit's healing energy."

Acise and the baby improved with each passing day. Ben and Miss Vivian were thrilled to hear they had a great-granddaughter and just as surprised as anyone to learn she had red hair and blue eyes.

"I can't wait to hold her," Miss Vivian said, "and to see Grayson. We still haven't seen him. I understand why, but oh, how I wish he were here."

"Grayson's wife is partly white. Somewhere in her background, there must be red hair and blue eyes."

"I'm sure we'll find out soon enough. I wonder what they will name her?"

They had named her I'Layah, and Oh'Dar sat gently cradling her in his arms. Her tiny fingers splayed out like the minutest stars, and she kicked her little feet now and then as if railing against the swaddling. He smoothed down the surprisingly abundant red hair and caressed her soft, smooth cheeks with his finger. Acise lay next to them, studying his face.

"I thought I had lost you," she said.

"And I thought I was going to lose you," he said.

"Yet here we are. And now little I'Layah has joined us."

"She is perfect. Just like her mother."

"Well, not just like her mother. Oh, Oh'Dar," Acise exclaimed. "So many times, I sat across from you at my family's night fire and studied you, just as I was doing a moment ago. I would dream of bearing your child and that it would have your blue eyes. And now—"

"And now you have your wish—and more."

I'Layah started to fuss, and Oh'Dar gave her back

to Acise to nurse. Though the wet nurse was still at the village to provide supplemental milk if needed, whatever Adia had done had also improved Acise's ability to feed her baby.

"What are we to do?"

"I wish I could say I count on the constable not coming back, but I cannot," Oh'Dar said.

"Can he really take us away? My mother, Snana, Noshoba, me? Our daughter!?" Acise was finally voicing her fears.

"This is private land, and that should provide protection. But I am not sure how far that protection will, in truth, extend."

Oh'Dar later explained to Chief Is'Taqa what had happened with the constable.

"No one can own land," said Chief Is'Taqa. "Only the Waschini would think of that. How can anyone own that which was created by the Great Spirit? We are only entrusted with its use to provide for our loved ones. But we are blessed that you understand the Waschini ways and have intervened to protect us."

"They can no longer drive you from here," Oh'Dar said. "But there is a potential threat to Honovi, Acise, Snana, Noshoba, and now I'Layah. I think it is best, once Acise and the baby are strong enough, that I take them to Kthama for a while.

"There will be no hiding her as we were able to do with you," Chief Is'Taqa said. "During the summer months, when the sun darkened your skin, only your eyes betrayed your true heritage. Her coloring is going to stand out among our people, even from a distance."

"As for Snana, Noshoba, and Honovi," Oh'Dar said, "I believe that they should come too, at least for a while. The constable is out to hurt me, and he might use them to do so."

Chief Is'Taqa nodded. "I will speak with them."

"I have brought more division," Oh'Dar said. "And now, the burden I grew up with has been passed to my daughter. An outsider, no matter where she goes."

"It is true that you stand in three worlds, Oh'Dar," said the Chief. "It is not that these worlds are being set further apart but that they are being brought closer together. Through you, and now, through your daughter."

It had occurred to Oh'Dar that I'Layah's coloring would be a delight to his grandmother. And, for however long she and Acise stayed at Kthama, having her great-granddaughter there would certainly brighten both her life and Ben's.

Constable Riggs was in the Millgrove office talking to Sheriff Boone, who was not pleased to see him back so soon.

"Grayson Morgan is correct. The land is private property now. You have no right to go back."

"I can if I have an official reason," Riggs quibbled. "I will stay here a few nights, then I am going to pay a visit to the governor. Maybe Grayson Stone Morgan the Third is out of my reach, but his wife and the Chief's wife are not. And, there is the fact that they must have harbored Morgan when he was an infant, even though you say you searched the village with your own men."

"It was a long time ago, Samuel, and there was no lasting harm done. You're not going to get a lot of public support on this one. In fact, it's starting to look like a personal vendetta. Things are getting tense with the locals, and this is not the time for you to create more problems than are already brewing."

However, the constable continued as if he hadn't heard a word. "That is a massive amount of land Morgan bought. Why so much? What is he hiding there?"

Ned could not get his visit to Miss Vivian and Ben Jenkins out of his mind. He replayed every moment of it over and over. The inclines, the turns. There were places where bushes scraped up against his arms, sometimes the sound of leaves under hooves, sometimes only the clip-clop on harder terrain. They had ridden a long time, with a couple of rests, but always traveling uphill. Then there was a long, even steeper incline before they dismounted and were led into an enclosure.

Ned could tell it was a cave—from the acoustics and his footsteps, an enormous cave with a high ceiling. Under his feet, the ground had turned from rocky soil to hard rock. It was damp inside, and he could hear dripping, so there had to be water somewhere. Then another walk across a stone floor. Though he could not see through his blindfold, he knew they were going through some tunnels. He had strained his ears as much as he could, trying to hear anything. He even held his breath at points, hoping that would help. The only sounds he heard were breathing and footsteps and then the loud scraping, which, when their blindfolds were removed, he realized had been a large wooden door being opened. It was lashed together with strips of cured hide or maybe vines; he was not sure which.

He pictured again the furniture that had been brought in, along with a mattress and linens that were on the bed. On one side of the room, the long bureau with a mantle clock sitting atop—it had chimed the hour while they were there.

Ben Jenkins was on the bed, partially covered up, and they both looked as he remembered, except that Miss Vivian's hair was not done up as she had kept it before. Instead of being piled on top of her head, it was pulled to one side in a long, thick, auburn braid that hung down over one shoulder. She had lost weight, which usually meant an illness, but she didn't look sick. He thought she looked happy.

Ned had kept turning his attention between the conversation and the whereabouts. They must be in a cave system and a huge one at that. One with tunnels and some type of water source somewhere. Obviously, others lived here with them. But who were they? If they were just another local tribe, why all the secrecy?

That was the deciding factor for Ned. Even if they wanted to keep the location a secret, then he understood the blindfolds. But making sure that they had no contact with anyone but Miss Vivian and Ben? What would be the reason for that?

Something very strange was going on. Something beyond his imagination, and Ned was unable to let go of it. Nothing else mattered any longer, not even his studies with Mr. Clement—at least not with the goal of eventually taking over the animal husbandry business when Mr. Clement retired.

Ned had touched the fringes of the unknown, and from that moment, the day-to-day world held little interest for him.

When word reached Kthama that Oh'Dar and his family might have to move there for some time, his old quarters were refreshed and an area prepared for the offspring. On top of the buzz of excitement over the upcoming High Council meeting, now there was the added stir of Oh'Dar's return. Also, word had spread that Oh'Dar's daughter was remarkable. Not as remarkable as An'Kru, but still. Everyone was intrigued by the idea of Waschini hair the color of a blazing sunset and eyes as blue as Oh'Dar's.

It would be some time before the young family could travel, so Adia distracted herself by keeping busy while she waited for them to arrive. Equally excited were Ben and Miss Vivian, the prospect of a great-grandchild to love and spoil filling them with deep happiness.

Miss Vivian set about sewing a little doll for her great-granddaughter out of a shawl she had brought. It was a considerable sacrifice, as she had been able to bring only so many things with her. With the left-over material, she also sewed a colorful bag to be hung out of reach on the wall to hold whatever other toys I'Layah would accumulate, keeping them up out from underfoot.

Miss Vivian continued to run the school, but other than that, they kept to their room. Ben was still unable to walk; his knee had swollen to twice its normal size, and the pain continued. His days of climbing on the scaffolding in the Wall of Records were over. Now what? How would he help them with their research? How could they unlock the key, if there was one, to their inbreeding problem?

Ben had not told Acaraho or Adia, but the fact was that unless there was some startling discovery, he did not see a way out. Though the numbers that made up their population were impressive, they were not limitless. Even adding in whatever variation there would be in the bloodlines of the People from the farthest communities, Ben had to agree. The original estimation had been right. They would be unable to safely reproduce in seven generations. Perhaps less.

Unless the Akassa were to disappear from Etera, they would once again have to dilute their bloodline with that of others. Yuma'qia and Bidzel had explained to him that further breeding with the Brothers was out as a solution; their blood had been intermingled long ago. Ben had to agree. That left only the Waschini. And that seemed out of the question. There was no way to introduce a Waschini bloodline without revealing the secret of the People's existence. And it would take more than one or two Waschini. Even if he could still father a child, how would his wife feel about that, and of course, would he want to do it?

It seemed to him that there was no way out. The Akassa were doomed.

CHAPTER 14

It was time for the High Council meeting. Acaraho and Adia were there to meet each of the participants as they trickled in, and it was an exhausting procession. Adia had left An'Kru with Miss Vivian, where he was safe and out of the fray. She knew he was a major attraction, and even those who had seen him before would want another glimpse.

Many who came brought gifts from their stores, so there was no shortage of food or other supplies. The spring weather was perfect for travel, and the travelers were grateful that the hot summer sun was not yet beating down.

Khon'Tor had arrived with Tehya and Arismae a couple of days early. As before, the People of the High Rocks were happy to see their former Adik'Tar. It was once more a bittersweet reunion for Khon'Tor, though the regret of the past that had tormented him had been healed at the end of the last High Council meeting through the gift given to Adia by the Guardian Pan. Tehya's seeding was showing by now. Her offspring was due with the onset of the cooler weather, and Adia's about a month after.

Tehya's parents had come with her to watch Arismae when Tehya wasn't able to.

Oh'Dar was still at the village with Acise and their daughter, though Chief Is'Taqa was attending the High Council meeting. All the Medicine Women had been invited to attend the Healers' meetings, but Ithua was aging, and Honovi decided to stay behind with her to tend to Acise and others in the village if they needed her.

As was customary for those traveling a distance, many came in a few nights before. It gave them time to settle in and enjoy socializing. After the events of the last High Council, spirits were high despite the somewhat foreboding future. Pan's speech about working closely with each other had fortified them with confidence that whatever happened, they would be able to face it together.

The question on everyone's mind was, of course, whether the Guardian Pan would make another appearance. While most did not expect it to become a matter of routine, they still hoped to see her.

The People were still assimilating their new history, slowly adjusting and replacing the one they had grown up with. All now knew that they were not formed wholly from the dust of Etera by the Great

Spirit. They had been created when the Ancients bred with the Brothers. There was humility in the revelation of their true beginnings, but there was something else—brotherhood.

As Pan had said, they were all one, truly. In their own ways, they were as diverse as the birds of the air or the flowers of the field, yet they had all been formed from the same materials by the same hand of the One-Who-Is-Three.

Wishing to avoid the pandemonium of bodies mingling, chatting, and hugging, Urilla Wuti was one of the first of the early arrivals. She was slower now than ever before. This was partly from age and partly from growing mindfulness about the preciousness of the moment. There was no need to rush to the next; the moment at hand was where life was lived.

Nootau embraced Acaraho and, as always, addressed him as Father. Adia knew she would hear more about Nootau's training when the Healers and Helpers were brought together after the next day's opening session, and for now, she was content just to be a family again.

After Tehya, Arismae, and the grandparents were settled, Khon'Tor sought out Acaraho.

"I must travel to the neighboring village where Ahanu was found. If I leave now, I can be there by dark. Then, if the Chief wishes to attend, I will bring him back with me. Iella says she has received no word from the Chief that he will or will not be attending, but I did say I would fetch him."

"Will you stay overnight in the village?" Acaraho was surprised that he might do so.

Khon'Tor laughed. "I have slept many a night out under the stars. It will be very pleasant."

"Do you want anyone to go with you?" Acaraho asked.

"I thought of that, but I am not sure. On the one hand, I do not want to overwhelm Chief Kotori. On the other hand, being brought into this assembly with the Sarnonn without any preparation would be too much. Maybe I should take one of the Sarnonn with me."

"You could take Haan," Acaraho suggested.

Khon'Tor thought for a moment. "That is a very good idea. I will speak with him. If he thinks it is wise, it may encourage them to see that the Sassen still exist."

"It is more than the Sarnonn's existence. Chief Kotori does not know what we have recently learned about our true origins and those of the Sarnonn. Or about the Guardian Pan and her visit at the last High Council meeting. All of this could be unnerving to him. And his people."

"It is best then that Haan and I spend some time before we head back to High Rocks explaining that to him. You are right, learning it all at once might be too much. I will make sure I talk to Haan about this also before we get to the Chief's village.

Khon'Tor and Haan set out for Chief Kotori's village. As the full moon was approaching, the Chief would have been expecting Khon'Tor anytime around the past few days, so they were not surprised when Pakwa was waiting at the outskirts of the village to greet them.

But Pakwa could not have foreseen who would also be present this time.

Khon'Tor stepped out from the treeline. "I have come as I said I would, and I have also brought an ally."

Pakwa opened his mouth. His eyes were fixed on Haan, who had seemed to appear out of nowhere, now standing just behind Khon'Tor. Khon'Tor towered over Pakwa and Haan towered over Khon'Tor.

"I have brought Adik'Tar Haan; he is the Leader of the Sasquatch community that lives close to us." Khon'Tor did not attempt to explain the relationship between Kthama and Kht'shWea.

"Sasquatch," Pakwa finally said. "Oh'Mah. Master of the Forest. We were not sure you still walked among us."

"My people and I still walk among you. We are

pledged to your protection, as are Khon'Tor and all the Akassa."

"You are called the Akassa?" Pakwa asked.

"Yes. But to ourselves, we are just the People."

"I have been waiting for days, watching for you. I will tell the Chief you have arrived. And that Oh'Mah has returned to our people." He turned and sprinted into the village.

Khon'Tor looked at Haan and grinned. "Well, that is better than having spears and hatchets thrown at us. I am glad they like you."

Haan smiled back, and Khon'Tor was reminded of how terrifying a sight it had been to him, the opposite of what was intended.

It was not too long before Chief Kotori and Second Chief Tawa, surrounded by what looked like nearly all the village, came to greet Khon'Tor and his guest.

"Each time you come, you bring a great blessing," Chief Kotori said.

It took Khon'Tor a moment to figure out what the first one had been, and then he remembered how Iella had commanded the animals to surround her to show that the visitors to the village meant no harm to anyone.

"Haan is part of our alliance. He and his people will be at the High Council assembly I spoke of. And there will also be other Chiefs of your people there. And more. Our Healers and the Medicine Women have all been invited."

Khon'Tor watched the faces of the Brothers as they took in both him and Haan, head to toe. At the back, he spotted Myrica, no doubt wanting news of Ahanu.

"Chief Kotori, have you made your decision about whether to join us this time? Haan and I are prepared to take you there tomorrow. You may bring whomever you wish with you."

The Chief looked around the people gathered behind him. He named his Medicine Woman, Tiponi. He then glanced at Myrica, now with entreaty on her face. "Myrica."

Several other women congratulated her. Presumably, it was a big honor to be chosen to go with the Chief.

"We will be back at first light then," Khon'Tor said. He had half expected the Chief to ask them to come into the village and stay awhile. "It will be at more than a day's journey at best, but you can travel light. Your needs for food, water, and shelter will be met while you are with us."

Myrica could barely hold back her excitement. Before she found Ahanu, nothing interesting had ever happened in her short life. Finding him had been a gift, she now realized. Not only did she get to experience the joy of having a child to love and raise for a while, but now enduring the heartbreak of giving him up would be rewarded with an adventure she could not even imagine the likes of.

Her friend, Awantia, rejoiced with her. "You are honored among women. You must remember every detail because I will want to know everything!" Awantia was nearly as excited as Myrica. "You must wear that light tunic, the one with the ivory beading around the collar."

"The one my mother was saving for me to be bonded in?"

Awantia gave her a look that said it all.

"You are right. Who knows when that will ever happen. What am I saving it for?" Myrica laughed, and the two friends clasped hands.

"You can always make another, but that one is so becoming on you," Awantia said. "After all, the tall one said there will be other Chiefs there, and no doubt they will bring some of their people with them too."

"The tall one who looks more like us, the one called Khon'Tor who allowed me to go with Ahanu? He was a great Chief. He carries himself in that way; you can tell that when he speaks, others listen."

"I could not stop looking at either one of them," Awantia exclaimed. "I know I will not sleep tonight. I wonder where the Sasquatch live—if they have shelters like ours? Or do they burrow?"

"Burrow!" Myrica couldn't help but laugh out loud, and then she pictured each of the hairy figures unearthing themselves from underground and rising up covered in dirt with leaves stuck to them.

They laughed so long their sides hurt, and when they had finally composed themselves, Myrica said, "Oh, that was too funny. But I know what you mean. I think you meant, do they live underground, as in *caves*! Like the People."

"I cannot imagine otherwise. They certainly seem too large to live in the trees!"

Awantia and Myrica were having so much fun, enjoying the excitement of the moment.

Oh'Mah has returned to us. That can only be an omen of blessings to come," Awantia said. "I am envious of you. But also so happy for you."

The mood shifted. "I hope you are right," frowned Myrica. "With the trouble the Waschini are giving us, I worry about our future."

"We all do, but look at the provision of the Great Spirit. Khon'Tor has offered protection. Their physical strength is greater, and I believe they have abilities we do not. Only good can come of this alliance."

Khon'Tor and Haan stretched out under the night sky. The night sky was clear, the full moon casting a soft light over everything. Khon'Tor pulled some fir branches over him.

"I miss Haaka," Haan said. "And Kalli."

"And I miss Tehya and Arismae," Khon'Tor said. "Peculiar, how a female can change your life."

"They are smaller than we are. They depend on us for protection and provision. Yet they are stronger than us in many ways, and they give us far more in return. They give our lives deeper meaning." Then Haan added, "Your offling is due at the end of the warm weather, is it not?"

"Yes," Khon'Tor answered. "A son."

They relaxed in companionable silence.

"Good night, Adik'Tar Khon'Tor," Haan said after a while.

"Good night, Adik'Tar Haan'Tor."

The next morning, Chief Kotori, Myrica, and Tiponi were waiting for them as promised.

The ground was wet with dew, but otherwise the weather was clear. Khon'Tor took his time, realizing the Brothers' stamina would be no match for his, let alone Haan's. Wanting to pace himself to their needs, he asked the Chief to walk beside him, with Haan bringing up the rear.

Once they were a short distance away, he asked them to stop as he wanted to share the truth about their past and the origin of the Akassa and the Sassen. Haan added his own pieces to the story to flesh out the parts as Khon'Tor told the story. Myrica was enthralled, while the Chief and Tiponi listened patiently, asking few questions.

When Khon'Tor had finished, with Haan adding his own pieces to the story, the Chief sat quietly a few moments.

"Oh'Mah has been part of our stories for many generations. To learn that the Oh'Mah of my great-great-grandfathers is not the Oh'Mah I see walking Etera now," and the Chief turned his gaze to Haan, "is information we would never have known had you not shared it. I thank you for your honesty."

Again, he sat quietly.

Then, just when Khon'Tor thought he was going to change his mind about going with them and turn back, Chief Kotori said, "Only a fool would close his mind to the truth, no matter how hard it is to accept. What was done is done. Those who sinned against us are long gone. We cannot hold the sins of your fathers against you. Let us move forward."

The watchers were set to alert Acaraho when the party approached. Knowing Iella had met the Chief when she joined Khon'Tor to find Ahanu, Acaraho made sure she was there to greet them.

The Great Entrance was cleared of everyone except Acaraho, Adia, and Iella. They saw the silhouettes approaching, and each said a silent prayer for a good beginning.

The Chief stepped into the entrance and immediately recognized Iella. Briefly scanning the great expanse, he greeted them all. "I am Chief Kotori, and we come at your invitation. I welcome a beneficial alliance between your people and mine."

"I am Acaraho'Tor, Leader of the People who live here. Welcome to our home, Kthama," and Acaraho waved his arm around to indicate the cave system. "This is my mate, Adia. She is the Healer to our people here."

The Chief turned to her. "This is Tiponi; she is our Medicine Woman, our Healer."

Adia extended her hand toward Tiponi. "You are welcome here. I look forward to learning from you how we can best help your people."

"There are others," Myrica said to her Chief. "This is not the cave system I was taken to with Ahanu."

"Yes. We have several communities spread out," Acaraho said, "and their representatives will be at the assembly taking place over the next few days. There are already many people here, and you will see them tomorrow morning. For tonight, I thought it best if we make you comfortable before subjecting you to all the commotion," he explained. "For the morning meal, we will seat you with the other Chiefs of your people and their guests."

High Protector Awan escorted them to their quarters. On the way, he explained the meal arrangements and that their personal needs would be taken care of; fresh water would be brought in and any discard or leavings removed, and someone would come to fetch them for mealtimes. The older offspring who were of age to participate, at least peripherally, in these types of meetings were ready to help the visitors find their way around.

Each was given their own sleeping space, though they were located close together and not far from the general eating area.

As the High Protector was leaving them to settle in, he pointed out a large, empty room just down the tunnel from where they were clustered together. "If you wish to meet with your people separately for any reason, please feel free to use this area."

Chief Kotori was not a man who showed a great deal of emotion, but he was overcome by what he had just seen. That these people lived in such organized fashion, came together in meetings for their mutual benefit—and all without detection by outsiders—was almost incredible.

He had been intimidated by Khon'Tor's size when he first met him. Now, seeing others of the kind and realizing there were perhaps hundreds of them here in this cave system alone, he was in a state of awe. However, there was also a feeling of slight unease. It was not fear of the People themselves; it was the fear of what the Waschini would do to the People if they were to be discovered.

The Chief was about to lie down when he heard Myrica call to him through the wooden door.

"Chief Kotori, Is there anything I can do for you?"

He opened the door and saw that Tiponi was with her.

"Rest, both of you. No doubt there are other wonders yet to discover here. It is no mistake that you rescued Ahanu, and it is no mistake that we are here. Whatever the next days hold, we must be mindful that we have been invited into a sacred brotherhood, and we must keep our hearts open to what this portends for our people and theirs."

Acaraho stood on the platform, preparing to address the sea of faces looking back at him. As at the last High Council meeting, Akassa, Sassen, and Brothers were all brought together in peace. Oh'Dar's grandparents had not yet made their appearance as Acaraho wished first to prepare the new attendees for the presence of Waschini among them, but they would be joining for a short time before the assembly ended.

Haan and Chief Is'Taqa joined Acaraho on the platform while he addressed the huge gathering.

"We come together as one people today. One people joined by our love and devotion to the Great Spirit. Joined by our love and devotion to our loved ones, our families, our way of life. Joined in peace. May the next few days deepen our understanding of each other. May we more fully realize that no matter the challenges ahead, we are stronger facing them together. May we form an alliance that no adversity, no disappointment, no enemy can break."

"But our alliance includes more than those of us who are here. More than the Brothers, the Sassen, and the Akassa. Our alliance must also include others whom we might not as easily welcome. For those who are joining us for the first time and have not heard it from others, our community here at the High Rocks includes three Waschini."

There was a muttering of comments among the handful of newcomers. "One of them is named Oh'Dar. He is my son in every way that counts. When he was a very new offspring, he was the only survivor of a massacre in which his parents were killed by their own kind—cruel Waschini riders rewarded to do so. He was overlooked and rescued to be raised by my mate Adia and me. And now, years later, we have welcomed his grandmother and her mate into our community. They have chosen to leave everything they knew before and spend the rest of their lives among us. Please, open your hearts and minds to learn about them as individuals. Do not hold against them the sins of their own kind."

As he had expected, before the groups dispersed for the rest of the day's activities, there was a great deal of discussion on the subject.

The day had been planned so specific groups could join together to discuss common matters. Urilla Wuti would be meeting with the Healers and

Helpers, while Chief Is'Taqa would lead the meeting of the Brothers' Chiefs and their guests. High Protector Awan had suggested that he meet with the other High Protectors to discuss advances in weaponry and fighting techniques, and Acaraho agreed that was a good idea. Toward the end, Oh'Dar and his grandparents would attend as Acaraho wanted them to address the group.

Urilla Wuti, Adia, and the Healers and Helpers were gathered in one of the meeting rooms. Once they were comfortably seated, Urilla Wuti opened the session by thanking the Great Mother for the opportunity for them to come together and for the blessings they enjoyed. She asked for strength to face future challenges and wisdom in knowing how best to handle them.

"The last time we were assembled, the Guardian Pan met with us. Some of us knew she still walked Etera; some of us have had conversations with her in other realms such as the Corridor, but this was the first time any of us saw her face to face. I, for one, was deeply affected by her appearance, as I am sure were all those of us who were there. Before she went, Pan said she was leaving us with a gift—that our abilities would be augmented. She also said that some who had not manifested any Healer abilities might notice them surfacing. So I would like first to focus on that discussion."

Taipa from the Great Pines stood to speak. "I was there. I, too, was astonished that the Guardian appeared. After I returned home, I started to pay attention in case anything changed. It was several days later when it did. At first, I thought I was imagining it, so I started spending more and more time alone to determine if it was possibly real. I can confidently say now that not only is my seventh sense much stronger, but I now have the ability to affect the weather."

A murmur spread through the group.

"I should explain. I was sitting down by the river on an overcast day. I was enjoying the solitude and the smell of the coming rain in the air. When it started to rain, I did not want to leave, but I also did not want to get soaking wet. I remember thinking, I wish it would stop raining long enough for me to get back home. No sooner had I thought that than it stopped, and I got up and went home. When I was almost inside, mostly in jest really, I said to the skies, you can release your blessing now. And I am not exaggerating; in that instant, it started to rain again."

"That is no less than amazing, Taipa," said Adia. "Please tell us more. What else have you experimented with?"

"All of it really, making the wind blow harder or softer. Coaxing the clouds away from the sun, clearing them from the night sky so I could enjoy its beauty. I have no idea of the use of this gift, but I am honored to have been given it."

A hand at the back was raised. "Yes, Eralato?" Urilla Wuti acknowledged the Healer from the High Red Rocks.

"I, too, have a new gift. Most of you do not know me, but I have always had a love of planting and harvesting. The smell of the rich soil, the sweet release of the fruit from the vine when it is ripe, seeing the little green heads of new shoots poking up from the ground. Perhaps my gift was given to me out of my love for Etera's bounty because I can coax the new growth to appear more quickly. And when a plant comes to full bloom, it is heartier and more robust than its neighbors."

"You can cause things to grow?" Adia asked.

"Yes. Plants and flowers. I have tested it by focusing on some and not others, and it is not my imagination. Considering the landscape surrounding our community, this is a rich blessing."

"Would anyone else like to speak?" Urilla Wuti asked.

Nepeta, Healer at the Little River, said quietly, "I may have a new ability. But I am not sure yet. I would like to remain silent until we meet again."

"I also have experienced a change," said Apricoria, a young apprentice Healer from the Deep Valley. "I would like to speak with you privately, though, Overseer, if I may?"

"Of course."

Then Urilla Wuti addressed everyone. "This is all very exciting. For the rest of you, I would not conclude that because you have not noticed a change, that one is not coming. And, if you have but wish to remain silent for now, that is also alright. This is a uniquely personal experience, and you will decide when you wish to share it with others."

Adia spoke next. "Taipa and Eralato, do you feel open to demonstrating your abilities to us? If not, I understand."

Both the Healers agreed, so the group went outside and down to the Great River. It was a beautiful summer day, and they excitedly chatted as they made their way down the winding paths.

As they arrived, Taipa and Eralato were very excited.

"I have an idea," Taipa said and leaned over to whisper something in Eralato's ear.

Eralato laughed. "Alright." She looked down the banks of the Great River until she saw what she wanted and called for the others to come to form a ring around a little khari plant so they could all easily see. Taipa stood next to her.

Next, Eralato knelt down in front of the plant. She closed her eyes and held the palm of one hand a little bit above it. Then she opened her eyes and sat back.

In front of everyone, the khari plant started to

wobble and wiggle. Then it started to rise up, new leaves peeking out from its thickening stem and then stretching out and unfurling new fully formed bright green leaves.

"That is enough," Eralato said. "I do not want to wear it out." She laughed. "Actually, I have no idea how much growth is too much, so I have only experimented with a little at a time."

"You next!" she said to Taipa.

Taipa smiled but remained standing. She closed her eyes. For a moment, nothing happened. Then, a gathering of moisture started to form above the little plant. It started to gain in density and became a small grey cloud. To everyone's amazement, a tiny rainstorm began, sending drops of water down to the little khari plant beneath it.

"By the Mother!" exclaimed one of the other Healers. "That is amazing; I would not have believed it if I had not seen it!"

Eralato stood up, and she and Taipa hugged each other.

"That was fun!" Taipa exclaimed.

"It was!" Eralato agreed. "I did not think about how our abilities might work together. That was the perfect demonstration."

"Indeed," said Urilla Wuti. "That is an important observation. Whatever gifts we are being given, we will no doubt be able to use them not only individually but in concert with the gifts of others. To what purpose, I do not know. Obviously, the ability to hasten crops and affect the weather will benefit us greatly in providing for our communities. As for Iella's gift of communicating with Etera's creatures, that gift is not so obviously put to use, though it was helpful in locating Ahanu."

Everyone nodded at this, having heard the story of how Iella had sent the hawk to find the Brothers' village where Ahanu was and how she had gathered the animals and birds around her to show the Brothers they came in peace.

"But Taipa and I are from different communities, so far away from each other. I wonder if our gifts can be developed to work over long distances?" Eralato asked.

"That is something to experiment with," Taipa agreed. "But how would we know since we live so far apart?"

The conversation led into what Urilla Wuti wanted to discuss next.

"Let us sit and get comfortable and continue our session here," she said. "A long time ago, I had an inspiration—that we needed to find a way to communicate with each other over long distances. Not being able to do so is a barrier to spreading news, asking for help, or, as Taipa and Eralato have just demonstrated, working together. Years ago, I started teaching Adia how to enter the Corridor. You all know what I mean when I speak of the Corridor?"

Heads nodded as they had all heard Urilla Wuti or other Healers speak of this before.

"The problem with entering the Corridor is that to bring someone there who has not themselves developed the ability requires opening a very personal connection between the two. It connects them at a deep level, a level at which some exchange of knowledge about the other is unavoidable, which can be troublesome as keeping thoughts private is our right. I know I have taught a few of you how to enter the Corridor at will, thinking that was the solution. But there is another way, one that I too casually dismissed and which I would like Adia to talk about."

"It is called the Dream World," Adia said. "I discovered it by accident, and Urilla Wuti helped me learn how to enter it whenever I want to. It is not the Corridor. Time passes the same in the Dream World as it does here on Etera. The experience is just like being here; everything looks the same, and it does not have the augmented beauty and vibrant aliveness of the Corridor. The only people in the Dream World are those who have also learned how to enter it, either by happenstance or through training."

Adia turned to find Nootau. "My son and I accidentally came together in the Dream World."

Nootau took this as his cue to speak, "Yes. No one was more surprised than I was. I have been trying to learn how to enter it at will and though I have not yet succeeded, I do feel I am close. The biggest problem is that I find I try to use my will instead of surrendering and simply allowing it to happen."

"That is a common problem for all of us,

Nootau," said Urilla Wuti. "You are not alone in that. Surrender is difficult, much harder than *trying*, to be sure."

"Patience. I have a problem with patience," Nootau said. "Allowing it to manifest in its own time. I feel a sense of urgency, which is not helping at all."

The Healers and Helpers spent the rest of the day learning about the Dream World and listening to Urilla Wuti explain how best to prepare for the experience to present itself. They agreed they would practice entering the Dream World, and then, at the next High Council meeting, they would try to enter it collectively.

Urilla Wuti and Apricoria were finally alone, and for privacy, were meeting in Urilla Wuti's quarters.

"You are the new apprentice at the Deep Valley, yes?"

"Yes," Apricoria replied. "I did not wish to disclose this in the group. I hope you will understand after I explain."

"That is fine; we are all learning because this is a new turn of events. You have a right to your privacy until you are ready to share whatever it is that is happening in your life, whether as a Healer or otherwise."

Urilla Wuti sat down opposite Apricoria, so their knees were almost touching.

"Our Healer was unable to come as she isn't well, so I am here on my own. I have little experience, so I was hesitant to share because I am so new, and the gift given to me seems too powerful for someone as untested as I."

Urilla Wuti waited for her to continue.

"I seem to be able to see things before they happen."

"Events?"

"Yes. It started immediately after the Guardian visited us at the last High Council meeting. That was my first trip to the High Rocks. I am still getting to know everyone and trying to find my place, so when this started happening to me, to start with, I did not believe it. But," she continued, "now I feel I have to admit it is real."

"Can you give me an example of what you saw coming that then happened?"

"It is just little things, nothing of any importance. One of the watchers came in to report that there is a piebald deer family living near us. Joyful news, to be sure. I saw them as if through his eyes before he came in to tell us about them."

"After you saw them yourself, how long was it before he came in to report the deer?"

"I would say a morning."

"Can you tell me of some other instances?" Urilla Wuti was not sure if Apricoria was seeing events before they happened or if she was seeing things at the same time they were happening to someone else.

"On the way back from the High Rocks, I knew that one of our expectant mothers had delivered. And before we got down to the Great River, I knew how Taipa and Eralato were going to demonstrate their abilities."

"An amazing gift, no matter what it is," Urilla Wuti said. "It seems from what you said about Taipa and Eralato that you are indeed seeing an event before it happens. I suggest you keep careful track of what you see and the time between when you learn of it, and when it happens, so we can determine exactly what ability it is."

"Thank you, Overseer. I was not sure myself, so I am glad to have you to consult. That is the other reason I did not wish to speak out. I thank you so much, and I will do as you said."

CHAPTER 15

The Chiefs and their guests, mostly the Medicine Men and Women from the various villages, had also elected to meet outside where they could enjoy the welcomed warmer weather.

Chief Is'Taqa opened their session by explaining who he was and how their village was not far from Kthama. He told everyone about the friendship that had initially developed between Khon'Tor, the Leader of the High Rocks at the time, and their prior Chief, Chief Ogima. He assured his fellow communities of the People's goodwill.

The Chiefs who had contact with the People's other communities agreed with Chief Is'Taqa. It was a beneficial relationship and one that Chief Kotori should welcome.

"Oh'Mah has returned to our people," Chief Kotori said. "It is good; it is a sign from the Great

Spirit, encouragement about the future. We have had grave concerns about the intentions of the Waschini because each time we assemble, we hear stories of their harassing our people. Even driving them from their homes to take their land, so this new relationship is very welcome."

Chief Cha'Tima, whose people lived not far from the Little River, agreed. "We, too, hear stories. The Waschini say one thing but do another; they do not honor the Great Spirit by their actions, and I fear for our people's future."

"An alliance with the People and the Sasquatch is a great assurance in that regard," stated Chief Is'Taqa. "The People have placed watchers along the edges of our territory, and as they are able to see further and travel faster than our own people, it has been a great benefit."

Chief Kotori was a bit skeptical. "Yes. A great benefit, I am sure. But as neither the People nor the Sasquatch can reveal themselves to the Waschini, the help they can provide has its limits. If it comes to a battle, we will be on our own. And we are no match for the Waschini's weapons."

"Then we must find a way to get Waschini weapons." The speaker was Chief Alosaka from the High Red Rock community. "Adik'Tar Acaraho said there are Waschini living here at Kthama—

Chief Cha'Tima looked across at Is'Taqa. "I know that a Waschini now lives among your people."

"His name is Oh'Dar, and he is the one who was

rescued by the Healer here, Healer Adia. He spends his time between the two communities as he is now bonded to my eldest daughter. They have just had their first child."

"A Waschini also living among you?" The Medicine Woman, Tiponi, spoke sharply. "And now with a part Waschini child?"

"Yes, he has been our ally, our advantage, in communications with other Waschini. But I hear the other words you are not saying. That it is a risk, especially in these times. That the Waschini would not take to having one of their own living among us, especially a child. We are aware that trouble may come of it; some already has. To that end, Oh'Dar and my daughter and their baby will be staying here at Kthama for a while. They will also be company for Oh'Dar's grandparents."

"How did the grandparents come to be living at the High Rocks?" Tiponi asked.

"It is a long story," Chief Is'Taqa said. "A long story for another time, perhaps. They have not been well, but you will meet them at the end of the assembly."

"They are not well?" Chief Kotori sounded alarmed.

Chief Is'Taqa was quick to answer, "It is not a contagion. Oh'Dar's grandmother is elderly, and his grandfather was hurt in a fall. But like the People and the Sarnonn, Oh'Dar and his grandparents are helping us. And there are others. Other Waschini who are not against us, who wish only to protect us and let us live our lives in peace."

"I would like to meet these others," said Tiponi.

"You must take my word that they exist," said Chief Is'Taqa. "For now, at least."

As one of the guests, Myrica hung on every word, trying to remember everything so she could share it all with Awantia when she returned. Though Larara had not come with Ahanu, Myrica was very happy to be there. It was exciting to see the other Brothers and have the privilege of listening to the Chiefs and Medicine Women discuss such important matters. She felt she was standing on the brink of something amazing, about to happen to them all.

Miss Vivian had just changed the bandage on Ben's leg. "It is healing so slowly. Oh, I wish we had something from Dr. Miller."

"But it is healing," Ben said. "It just takes longer because of my age. I doubt anyone could provide better care than Adia and Nadiwani. Their remedies seem very effective."

"Oh, I didn't mean that. I am just worried, that's all."

"Come and lie down here then," Ben said, extending his hand to his wife. "We can talk about what is to come. Very soon, our great-granddaughter will be here, and then you can fuss over her instead of me." He smiled.

Miss Vivian took his hand, and he gently pulled her down to lie next to him.

She laid her head on his shoulder and placed her hand on his chest. "How can we ever repay Grace and Ned?" she asked.

"Oh, they do not want anything in return; they did it out of the kindness of their hearts. Can you imagine? Setting out by themselves with only a map across such open territory. Such courage, such strong hearts."

"It was good to see other people—oh, you know what I mean."

"I do, honey. I do," replied Ben.

Acise grew stronger every day. Oh'Dar left her side as little as possible, and Pajackok helped provide food for them. Snana and Honovi visited frequently.

One morning by the fire, Honovi said to Oh'Dar, "I did not know you brought harmonicas back on your last trip."

"I did. I bought a ridiculous number. The storekeeper thought I was mad, no doubt. I had them in a sack in the wagon, but I thought better of it and took them away. Noshoba must have found them before I did so. It was foolish on my part; my experience with the Waschini is very limited, and I let my guard down about my presence here, not thinking of the possible repercussions. And now look where we are."

Oh'Dar threw a piece of cooked meat to Waki, who snapped it up mid-air. Waki, the wolf cub given to him the day he and Acise were bonded. She was now a beautiful adult, particularly devoted to Noshoba who had cared for her during Oh'Dar's absences.

"Trouble was bound to come anyway," said Honovi. "We have heard too much about it from other tribes to think it would pass us by."

Oh'Dar nodded slowly. "I can take Acise and I'Layah to the High Rocks, but what about you? And Snana? And Noshoba? Yes, this is private land, but there are ways around that, and the constable seems to have a personal vendetta against me now. I think you should all come with me."

"Is'Taqa told us about your conversation. I know it is impacting us personally, but it is bigger than our issues with the one Waschini. There are others like him, many of them. I fear for the future of every village. But none of us can leave. I must stay to help Ithua, and should any Waschini visit, to translate. Pajackok wants Snana to go, but she refuses. And you know Snana; she is going to do what she wants to do, to the point of returning if she is forced to go—and we cannot keep her prisoner." Honovi shook her head and sighed. "As for Noshoba, I am afraid he would be frightened among all the People and the

Sassen. I do not believe the situation is urgent enough to put him through that right now."

"The High Council meeting is now underway and will be over in a few days," Oh'Dar said, thinking out loud. "I promised Acaraho that I would be there for the last day, but I do not like to leave you while Chief Is'Taqa is also away."

"Acise is well enough for you to leave; Pajackok and all the other braves will watch over us. I think it is important that you be there," insisted Honovi. "The watchers are here, and if it comes to it, I am certain they will find a way to make sure we don't get hurt."

Oh'Dar realized what she was saying was true.

"I know you are right. But in an altercation, the Waschini would have guns."

"Oh'Dar," Honovi said, laying her hand on his wrist. "If the Waschini have guns and intend to use them against us, your being here will make little difference."

He looked at her for the longest time. Then he placed his hand over his heart. "We cannot live in fear, but we must be prudent. I will attend the High Council gathering, and when I return, I hope Acise and I'Layah will be strong enough to go back with me to the High Rocks—at least for the time being."

Oh'Dar was greeted warmly, and word was sent to Acaraho and Adia that he had come home. They were disappointed he had not brought Acise and I'Layah, but he gave them an update on their progress. They hung on every word as he described all the events, including Grace Webb's testimony and how it had turned everything around. They would have more time to talk later, but having that much out of the way, Oh'Dar went to visit his grandparents.

Miss Vivian practically leaped off the bed where she had been sitting next to Ben. "Grayson!"

He leaned down to wrap his arms around her in a warm, strong hug.

"So, Ben, I hear your climbing days are over," Oh'Dar said, hugging him next.

"Yes, it's time to leave the tricks to the younger folks, I guess. How are you? Where are your wife and daughter?"

"They need a few more days, then I will bring them here. I cannot wait for you to see your great-granddaughter."

Miss Vivian chuckled. "Oh, my, that does sometimes make me feel old!" Then she became more serious, "After your father and mother were killed and you were lost, Louis and Charlotte seemed estranged, always arguing, and I had little hope left of having a proper family again. Then you appeared, and my world was reborn. And now, really just a handful of years later, I have you, your lovely new wife, and a new great-granddaughter."

Then she turned back to Ben. "And my loving husband."

"We haven't seen you since you got back. So much has happened," Ben said. "We know, of course, that the letter Miss Vivian wrote must have done the trick."

"Can you stay and talk to us, or do you have to be somewhere?" Miss Vivian asked.

"First, do I need to bring you something to eat?" Oh'Dar asked.

"Oh, no," his grandmother answered. "Mapiya has taken care of that all along. Sit and enjoy our time together."

Miss Vivian took her place next to Ben, and Oh'Dar pulled the brocade chair closer, the one that looked so like some of his grandmother's chairs at Shadow Ridge. He told them all about the trial, about the troubles caused by the man named Snide Tucker.

Ben remembered seeing him at the village and mentioned that he'd immediately taken a dislike to the man.

Oh'Dar then talked about how Tucker had accosted Grace and how he had ultimately been taken to the jail in Millgrove. Then he went over the trial in as much detail as possible and spent a long time talking about what took place when Grace returned with the letter.

"It was a stroke of genius, Grandmother," Oh'Dar said.

"When Grace told me who the judge was, I knew exactly what to do," said Miss Vivian. "Of course, your great-grandfather knew most of the people who had any standing, but in this case, there was a more personal relationship as Judge Walker and your grandfather, my first husband, also grew up together. It was just a stroke of luck that I remembered about the gavel and the inscription."

"I wish you could have seen it unfold. It was amazing," Oh'Dar said. "And Grace, she couldn't have handled it any better. She had a retort ready for each of the prosecutor's counterpoints!"

"All those years of listening to your grandfather talk about business; well, I guess it taught me a thing or two about strategy," Miss Vivian said. "And what of Grace and Ned? Your parents took great pains to make sure that they saw nothing outside of this room. I know you would have been worried about that."

"Yes, and I understand why it had to be done as it was. But Ned is a curious fellow, and he couldn't stop talking about it. He approached me about coming here."

"Here?" Ben said.

"Yes. He is smart. He knows that no one goes to that amount of trouble to hide another village of locals. He knows there is a mystery here."

"Oh, he would be quite the asset, though," Ben mused, "with what he has learned about animal care. I could teach him what I know about breeding."

"Oh, Ben, it is out of the question. He is too young. He doesn't even know what he is suggesting. I do know; I lived the life of an Outsider, the only Waschini among the People. Even with the Brothers nearby, the time I spent with Chief Is'Taqa, learning their ways, wasn't the same. I was not one of the People, and I was not one of the Brothers, either. And, in time, I am relatively certain he would find he misses his family and his future prospects more than he thinks he would."

"Yes, but we are here now," pointed out Miss Vivian. "He would have us, and you, and Acise—and little I'Layah. And so many of the People here can now speak with us enough to get by. It is a different world than the one you were thrown into."

"I can't think about that now, really, Grandmother. There is too much else going on. My hope is that his enthusiasm will wane, and the next time I see him, it will not even be a topic of discussion."

"We understand, really we do," Ben said.

"Yes, oh, and there is more. Storis and Grace were married."

"Really?" Miss Vivian thought a moment. "I can see it; despite the age difference, I think they would be good together."

"He bought a little house not far from the Webbs. Judge Walker married them before he left town, and they seemed very happy together. She is a brave and strong young woman, that one. I owe everything to her, Ned, and you. I would not be standing here today if it were not for what they did."

"But something else is on your mind, I can see it," Miss Vivian said.

Oh'Dar explained about the run-in with the constable who was now going after the land the Brothers lived on. Then Oh'Dar explained that he had seen this coming and had Storis buy up all the surrounding land possible. "From here to the Far Flats, and from the Great Pines to the Little River, and beyond, the People and the Brothers are at least safe from being driven off their land."

"That is a tremendous amount of land, sure to draw attention from someone," Ben said.

"Seems like every move has a drawback, but it is owned by the Morgan Trust, on the pretext of land management."

"Land management?" Ben repeated.

"Yes. Timber. Lumber. A very legitimate cover, Newell assured me."

"So, yes, we will put that out of our minds for now," agreed Ben.

"Tell us about little I'Layah, please? Your mother told us she has my red hair and blue eyes!"

"Yes, she does. She is really small, but she and Acise are doing well, and so far, she is a very calm baby. I expect they will be able to travel by the time I get back. Everyone is astounded at her red hair, which is another reason I want to bring them here. Acise was just giving birth when the constable was leaving, but I am sure it was not lost on him. He will most likely be back, and she— She will never be able to blend in with the Brothers."

"She will be safe here, and we will also do our best to make Acise feel at home."

"Somewhere in Honovi's past, there must have been a relative with blue eyes," mused Ben.

"There was. Honovi's grandmother on her father's side."

Just then, outside, there was the clack of the announcement stone, and Mapiya had arrived with their dinner.

"I will leave you to eat. I want to talk to my father and Chief Is'Taqa if I can find them before the High Council reconvenes."

Oh'Dar left to find Acaraho. He and Adia were talking with High Protector Awan, who excused himself as Oh'Dar joined them.

"I am glad you are here. And we need your representation in the High Council meeting," Acaraho said.

"I also want to address the High Council meeting, if I may," Oh'Dar said. "I keep hearing about the Waschini threat, and I am sure the Brothers from the other villages are also worried about it. They need to understand that not all Waschini are bad."

"I am sure they realize that, son, but I agree that it would be good for them to meet you."

"I think I will wait to bring Acise and I'Layah here until after the assembly is over, so there is less commotion."

Then he added, "I'm sure nothing can come of it, but you should know that Ned, the male who came here with his sister, Grace?" Oh'Dar said. "He has become enamored with the mystery of what he experienced. He says he wants to come and live here. Before you say anything, I agree that it is impossible. Ben was excited about the idea as Ned had been studying similar things. But Ned is too young to make any such decisions, and I hope his enthusiasm will die down."

Acaraho let out a long breath. "I knew it was a risk of bringing them here. We took great care to hide as much as we could. But that in itself triggers curiosity."

"Father, I know the life that would await him here, even if he does not. You know I will always be grateful for your giving me such a wonderful life. But it is different for Ned. He has no idea of what he would be sacrificing."

"I know you will handle it," Acaraho said. "And, I imagine it also presents a possibility of bringing in the Waschini seed that the High Council once considered as a way of preserving the Akassa line. Still does, perhaps. But wanting to live among us out of curiosity is not the same as agreeing to have your seed used to help father a new generation."

"Yes, and there is no way to broach that subject without revealing far too much," Oh'Dar agreed.

"The individual groups are still meeting, but tomorrow we will reconvene to close the session. Your grandparents have agreed to be there."

"I need them there when I speak, so that works well."

Adia had to talk to Urilla Wuti again. Learning that there was even a possibility of another Waschini coming to live with them, however remote a chance, had stirred up her idea about how the Ancients might have interbred with the Brothers using the Dream World.

She was glad to find her alone.

"We have hardly had any time to talk," Urilla Wuti said, embracing her former student, now friend.

"Remember our conversation about the Dream World and that perhaps it is how the Ancients did it? That they harvested the Brothers' seed through the Dream World and used it to impregnate their females, and that perhaps we could do this using Waschini seed."

"Of course, the obvious problem is that the only Waschini males we have are Oh'Dar and Ben. And

Ben may be too old," Urilla Wuti continued. "Or he and Miss Vivian could be unwilling. So might Oh'Dar; he also has a mate, after all.

"Yes, it is an extremely personal issue."

Then Adia told Urilla Wuti the story of Oh'Dar's arrest and imprisonment and how two Waschini friends of his found the Brothers' village and took back a letter from Oh'Dar's grandmother, which had freed him. And that, though there was no expectation that this would happen, the male Waschini wanted to come to live among the People.

"I wonder if this is how it starts," Urilla Wuti mused. "With one volunteer and then another. For diversity, though, there would have to be more than the seed of a few Waschini."

Adia put her face in her hands and sighed. "I cannot imagine Oh'Dar being involved in it, but he is a logical possibility."

Urilla Wuti put her hand on Adia's shoulder. "You are tired. Overwhelmed. It has been a trying time ever since the Guardian came. Come here and let me see how your offspring is doing."

Adia went over to the sleeping mat and lay down. Urilla Wuti knelt next to her and put one hand on Adia's belly and the other on Adia's head. Then she quietened her own soul.

Adia felt a stirring in her belly, not unpleasant, just reassuring of the new life growing within her. She opened her eyes when Urilla Wuti removed her hands.

"Everything is fine. But, my dear friend, you are carrying not one offspring but two."

Adia sat up. "Again? Twins again?" Her mind flew back to the moment after she had finished delivering Nootau when Urilla Wuti told her there was another yet to be born.

"Yes. There is no doubt."

"Oh, Urilla, how am I to raise two offspring in addition to An'Kru? I know I will have help, but right now, the idea is too much."

"Acaraho will be pleased, no doubt."

Adia felt a check in her spirit; she had not even thought about Acaraho. "Yes, no doubt he will. I should rejoice because our family is growing so very quickly. And after the contagion left so many of our males sterile, it is good for the community to have new life coming in. In everything, I have been given so much more than most. I have a loving mate who I never expected to have. A family. A position as a respected Healer helping her people. I have been shown that life goes on despite our challenges, and I have been blessed to visit my mother in the Corridor. Yet here I am expecting twins—"

"A male and a female," Urilla Wuti said.

Just like that, Adia's agony at giving up Nimida came crashing back in.

"It is as if I am back where it all started."

"It is not the same as then," Urilla Wuti said, sitting down on the edge of the mat. "You have Acaraho, and you have grown in wisdom and maturity. You have weathered so many challenges that I do not see this one as more than you can handle. But it is not just about having twins again, is it?"

"No. You know what it is. It is the guilt that I have still not told Nimida the truth about her birth."

"I have watched you struggle with it for years," Urilla Wuti said.

"You know I have looked for an opportunity. But there never seemed to be one. I almost told her when she and Tar were paired, but then there is the whole truth of how I became seeded. To tell half of it, to let her think Acaraho is who seeded her—and Nootau—would still be keeping the truth from her. So much is still at stake."

"This is bigger than you, Adia, it always has been, and that is what has kept you from telling her. It is not just between you and her; it potentially impacts our entire community, even all the People. That has been and still is a great stumbling block."

"I try to weigh her right to know against the devastation that might result, and then those two aspects against the repercussions for her of never knowing. There is no good answer," Adia said.

"No, there is not. It was a terrible situation all around. Not only for her, as an innocent offspring, but remember it was and has also been for you. You suffered for something that was unfairly done to you and which had far-reaching consequences. A crime committed against you, for which you alone had to bear the fallout. And the High Council would not

have let you keep her, most likely giving her to
Hakani to raise along with Nootau, whom you had
already had to forfeit. In the end, the decisions you
made gave her the best life possible, one free from a
stigma which would have followed her forever."

"I doubt she will see it that way."

"You speak as if you are ready to tell her," Urilla
Wuti said.

"I still fear the outcome, but in my heart, I feel I
have stalled enough."

The final day had arrived, and Acaraho, accompanied by the Overseer, Urilla Wuti, took his place at
the front to address the assembly. The sessions he
attended and the reports from the other groups all
left him feeling it had been a very productive gathering. Great strides toward understanding and creating
cohesion between the different participants had
taken place. Adia would soon be arriving with
An'Kru, as they knew everyone wanted to see him.

"As we prepare to return to our separate lives,"
Acaraho said, "I ask that you nurture in your hearts
the feeling of brotherhood we have established
between ourselves these past few days. I am encouraged, as I am sure you are too, by what we have
accomplished so far. I know we have many challenges to face, some of which seem insurmountable.
But our faith in the love and guidance of the Great

Spirit has gotten us this far and will lead us the rest of the way. Of this, I am sure. Haan?"

Haan stood to speak. "As Adik'Tar of the Sassen, I wish to offer to each of the Chiefs my peoples' services as watchers within your territories. Not to replace your own security efforts but to augment them. Even just one of my people can cover a vast area. Please speak with me before leaving if you believe this would be of value to your village."

Chief Is'Taqa stood next. "Much has been learned about the true past of each of our peoples. We are encouraged to know that Oh'Mah still walks Etera. But out of respect for Haan's people, I suggest that within our group here, we should refer to Oh'Mah as they refer to themselves, as the Sassen."

There was much murmuring of assent, to which Haan expressed his appreciation for the consideration.

Chief Kotori then spoke, "We are honored to be included in this assembly. I wish to thank the People and Adik'Tar Khon'Tor for including us and making us feel welcome. Our people have heavy hearts because the Waschini threat grows with no sense of abatement. We have heard that the Waschini who live among you have tried to help our people, to prevent us from being driven away from the land that nurtures us. I also wish to thank them."

As if on cue, Oh'Dar and his grandparents entered, Ben walking very carefully, supported under one arm by a crutch Oh'Dar had fashioned out of a forked tree branch and some padding. Oh'Dar supported him on the other side. All heads turned as they entered.

Oh'Dar helped his grandparents to the seating in the front that had been set aside for them. Once they were safely positioned, he turned to face the assembly.

"I am Waschini by birth. My mother, the Healer Adia, rescued me and raised me here at the High Rocks. This is and always will be my home. My father, Adik'Tar Acaraho, taught me everything I needed to know about being one of the People. His wisdom and guidance, as well as my mother's love and devotion, have made me who I am today. But I was doubly blessed, as I also lived among the Brothers. Chief Is'Taqa and his life-walker, Honovi, also helped raise me. So I benefited from the wisdom and teachings of two worlds."

He walked over to stand next to his grandparents. "But my heart was troubled. Part of me longed to discover my blood roots. And so I left Kthama, leaving behind everything and everyone I knew. By the grace of the Great Spirit, I found my birth family. My birth mother and father had long returned to the Great Spirit, but my grandmother and Ben welcomed me into their lives as well. As you can see, my grandparents now live among us here at Kthama. Shortly, my life-walker, daughter of Chief Is'Taqa and Honovi, will join me here. My newborn daughter will grow up as I did, with the love and guidance of all these peoples. She will live a life of wonder, but she will also face the difficulties I did in trying to bridge different worlds.

"I was fortunate to find harmony between the three worlds I belonged to, but that is not the case for everyone. I have just recently returned from the Waschini world, a long story I will not tell here. But during my time there, I heard firsthand from the Waschini about their intentions to remove the Brothers from the land that has supported them through the ages. To that end, I used the—" Oh'Dar searched for the words "—the system of the white world to lay claim to the land we inhabit. It will protect the Brothers from being forced from your villages, but it will not protect all the Brothers throughout Etera."

Acaraho thanked Oh'Dar and then said, "My people here face a terrible challenge. We are in need of new blood in order to continue the Akassa line. Care has been taken to allow mating of only those from families who share little family history. But the combinations are dwindling."

Ben, Yuma'qia, and Bidzel then stood to address the council.

Ben struggled to his feet and hobbled to stand next to the two researchers. "I, too, along with my wife, am blessed to be accepted among the People as well as the Sassen and the Brothers. For this, we are both grateful; we have been shown hospitality and forbearance that my own kind has not returned. For that, I deeply apologize.

"In the Waschini world, I learned about bloodlines, how to identify impurities, and to make combinations that would minimize their impact. I have brought my experience here to work with researchers Yuma'qia and Bidzel, using a huge historical record housed within Kht'shWea where Adik'Tar Haan and his people live." He sat down again.

Haan then spoke. "The blood of my people facilitates the flow of the life force of the Great Spirit in and out of this realm. Though diluted by the Ancients' interbreeding with the Brothers, enough has remained to keep Etera from deteriorating. The Akassa's blood is not as strong, but because of the limitations of our population, the choices for continuing to produce healthy offling are narrowing. I believe this has already been explained to the Brothers?"

"Yes," Acaraho said. "We all understand the challenges facing the Sassen and the Akassa."

Then Urilla Wuti spoke in her position of Overseer. "It is with a heavy heart that we feel we must be honest with everyone. Despite all the work of Yuma'qia and Bidzel, along with the help of Ben Jenkins, we can find no combinations for either the Akassa or the Sassen to safely continue to reproduce past six or seven generations. It appears that our time of producing healthy offspring will be coming to an end."

Chief Is'Taqa rose to speak. "If the Akassa and the Sassen no longer walk Etera, then we will all perish. It is their blood that keeps Etera alive. It is their blood offsetting the negativity of the Waschini."

Silence.

Nootau, who was sitting in the second row back with Iella, couldn't help himself. "Oh."

His involuntary reaction caught everyone's attention.

"What is it?" Urilla Wuti asked quietly.

"I would like to address the council, please."

"Of course, Nootau, please do so," Urilla Wuti said.

Acaraho searched the back of the room for Adia. He hated for her to miss this conversation and also was concerned about where she was.

"For our new members here, I am Nootau, son of Acaraho, Leader of the High Rocks, and son of Adia, our Healer. There is so much wisdom and humility in this gathering. As I listened to each person speak, my heart became heavy; surely there is a solution to every problem? We serve the Great Spirit, the Three-Who-Are-One. We have been brought here through a series of miraculous events, surely not to come to a dead end?

"The blood that circulates in the Sassen is instrumental in keeping Etera alive; this we understand. But there is no reason to believe that it is not sufficient to carry us until we find a solution. The negativity of the Waschini is part of the root problem here. It is that which is contaminating the life force circulating within Etera. We have been focusing on increasing or at least maintaining what is left of the original Mothoc blood. But that is only half of the picture. The other half is the self-centeredness of the Waschini.

"My brother, Oh'Dar, has lived among the Waschini at least part of his life. His grandparents, Miss Vivian and Ben, have until very recently lived all of their lives among the Waschini. They can help us understand the distortions of their culture. The root, the beginnings, of the negativity that is causing strife, division, animosity, greed, all the elements that must be corrected if Etera is to survive. If we can teach them to live in harmony with the Great Spirit instead of leaning into their own ways, perhaps that is the path forward."

Ben stood up again, "Yes. Yes, there is the problem of the Mothoc blood. But there is also the problem Nootau points out. The caustic culture of my people. A culture of competition and division. As much as Etera needs the blood of the Akassa, the Mothoc, the Sassen, she also needs the Waschini to live in harmony with her creatures, not dominating them and squandering her resources as they do now. My people must be shown how to come back into alignment with the Great Spirit. My people need teachers. Way-showers."

Urilla Wuti spoke. "All this is true. Of course, we are worried about our own cultures, our families, our loved ones, our future generations. But it is the negative distortion of the Waschini that will lead to Etera's destruction."

Acaraho commented. "We cannot directly help the Waschini. Nor can the Sassen. There is only one group that could move among them, teach them how to live in harmony. And they are here among us now."

He looked around at the various Chiefs present. "The hope for the future lies in the Brothers. The Guardian Pan told us this at the last High Council meeting. How did I miss it? How did I not hear the importance of what she was saying? She told us that the Brothers are one of the greatest gifts to Etera. You, the very people whom the Mothoc betrayed at the deepest level, the hope for the future of Etera lies within you. Those were her very words. You are the key somehow. Yes, somehow, you must become the Waschini's teachers."

Chief Is'Taqa had nothing but the greatest respect for Acaraho, so he chose his words very carefully in order not to diminish the power of what the Leader had just said. "I hear the wisdom of the words spoken here. I feel the goodwill and the movement of our souls to seek and receive answers. A tremendous challenge to be overcome is this, though; how are we to get the Waschini to listen to us? They see us as inferior, as savages, even. Yes, how are we to get them to listen to us?"

"I do not know," Acaraho answered. "I only know

in my heart that this is the answer. I understand what you are saying. I understand; to get them to listen to you, those whom they persecute and look down upon—it would take a miracle."

Just then, Adia entered the room holding the silver-haired An'Kru, and a sudden chill passed through Acaraho.

CHAPTER 16

In the flickering light of the evening fire, Acise threw her arms wide to embrace her life-walker. "You have come home. My heart sings!"

After hugging him, Acise pulled Oh'Dar down to sit next to her.

Honovi, rocking I'Layah in her arms, smiled profusely. "Is'Taqa arrived earlier and told us all about the assembly. It seems momentous progress was made, though I am also perplexed at the concept of our influencing the Waschini's distorted thinking."

"I also do not know how it would happen," Oh'Dar said, placing an arm around Acise's shoulder. "But we have a direction, and sometimes that is half the battle. Has there been any more trouble from the Waschini while we were away?"

"No," said Pajackok, sitting across from them next to his life-walker, Snana. "We have been watching the area with great dedication."

"Haan made a generous offer to place some of his watchers around the area," Oh'Dar said.

Just then, Chief Is'Taqa and his sister, Ithua, joined them.

"Welcome home, Oh'Dar," Chief Is'Taqa said. "We welcome Oh'Mah's help. Even if we do not see them, knowing they are there will be a great comfort."

"It is peculiar to me," Oh'Dar said, "that more dire our circumstances, the more my faith seems to be strengthened. When Grace and Ned Webb brought my grandmother's letter, it restored my belief that everything is happening as it should. I truly thought I would never see any of you again, but instead, I have been blessed to intervene with the Waschini in support of the Brothers. I feel I must leave again and take Acise and I'Layah to Kthama, but that also feels to me like the will of the Great Spirit."

Acise leaned her head against Oh'Dar's shoulder. "I know we need to go."

Oh'Dar turned so she could see his face. "I am so sorry. I know this is not the life you envisioned when we were bonded. I know the hardship of trying to live in two worlds, and now I have brought that burden to you and our daughter. Your love for me has cost you the joy of living among your own people, even if temporarily."

"Your people are my people," Acise answered. "I am your life-walker. I walk this life with you wherever it leads. My place is at your side, and I come with you willingly with joy in my heart. As for our daughter, her life will be richer for it; she will enjoy the blessings of many worlds. It is not as if we will never return here, and your grandparents are getting older; she needs to know them and benefit from their love for her. I count none of this adjustment as loss, but all of it as gain, my love."

"But there is also the issue of your mother and Snana and Noshoba," Oh'Dar said.

"The most urgent issue is your baby and Acise," stated Chief Is'Taqa. "I believe we have time to determine what to do next, and Honovi and Snana have made it clear that they and Noshoba will be staying here for the time being."

"When will you be leaving?" Honovi asked.

"I do not believe there is any immediate threat, so whenever Acise is ready," he said, looking at his lifewalker.

"I believe we can travel tomorrow."

Goodbyes that were not goodbyes were said, and the following evening, Oh'Dar, Acise, and their daughter arrived at Kthama.

After much greeting in the Great Entrance and much showing off of I'Layah, Oh'Dar and Acise were finally able to present Miss Vivian and Ben with their great-granddaughter.

"Oh, my," exclaimed Miss Vivian. "You were not exaggerating about her coloring. Oh, she makes me think so much of when my mother described how I looked as a baby. The shocking red hair, the bright blue eyes. Of course, many babies start out with blue —" then she stopped herself, wondering if that was true for the Brothers.

"Well, whatever happens, she is beautiful," Ben said.

Her full name is beautiful, too," Oh'Dar replied. "I'Layah Elizabeth Morgan."

"Oh," Miss Vivian exclaimed. "Oh!"

They all laughed.

"You did not expect her to have a Waschini name as well?" Oh'Dar asked.

"You named her after me. My middle name."

"Of course," Oh'Dar said. "She is a Morgan. She is a part of both worlds."

Oh'Dar's grandmother searched for a handkerchief to dab at her eyes.

Acise waited for her to finish and then extended I'Layah for her to hold. Miss Vivian cradled her great-granddaughter and looked down at her with the deepest love in her eyes.

"You came just in time," she said to the baby in her arms. "In a way, you represent the hope for all our people. The hope that we may move forward into a future of peace and harmony joined together as one brotherhood."

"That is so much of what I felt when I first held

her," Acise said. "A sense of hope."

Just then, little I'Layah stretched out her tiny arms and yawned, and they all smiled at how precious she was, so innocent and apparently so unimpressed with their philosophical musings.

Summer came and went. The fall leaves had turned and were littering the hills and valleys with their beauty.

Tehya's seeding had progressed without issue. It was time for her to deliver, and Urilla Wuti and Iella were there to help. Khon'Tor, holding Arismae, and her parents and others were outside, waiting. What a contrast this birth was compared to the trauma of Arismae's.

Though he was bigger than his sister had been, Khon'Tor and Tehya's son was born without incident, and Tehya was cradling him when Khon'Tor was brought into the room.

Tehya tilted him for his father to see. "He has your markings! He is perfect." She played with his little fingers as she spoke.

Khon'Tor looked into the eyes of his son. Not his first son, but the first he could claim and raise as his own.

He shifted Arismae's weight on his chest. "What will you name him?"

"I was thinking Bracht—if that pleases you."

Khon'Tor smiled. "Bracht'Tor. It pleases me. Are you alright?"

"Yes," Tehya smiled. "This time, I am fine."

"Your parents are outside and anxiously waiting to come in. Do you need to rest, or do you wish to see them?"

"I am tired, yes, but oh, if I do not let them come in, I will never hear the end of it," she laughed. "Of course, please bring them in."

Tehya's parents were thrilled with their second grandchild and approved of her choice of name.

"We must send word back to the High Rocks," Khon'Tor said. "And Oh'Dar; having just experienced the birth of his own offspring, he will also be happy to know all is well."

"And Adia will be next to deliver," exclaimed Tehya.

"The Great Spirit has blessed us with so many offspring," said Iella, somewhat wistfully.

Nootau put his arm around her waist and murmured, "It will happen for us, I promise."

When the time approached, Urilla Wuti traveled to the High Rocks in preparation for Adia's delivery. She had planned on going anyway, but knowing Adia was having twins made her presence all the more important. Urilla Wuti had no doubts that as happy as the event would be, it would cause a flashback to the time of Nimida and Nootau's birth. Not sure about Adia and Nadiwani's storeroom, she had brought some medicines with her just in case.

Now, Nadiwani, Urilla Wuti, and Adia were in the Healer's Quarters. Acaraho was outside with Commander Awan and Oh'Dar. They had been there for some time and were sitting with their backs against the rock walls.

"This waiting is excruciating," Acaraho said.

"I know. But Urilla Wuti is with Mama, as well as Nadiwani," replied Oh'Dar. "She is in the best hands."

They chatted to pass the time.

"Tehya sent word she is ready for visitors," Oh'Dar said, "so Acise and I are going to take I'Layah to see her at some point."

"She will be thrilled to see you all. And so will Kweeu," Acaraho said.

"You are both blessed to be paired and have families." Awan sounded wistful.

"There is still time for you," observed Acaraho.

"Do you have your eye on someone?" Oh'Dar asked, smiling.

"Perhaps, but it is such a big change. I am taking it slow."

Acaraho smiled. "That is for sure."

"That being paired is such a big change?"

"No, that you are taking it slow."

They all laughed.

"Point taken. Perhaps I should move it along."

"Wait. Wait! Who are we talking about?" Oh'Dar asked.

"Apparently, an attraction has arisen between Awan and Nadiwani," Acaraho answered.

Oh'Dar thought a moment. "Yes, I think you two would be a good match. You should ask Yuma'qia and Bidzel to look into it."

"We have both been unpaired for so long; perhaps it would be too much of an adjustment to make." Awan sighed.

"Change has always been hard for the People," Acaraho said. "But that does not mean it should be avoided. A loving partner is a tremendous blessing."

Just then, Nadiwani stepped into the hallway. "Acaraho, you have a son."

Awan leaned over and slapped his Leader on the shoulder. "Congratulations!"

Nadiwani waited a moment for them to quiet down before adding, "And a daughter!"

"Two?" Oh'Dar exclaimed, then turned to Acaraho. "Did you know this?"

"Yes," Acaraho said, rising to his feet. "Urilla Wuti sensed it. We did not tell anyone, though. May I see them now?"

"Of course. She is waiting for you."

Acaraho stepped into the room and was immediately taken back to when he had once before walked in and seen Adia with two newborn offspring. Nimida and Nootau. The situation was entirely different, but he knew if he was thinking about it that his mate would also be. So many mixed emotions. Happiness that Adia and the offspring were all well, joy at having another son and a daughter of his own, concern over Adia's state of mind.

Adia was leaning back with a bundle in each arm, and Urilla Wuti was standing not far away. He sat down beside his mate.

"Meet your son and your daughter," Adia said, and Acaraho leaned over and peered at each one closely.

"Which one is which?"

Adia laughed, which lifted his spirits. "This is Aponi," she said, slightly raising the one in her left arm. "And this is your daughter, Nelairi. Do you approve of the names?" she asked as she looked down at first one bundle, then the other.

"Yes, very much so." Acaraho reached over and touched Adia's cheek. "Saraste', how are you doing?"

She looked over at him. He could see tears in her eyes but did not know if they were tears of happiness or sadness. Or both.

"Conflicted," she said. "I should only be happy, but my heart is so heavy with sorrow and regret."

"I know. I understand; I do. How can I help you?"

"Just be here for me, as you always are. This is mine to solve; I knew this day would come. I wish I had faced it earlier but, as you know, it never seemed to be the right time. As bad as the timing may be, just having had our own twins, I believe now I have to do what I can to make it right, as much as I can."

Acaraho knew she was speaking of Nimida and Nootau.

"But let us put that aside for the moment. We have a new family to raise, my love," she said.

"You have a crowd waiting outside."

"Send them in; I am ready."

Oh'Dar was brought in first. "They are beautiful, Mama. I am so happy for you both," Oh'Dar said. "And they are blessed to have such parents as you."

Adia sighed. "With An'Kru being barely a year old, I hope I can be the mother they deserve. Acaraho has his own duties to attend to."

"You know I will help you however I can," Nadi-wani said.

"You helped me raise Oh'Dar and Nootau. And now An'Kru. I know you will."

Everyone else was brought in, and when they and Urilla Wuti had left, Acaraho and Adia were finally left alone with their two new offspring.

"I know what is on your mind. Please, Saraste', let it go for now," Acaraho said. "There is plenty of time to tell Nimida and to let Nootau have the full truth."

"Something tells me Nootau already knows about Nimida. When he told us he knew that Khon'Tor seeded him, he implied there were other things he also knew. For my own selfish reasons, I hope this is true. Firstly, it would mean he knows and has not rejected me for that decision to give his sister away. And secondly, because he is such a stabilizing force for good, I believe he could help Nimida through this. I imagine it is going to be a tremendous blow to her."

"Are you going to tell her all of it?"

"You mean including who seeded her? If I do not, then a part of the truth is still being kept from her." Adia fell silent. "But you are right; I need to set it aside for a few days at least. Let us bask in our happiness over the new additions to our family."

As if somehow knowing that Adia would need him, Nootau showed up at Kthama a few days later.

"They are both beautiful," he said. "They look strong and healthy."

"They are," Adia agreed from her place on the sleeping mat. "I am so glad you are here. How did you know to come?"

"I was told it was time," Nootau answered.

"By?"

"It was not Pan. It was just given to me as it sometimes is."

Nootau stepped closer to his mother and crouched down next to her.

"I know more of the burden you carry than you realize."

Adia waited for him to continue, praying that he

would tell her what she had been hoping was true.

"I will not make you guess, Mama. I know about Nimida. I know she is my sister. And I know why Urilla Wuti sneaked her away to be raised at the Great Pines."

He continued, "I also know about the High Council, how they forced you to give up one of us, either Oh'Dar or me. And I know and understand why you decided you had to raise Oh'Dar yourself. For what it is worth, I would have made the same decision."

Adia realized she was holding her breath and that tears were ready to run down her cheeks.

"And I know that when Nimida was born, you feared the High Council would force you to give her up, too. Perhaps even to Hakani, who later tried to murder me when she attempted to take her own life."

Against Adia's will, the tears fell.

"This time, it was different, though," Nootau explained. "This time, it was not just information that was given to me, but an entire flood of direct experience. I felt, actually felt, your dilemma. I felt your anguish over having to pick who would go with Hakani and who you would raise, Oh'Dar or me. Your very real fear of the High Council, and then the horrible realization that Urilla Wuti was right; Nimida would have a better chance at life elsewhere. And I also know how that decision has haunted you every day of your life. So when I humbly say I understand, believe me, I truly do."

"It helps to hear you say that, though I am sorry that you had to feel all that I went through."

"I came here not only to comfort you, Mama, but also to be here to help Nimida. I know you are planning on telling her the truth." Nootau paused a moment before adding, "All of it."

"She has a right to know," Adia said softly. "I feel there is no excuse for taking so long to tell her. But I do not think I will tell her everything at once. I know it will be a blow to her, in many ways that I can imagine and in many ways I cannot."

Nootau leaned forward and brushed his mother's tears away before kissing her on the cheek. "I am here for you, Mama. Always."

After Nootau left, Adia felt a sense of relief and gratitude. Somehow he had experienced what she had gone through as if living it himself. She recognized what he had described; it was exactly the kind of experience she had when she formed a Connection with someone. Yet he had said nothing of a Connection with another.

What was happening? What was happening to her son, and to others? The new abilities of the Healers, their Helpers, and their apprentices. Those were wondrous, it was true. But to what point? Of what day-to-day use were these new abilities? Were they all being prepared for something that was going to happen, perhaps something more far-reaching than any of them could imagine?

CHAPTER 17

Adia knew she could put it off no longer and sent for Nimida. After Nimida had met and admired the twins, Adia asked her to sit down.

"There is something I need to talk to you about. Something I should have brought up long ago. Something for which there is no excuse that I have taken so long to tell you."

Curiosity crossed Nimida's face. "Please, tell me, whatever it is."

"You know about Oh'Dar. I rescued him as a tiny offspring and had to fight very hard to keep him. For all the time before you were born, Healers and Helpers were not allowed to be paired or have offspring. We were expected to devote ourselves entirely to helping our people, but there was also the fear of losing a Healer in the birthing process. There were so few Healers, you see. Oh, there is so much to tell you."

Adia paused, searching for the right words.

"During this time, something—happened—and I became seeded. I went to the High Council and told them. They were unmoved by my situation and told me I had to give up one of my offspring—either Oh'Dar or the offspring I was carrying. It was the hardest decision of my life. Oh'Dar was so fragile, so helpless. And it was my responsibility to protect him, to make a way for him to live here. Not everyone approved of him, you see. And so I had to make a decision no mother should ever have to make—I had to give up one of my offspring to be raised by someone else."

Nimida's eyes grew wide. "Are you telling me— Are you trying to tell me that—"

"Yes, Nimida. You were that offspring. I am your mother."

"No, that cannot be."

Adia took a deep breath and paused again before continuing.

"It was the hardest decision I ever had to make. I loved you from the moment I saw you. I was advised not to hold you, not to name you, because it would make it that much more difficult to give you up, but I could not do that. I held you, and I gave you your name. There is so much more to it that I do not want to burden you with right now. I realize it must be hard enough for you just to hear this."

Nimida looked away, then back at Adia.

"Why are you telling me this now? You have kept it secret all these years—"

"There were many times I wanted to tell you. Many times I almost did. I was so torn. Seeing you happy here, pairing with Tar. I did not want to hurt you by telling you the truth."

"So why now? What has changed?" Then Nimida looked at the twins. "Is it because you have had more offspring?"

Adia closed her eyes and prayed to the Great Mother for strength and wisdom to say the right thing.

"In a way. It is because I have had twins—again. Because there is more. You were one of two offspring born to me. You have a brother."

Nimida rose and walked over to one of the walls. She bent her head forward and let it rest against the cool smooth rock. She took a moment before turning back to Adia.

"I do not think I want to hear any more right now."

"Please take some time, but when you are ready, I must tell you the rest. I owe it to you; I have for a long time."

After Nimida had left the room, Adia let her tears fall.

Acaraho entered a few moments later and saw the expression on her face. "Did you tell her?"

Adia nodded through her tears.

He hurried across the room and held her tight. "I should have been with you; please don't go through any more of this alone. I am as responsible as you are."

"No, no, you are not. You were there when I needed you most. I understand what you are saying, that you went along with the cover-up, but you are not the villain."

"Neither are you, Saraste'. Try to remember that."

Nimida did not know where to go. She was drowning in feelings of betrayal, anger, and disbelief. She wanted to be anywhere but there, but there was nowhere to go. Nowhere to go to get away from the pain she was feeling. *How could she give me up?* How could any mother give up her offspring? Nimida knew she would never give up any of hers. She would find a way to keep them, somehow. Even if she had to run away.

Finally, she sought out Tar. Her mate listened carefully and held her close, but there was not much he could do to console her.

"I do not know what to believe in anymore. Someone I looked up to, someone I wanted to be closer to— This has changed everything."

Nimida spent several days trying to deal with the flood of overwhelming feelings and finally pulled herself together enough to face whatever else Adia wanted to tell her. No matter how hard it would be, she needed to know it all. Uncertain of how to proceed, she asked Nadiwani to set up the meeting.

Adia arranged with Acaraho to join them, and so it was that Nimida arrived at the Healer's Quarters to find two people waiting for her.

"Why is he here?" she asked.

"It involves him."

"Are you my father? Is that what happened; you and the Healer fell in love, and I was the result?"

"Nimida," Adia interrupted. "Let me try to tell it to you in as orderly a fashion as I can. I told you that I was allowed to keep only one of my offspring. Either Oh'Dar or the one I was carrying. The High Council had decided the offspring I did not keep would be raised by someone else. That female was Khon'Tor's first mate. Her name was Hakani, and she hated me for reasons I only later found out. Oh'Dar had such special needs, not being one of us, and Khon'Tor was not accepting of him at that time. As horrible as it sounds, having to choose, I felt that I had brought him here, and I feared that only I could provide the protection Oh'Dar needed. So when it came time to give birth, I already knew I could not raise the one I was about to have. Only, unbeknownst to me, I was not carrying one. I was carrying two. I had twins."

Adia waited a moment and added. "You and Nootau."

"Nootau is my brother? But—but Nootau was raised here with you." Then she looked at Acaraho, "And you."

"Yes, but he was only returned to me after a terrible series of events, which ended with Hakani stepping off a cliff into the Great River. As for you— Well, I knew the High Council would not let me keep you, and the Mother only knows who they would have given you to. So I had to hide your existence from them because that was the only control I had over where you ended up. So the Healer who was with me took you away with her and placed you with your family at the Great Pines."

"So you raised my brother but gave me away," Nimida said almost in a daze.

"Nootau was born first, and then you. I had only a short time to decide which of you to let go to Hakani. Because you were a female, I had particular concerns for your welfare because of things I haven't told you yet. So Hakani was notified that my offspring was a male. My worst fears came true not long after when Hakani tried to kill herself with your brother in her arms. She was going to take him over the cliff with her to the Great River below, so great was her hatred of me. But at the last moment, with Acaraho's help, I was able to get him away from her before she went over the edge."

"So when Nootau was returned to you, why did you not send for me? Bring me home and raise me with my brother?"

"The High Council would not have let me keep you. I knew very well they would have sent you away again. I had faith that Urilla Wuti would find you a good home."

"It was, until my mother died," Nimida said with tears in her eyes. "When I first came here, you were so kind to me. I was missing my mother—my *mother* —so badly. There was so much love here, between you and Acaraho and Nootau and Oh'Dar. Many times I wished I was part of your family. And now to find out that I was. *Should have been.* So my daydreams about the life I missed were all true. I do not know what is worse, having them only as daydreams or knowing that they could have come true but did not."

"There is more, Nimida. So much I need to explain. I want you to know all of it."

With her heart breaking, Adia looked across at her long-unclaimed daughter. "But if it is too much all at once, I understand."

"I am trying. I am really trying. If I did not know you, had not been around you all these past years, by now I would have left Kthama with Tar and gone— anywhere. But I do know you, and I know your heart is good. But it hurts. I could have been raised here with my blood mother and father. And my brother."

Adia closed her eyes, trying to keep her composure. The last thing she wanted to do was to break down and have Nimida feel sorry for her. And now, she had to tell her the rest of it.

"Acaraho did not seed you and Nootau. I was seeded Without My Consent."

Nimida's face constricted into a frown. "A male forced himself on you?"

"Yes."

"Do you know who it is? Where is he? He must have been punished. Surely the High Council punished him?"

"I did not tell the High Council. For reasons I hope I can make you understand. If it had come out, it would have destroyed the community. Perhaps even had repercussions across other communities. It was a time of great turmoil within the leadership here, so I told no one, and I lived with it. The shame. The talk. And Acaraho— Well, he found out, and he intentionally took the blame for seeding me. A Healer who was not permitted to pair, least of all to mate. A maiden. As far as everyone else knew, I had failed at my calling, and he bore the shame with me, though none of it was rightfully his to bear."

"Is he here? At the High Rocks? The male who took you Without Your Consent?"

"No."

Nimida let out a long breath, which Adia took as a sign of relief.

"Who was it—*is* it?"

"I will tell you in time, Nimida, but I am concerned now about how much I have already laid on your shoulders. I know there is nothing I can do to make this not hurt; I can only apologize that I did not tell you sooner. I have thought about you every single day for your whole life."

"Does Nootau know who our blood father is?"

"Yes."

Nimida looked off wistfully. "I want to talk to him."

"I understand. Perhaps you can help each other through this."

It was as if Nootau knew Nimida was coming to find him. He was outside in one of the most beautiful areas around the High Rocks. He had told the guards he would be, so she found him easily.

"Nootau," Nimida called out softly.

He turned and greeted her.

"I would like to talk to you, please."

They sat down together.

"I do not know how to start," she faltered.

"Is it about Adia and Acaraho—and you?"

"Yes." Then she added, "and also you."

"I understand."

"How long have you known?"

"Only a short while. I grew up believing Adia and Acaraho were my parents. And they were, in all matters that count. I only recently found out otherwise. I imagine it is harder for you as you did not have the benefit of growing up with them. Though you and I have never really talked much about what your life was like at the Great Pines."

"I suspect it was like most lives. Like I told you, my father was not the easiest person. But my mother was very loving. She shielded me from most of my father's problems. I did not have any worries, really, despite my father's gruff exterior, until my mother passed. Then tensions rose between my father and me. My aunt stepped in and let me go and live with her, but she was cold, like my father. As soon as I reached pairing age, I asked to be paired to escape my life there."

She put her head forward. "I do not know what to do. I am so angry. And hurt."

"I had to work through it, too, though I think my situation is not nearly as hurtful as yours. I still struggle at times. My head knows they had their reasons, but my heart hurts. The people I called my parents lied to me my whole life."

Nimida looked over at Nootau, "The adult in me is not in control right now; otherwise, I would be able to understand how hard Adia's situation was. I guess I am not ready for that."

"Adia would not want you to feel anything but what you are feeling. If anyone knows about how hard life can be, she does."

"You know who seeded us," she said.

"Adia did not tell you?"

"She said she would later."

"I do not want to sound as if I have this all figured out," said Nootau slowly, "because I do not. I am just a little ahead of you, and I do not have as much to deal with as you do. But if she said she will tell you later, then she believes that is what is best for you. She is the least selfish person I have ever known, other than Acaraho. She will tell you if she said she would."

"I hope so. I do not want to be looking at every male, wondering, is it him? Is it him? But she did tell me he is not at Kthama." She continued, "Maybe this is an unfair question, but do you wish they had not told you?"

"Do I wish I did not know the truth?" Nootau paused. "Sometimes. I was more innocent before. The world is a little uglier now; imagine a male taking a female Without Her Consent."

"I do not even want to think about that. And what it means for us." Then a little light began to shine deep within Nimida. "I am glad to have a brother, though.

"Oh, no!" she exclaimed.

"What?"

"How I got here in the first place; the pairing ceremony. The High Council matched us together, remember?"

"Yes, I do. The Overseer of the High Council asked me to back out of the match. He said he could not explain why but that I would at times be asked to do things without being given a reason."

"Your—our—mother collapsed. I thought that was the reason, but now we know."

Nootau pulled at a clump of moss and handed it to her to dry her tears.

She accepted it with a bleary smile. "I know you, and we have been close since we met, probably even as close as brother and sister. But it would have been great to know all that time that you were my brother."

Nootau put his arm around her. "I know. I have thought the same thing. But we know now, and we do still have years to live. And I am only up at the Far High Hills. Maybe the four of us should get together when you are ready. Iella, you, Tar, and I. Have you told him?"

"Yes. He was kind and understanding."

"Well, you and I can also lean on each other. There is a lot to sort out. Who do we tell? *Do* we tell anyone other than Tar and Iella? Adia and Acaraho had valid reasons for keeping it all a secret. And what do we tell our offspring when they come? Do we let them know from the start when they are little or do we wait until they are adults to tell them the truth?"

"That one of their parents is a product of a crime?" Nimida said. "What a horrible thing to have to live with," she said wistfully. "What good would it be for them to know that?"

Then she stood up and turned back to face

Nootau. "Thank you for talking to me. If you want to talk more, just let me know. I do not know when I will go back and talk to Adia. I am going to take some time to sort it all out in my head before I do anything else."

CHAPTER 18

The Sassen Guardians were busy. Four of the six females had already had their offling. Three males and one female. The remaining two would not be long having theirs. All Kht'shWea was alight with joy and wonder because the four offling were all marked by the same silver-white coat—that of a Guardian.

But unbeknownst to the Sassen—or the People—across the verdant hills and valleys of Etera, a lone figure was making its way toward Kthama.

PLEASE READ

As Series One starts to wind down, I encourage you to read Series Two: Wrak-Wavara The Age of Darkness. You can find it by searching for The Etera Chronicles by Leigh Roberts. Some readers have been hesitant to read it, not wanting to leave the characters in Series One. But, hopefully, you will fall in love with them too, and you will gain a lot of insight into the background of Series One and the events that led up to the great division between the Sassen and the Akassa.

The next, and probably last book in Series One, will be Book Thirteen. Once that book is put to bed, I will launch Series Three: Wrak-Ashwea The Age of Light. It will follow the journey of Pan, An'Kru the Promised One, as well as other characters in this series whom you have grown to love.

I published Book One: Khon'Tor's Wrath on September 30th, 2019. Since then, I have released twelve books (soon to be thirteen) in Series One and five books in Series Two. I don't know how many will be in Series Three. It depends on what the characters decide!

This has been a considerable undertaking, and I have loved every moment of it. I could not have done it without my dear, dear editor Joy. Joy started out as the exceptional professional she is, and shortly along the way, she became a cherished friend. When we started this together, she promised to stay with me for the long run—and she has.

If you look back in Book One, you will see a quip about picking out a red dress. When I published that first book, I had daydreams of us standing together on some award ceremony platform, both in fancy red dresses. I still do. Who knows, it could still happen. Perhaps someday, the stories will 'catch fire', and we will be on our way. One thing about life, you never know what is around the corner. But if they do catch fire and take off, it will be because of readers like you who tell their friends and family about The Etera Chronicles. Word of mouth is the most powerful advertisement. So, if Joy and I ever do end up on a stage someday, we won't forget who helped us get there. And know that we are always very grateful for your support.

How to stay engaged with me:

Follow me on Amazon on my author page at https://www.amazon.com/Leigh-Roberts/e/B07YLWG6YT

Or you can subscribe to my newsletter at: https://www.subscribepage.com/theeterachron-clessubscribe

I also have a private Facebook group at The Etera Chronicles

If you enjoyed this book, please leave a positive

review or at least a positive rating (stars without writing anything). Of course, five stars is the best.

If you found fault with it, please email me directly and tell me your viewpoint. I do want to know. But a negative rating truly hurts an author.

You can find the link to leave a product review on the book link on Amazon, where you purchased or downloaded the book.

I also always appreciate positive reviews on Goodreads.

Until Book Thirteen!

Blessings—
    Leigh

ACKNOWLEDGMENT

Peeper frogs in the spring, twinkling stars overhead. Crickets, butterflies, hummingbirds. Lighting bugs, praying mantises, bees, and dragonflies. Flowers that push their faces up through the warming soil, reminding us that life is returning after a long winter, as promised. All these gifts, these miracles of creation that we take for granted in our rush to get - somewhere else.

Made in the USA
Las Vegas, NV
09 February 2024

85513254R00208